HOT
TYPE

HOT TYPE

by *Marjorie Lipsyte*

1980

DOUBLEDAY & COMPANY, INC.

GARDEN CITY, NEW YORK

Library of Congress Cataloging in Publication Data
Lipsyte, Marjorie, 1932–
    Hot type.
    I. Title.
PZ4.L7677Ho   [PS3562.I63]   813'.54
ISBN: 0-385-15798-3
Library of Congress Catalog Card Number: 79–8502

For Bob

1

Each morning when I walk into the city room my nostrils twitch, my blood rushes. I come alive. Really. It gets me every time. From the day's slow beginning to the late afternoon buildup, I love the almost visceral excitement of capturing fugitive strands of the planet's happenings and twisting them into the sleek morning newspaper that is considered, especially by the people who work for it, the best in the world.

I love The Paper but of course I see its imperfections. That's only natural, I suppose, and part of my love for it. All those who love The Paper complain about its warts incessantly, the way it looks too much to the past; the way it is changing for the worse; the way it allows the wrong people to hold positions of power; the way it lets talented people slip away. If only these unsightly warts were removed—with modern 1960 surgical techniques, some say; with good old-fashioned remedies, say others—The Paper would then be as it should be, perfect.

As secretary to the Cultural News Director I am only an

appendage to the men who produce The Paper, a small cog, as they say around here, in a great wheel. I have no part in deciding what is news on any given day, I have never seen my name in print or even stayed for the climax when the first edition goes to press. I have only heard about the great rumble from the sub-basement at press time when the giant machines ejaculate their nightly load into the waiting city. Still it gets to me. The ink must be in my veins now, rushing through my circulatory system, giving me that special news-paperman's high I feel when I arrive at work each morning.

Yes, I'm still a secretary, even though when I returned from Europe I vowed that I would not be a secretary, ever again. But of course this is so different. It really is this time. Working for a newspaper is certainly not like working for the government. The Paper is a warm, friendly place and since I moved down to the news floor it's been interesting and stimulating and fun. Most of the time. Newspapermen are fun. And I have learned that it is sometimes possible for a secretary to advance to a writing job on The Paper despite what Mr. Purledge told me.

Usually I feel exactly like so many people around here, thankful to be lucky enough to be working for The Paper. But there are times, I must admit, when I get completely honest with myself and I look at my situation for what it is, stripped of the aura of excitement that surrounds me daily. Then, like a lot of the others here, from clerks to editors, I check the course my life is on and I see that The Paper can be a real dead end. Two months ago I hit twenty-six. The fifth anniversary of my graduation from college was two weeks ago. These are milestones you have to be pretty foolhardy to ignore. The bald truth is that here I am with-out a husband or a career and no different really when you come down to it from all the other aging single secretaries I see around me.

But these are mostly night thoughts, thank goodness, thoughts that intrude when I am unable to sleep and I pace my studio apartment, smoking one cigarette after another, furiously spinning the radio dial, tuning in the clear, yearning music of the Milkman's Matinee, dipping and sliding over the polished hardwood floor, aroused as I ever was at a fraternity house mixer or a "Y" dance or lying with Allan in his room.

Night thoughts are far away now, this sultry June morning. As the Man in Bronze downstairs says, EACH DAWN A NEW DAY, EACH DAY A NEW BEGINNING. Corny as it is, I believe it and every morning when I read the words, inscribed in marble on the wall behind the Founder's bust, I agree. Like The Paper itself, my day will be filled with the usual facts and fictions, the mundane minutia microfilmed on my brain while I, like The Paper, wait expectantly, eternally prepared for the cataclysm—a disastrous earthquake or an earth-moving love.

Isabelle Lipton is in front of her locker fluffing her wispy red hair. Half-crouched, she squints into a small mirror that hangs inside the locker's door. I once asked her why she used that little mirror instead of the large wall of mirrors above the sinks in the washroom. "Is it to gain sustenance and inspiration from your gallery?" I teased, referring to the news pictures and headlines she has taped around the mirror. "If I step back," I had said, "I can see you in that *Time* magazine cover of the Suburban Wife."

"That's a crime?" Isabelle had answered testily. "Who you kidding? You're dying to be married and living in a nice suburban home like everyone else."

On some days this was definitely a true statement about me. But not the part about the suburban home. I wanted to be married, of course, like everyone else, but I wanted to stay just where I was, right in the middle of Manhattan. Maybe when the kids came, a house in the suburbs.

"How was your date with Bob Mann?" Isabelle asks me. She is now millimeters from the little mirror, stretching her lips wide over large white teeth. If the chemists at Revlon are accurate, her lips are turning the color of a Persian melon.

"I wonder what a Persian melon tastes like," I say.

"Don't evade the question. How was your date?" Isabelle turns and looks at me demandingly through heavily mascaraed lashes.

"You don't miss a thing do you?"

"I saw you sneaking down the back stairs. Is it a secret?"

"No," I answer slowly. "It's not a secret. We weren't sneaking. It's not anything." I'm at my locker now, getting the gray cashmere cardigan that I keep there to throw over my shoulders when I need it. Today I am wearing a sleeveless linen sheath, perfect for the street and subway and the office in the afternoon, but inadequate for the early morning polar blasts from the air-conditioning ducts above my desk. It's really incredible how bad the air quality is in this building and how docilely these supposedly sophisticated people accept it. In the morning it's quite cold and by the middle of the afternoon it's like a steambath. Everyone agrees that something should be done. "You're right, Arlyn," they mutter. Then they just bury their heads in their typewriters again.

"So?" Isabelle is waiting for an answer.

"I went for a drink and dinner with him. It's not exactly big news."

"How about maybe for *Overset?*" Isabelle cracks, slamming her locker shut and heading toward the washroom, her full skirt bobbing behind her.

"I'm afraid not," I say, following her.

"You didn't like the latest heartthrob of the city room," Isabelle calls over a toilet booth, "the best catch all year. It's him or you're so particular?"

I don't answer, but as we wash our hands Isabelle, undaunted, nudges me in the side with her elbow. "You'll tell me. How about lunch?"

"I'm busy for lunch." It's a lie, but I just don't want to have lunch with Isabelle today and talk about my date.

"And it's not Bob Mann," I add when I see her eyebrows rise as she gives me that so-things-are-really-happening look.

"So, he's a real phony or he's nice?" She is relentless. "Tell me so I know whether to be interested. Not that I have a chance, he's so remote. But I do find him cute. I kind of like that cool, continental look."

"He's okay, I guess," I answer. "He's a connoisseur of French wines. You should have seen the way he ordered dinner. A different wine for each course." I'm not about to tell her what really happened. Mann had caused a major stir among the secretaries when he reappeared in the city room last week after a two-year tour in Southeast Asia. Those who had known him before swooped around him welcoming him back, laughing and flirting. I heard about a few different girls he took out, but he's hardly sweeping his way through the news floor as it is bruited about mostly by envious, married men.

I kind of brushed by his desk whenever I could, too, and my turn came last night. I must say that I wasn't that surprised at the disastrous turn the evening took. It's a myth that newspapermen are different when it comes to women. In that respect I'm afraid they're just like most other guys. I did expect a Foreign Correspondent to be different though.

My key was barely out of the lock of my apartment door when he pushed me through the door and kicked it closed behind him. A bad sign. "Sit down," I said. "Would you like something to drink?"

He answered by grinning broadly and grabbing both my wrists with his long, spidery fingers. I tried to pull back, pressing my feet to the floor, but he suddenly let go of my wrist and gripped my upper arms. In an instant he had pulled me to him. He encircled my back with his arms and dragged me down with him onto the couch. He twisted and lunged on top of me, covering my face with hot, wet kisses.

"You're so beautiful," he murmured, spittle dripping as he licked my neck. "I can't control myself." His hands were braced against my shoulders and with jerky motions he was grinding his pelvis against me, jabbing his erection between my linen sheathed thighs. He was heavier than he looked. I tried to thrust him off me but he wouldn't budge. Then he stopped grinding a minute to push my skirt up.

"You're sensational," he said. "I've been waiting to be with you like this all night." Through all the wine, I thought as I heaved forward slightly. I still couldn't budge him so I took my arms and wrapped them around his back, dragging my fingertips over his collar until I found the bare skin on the back of his neck, that patch that the barber runs the clippers over. There. I circled slowly, like that. It gets them every time.

"Ohhhh, ohhhh." He shifted in pleasure and I placed the palms of my hands against his shoulders and pushed with all my might. He topped off me, landing on the hardwood floor.

His clean-cut, chiseled features wrinkled in disbelief. I stood up and looked down at him, the elegant Foreign Correspondent Robert Mann, flat on his can, his crisp summer suit rumpled, his Italian silk tie askew.

"Please leave," I said in my sternest tone. I felt saddened though. Again I had won the battle, but I was still losing the war.

"You're kidding!" He pulled himself up from the floor and sat down on the couch. "I sure read you differently. Let's talk about it."

"Not now," I insisted. "Please leave."

He ignored my words, leaning back on the couch, plumping a pillow. He patted it into place and indicated it was for me to lean against. "Sit," he said. "I won't try anything. Scout's honor." He held up three long, skinny fingers. "Seriously, I'm sorry. I just read you wrong. You're not a kid."

Suddenly I felt bone-tired. I have to be alone immediately, I thought, I have to be in the bathtub in three minutes or I'll scream. I walked quickly to the door and opened it wide. Bob Mann sighed in exaggerated resignation and came toward me. Straightening his tie he looked at me with an expression of wounded innocence. "Just tell me what's wrong. I thought things were going rawther well with us." When I first heard the prep school rawther it surprised me as did certain other inconsistencies in his speech. But I didn't question him about it.

"I don't like to be pounced on," I said, as matter-of-factly as I could.

"Pounced on? You're joking?" The wounded innocence gave way to laughter. "Look, we've got to talk about this." He reached out for my hand and tried to lead me back to the couch.

I yanked my hand from his grasp. "Not now. Please leave. I'm exhausted." Why get into it, I thought. Let him think it was because I was tired.

"Can we try again sometime?" Mann asked softly. Now his expression was open, his blue eyes friendly, his thin, well-shaped lips warmly smiling. I was mortified. Had I overreacted again? "We'll see," I whispered, not looking into his face as I closed the door.

Isabelle's Persian Meloned lips are moving. "So after dinner, then what?" If she only knew what really happened.

"Nothing." I try to be as offhanded as I can. "We just went back to my place and had a drink." I continue describing the chic, East Side restaurant, talking about its extensive menu, the wines, the glowing women and the polished men. It was an old trick, telling a girlfriend about a date without telling her about a date.

"Did he tell you there's talk of sending him to India? But I heard he doesn't want another foreign assignment now." Isabelle is showing me there are still a few things around here she can tell me. "I heard he wants to stay here and cover the convention and campaign and the next administration. He's sure Kennedy will get the nomination and it will be a very exciting time." Isabelle discusses Bob Mann's career in a lowered voice, even though we are the only two people in the entire Ladies Lounge.

As secretary to Judd Trent, a city editor of the Ancien Régime now idling his time until retirement as one of a half dozen assistant managing editors, Isabelle has her desk in the secretaries' row, directly in front of his in the executive bullpen. It is a central location and does keep her up to the minute on all the shifts of Foreign Correspondents' Assignments, a subject endlessly fascinating to everyone on The Paper, it seems. Me included.

Who doesn't get a vicarious thrill just thinking about the life of a Foreign Correspondent, especially after a particularly thrilling behind-the-scenes memoir in *Overset*, The Paper's house organ which we read more avidly than The Paper.

It was often said, though not in *Overset*, that being a Foreign Correspondent enabled a man with a family to live as though he earned sixty thousand dollars a year instead of twenty. All those perks. And the currency exchange was usually favorable. Maybe not in Europe anymore, but certainly in other places. Mann had alluded to this at dinner. After only a two-year tour in Indochina he was very nearly a rich man, he said.

Sometimes I'd imagine myself married to a Foreign Correspondent in Rome or Paris or London. I think I'd enjoy living in Europe again—as a wife. But of course if my husband were assigned to one of the developing countries in Africa or some other place on the prickly heat beat, as Bob Mann called Southeast Asia, would I like that? The loyal native help, the cooks and chauffeurs and nursemaids, shopping with an interpreter, spending the day learning the language and arranging dinner parties that would yield exclusive front-page stories? My picture in *Overset*?

In a way I must admit I was disappointed when Bob Mann turned out to be just like most of the other availables around these days, an egotistical bore at the beginning of the evening and a boar at the end of it. But one good thing about working on The Paper, there is always another desirable man just around the corner, even another Foreign Correspondent.

"I don't remember him saying anything about India, I thought he mentioned Israel."

Isabelle dramatically elevates her eyebrows. Now she has me. "That's impossible, you must have misunderstood him," she says. "He can't be assigned to Israel. They never send Jews there, even a goyisher Jew like him."

She waits for my reaction but I just laugh. I'm not going to get started with her again on that subject. Isabelle has a lot of trouble accepting my Jewishness, or lack of it.

"Maybe he said they wanted him to go to India," I answer.

"Hi, who's supposed to be going to India now?" It is Kit Rockwell, the Foreign Editor's secretary. She had silently slipped into the Ladies Lounge and is leaning nonchalantly against the opened door of the washroom.

Isabelle, who is obviously embarrassed to be caught by Kit spreading a Foreign Desk rumor, particularly one that might not be true, rushes past Kit sputtering, "Is Mr. T in yet?"

"No," Kit calls after her, rolling her eyes at me. I feel uncomfortable. There's not a lot of love lost between Kit and Isabelle. I hate to be caught in the crossfire of these things.

"I'd better get out of here too, Kit." I jam my comb into my purse and rush past her. "Early birds like you give us lateniks a bad name."

2

Sharipp. If I were writing a story of my day that is the word I would use to describe the sound of the miniature pewter dirk slashing open each envelope. The sound travels through the almost empty Cultural News Department and echoes in my head. *Sharipp.* Of all the secretarial duties, opening mail has always been the most onerous to me. When I worked upstairs in the Publisher's Suite, Maggie would trust me only with the obvious garbage mail and in Bonn all the mail for the Colonel was brought to me already opened by special machines designed just for that purpose. The letters were flattened out and placed neatly in manila folders by a mail clerk. At the Gladstone Agency I thought there was a lot of mail, but here, every morning, I have to open a stack of envelopes a foot high. And no one ever heard of electric letter openers down here. I can hear Ashley if I were to bring it up: That sounds like something for an insurance company, Arlyn, not a newspaper.

FOR IMMEDIATE RELEASE. EXCLUSIVE. FLASH. There are mornings I want to scream. I'm drowning in Press Releases.

Boring, pretentiously written, repetitive, untrue—no matter, every release must be placed in its proper place: For AF; CALENDAR; FUTURES FILE. And then of course there are the tickets. I must open each envelope carefully. You are never sure when one of those magical pink or green or lavender pieces of cardboard will fall out.

Before I came to work in the Cultural News Department each critic received and disposed of his own tickets. There were abuses, of course, but for the most part, everyone says, the system worked well. Doling out seats for standing-room-only shows to superiors and colleagues and friends around the office is considered shrewd and sensible and the decent thing to do in this backscratching world we live in. Bestowing tickets on one's auto mechanic, dentist, or doorman's daughter is accepted as a reasonable way to grease the gritty wheels of life. And don't forget the printers. The Paper could not exist without printers. Everyone knows that. Printers themselves tend to prefer sports events and high-decibel hi-fi shows to opera or ballet or theater, but apparently their children are developing a taste for the arts.

Just before I transferred down here the time-honored practice of individual ticket dispersal had finally gotten out of hand. Though he vehemently denied it, one of the music critics was suspected of giving his pair for a Milk Fund Benefit of *La Traviata* to a Times Square Lady of the Evening in return for her services. Despite his continued insistence that he had no idea how the two rouged and robust women of the street came to be sitting cheek by jowl with the rouged and crepey grandes dames of Park Avenue in the seats assigned to him at the poshest benefit of the year at the Metropolitan Opera House, a directive, nevertheless, came down. Memos flew, even a dreaded Lime Note, a missile fired directly to the Managing Editor from the Publisher's Suite. I don't remember typing that one. Perhaps it was a morning I had a chore out of the office and Maggie took the memo off the Publisher's overnight Dictabelt herself.

Now only one pair of tickets for each event is sent to the office. And I carefully log the arrival of each ticket in a special notebook and lock the precious piece of cardboard in the Ticket Box. When a critic wants to take care of his auto mechanic, dentist, or doorman's daughter, not to mention his superiors or colleagues or printers and, I might as well add, a secretary, he must telephone the press agent and specifically request the free tickets. Some of the younger critics are outraged, but the old-timers are more philosophical. It will pass, Arlyn, they tell me. Like all directives, it will pass.

Sharipp. Sharipp. Ashley Franks bought the dirk in Scotland on his cultural swing through the British Isles in May. It was really very sweet of Ashley, it was his first trip abroad and the letter opener made a lovely gift.

Sharipp. Sharipp. Dinnnnnnggg. Damn! Phones already! They seem to be starting earlier and earlier these days. And once they start there's no end. Fifty telephones on as many desks, insistent lights flashing and harsh, stabbing rings. All day long.

"Cultural News, please hold . . . Cultural News, please . . ."

"Mornin', doll." It is Lew James, the Press Agent's Press Agent, dronin' on. He knows that Ashley won't be in before eleven-fifteen. Why does he do this, call several times every morning? Does he think his messages piling up will have a subliminal effect on Ashley, or is it a habit from the days when he was a small-time hustler and had trouble reaching even unimportant editors on the telephone? Surely he must know that Ashley—and everyone else in the Cultural News Department—is always available to him. He always has tickets for even the most distant out-of-town relative and everyone agrees that the quality of booze in his Christmas basket is consistently the best.

"Sorry to keep you," I say to the woman waiting on the other extension when I finally extricate myself from Lew James.

"Something is wrong," she warns me. "Dylan Thomas is supposed to be reading from *Under Milk Wood* on the Gems of the Spoken Word and instead e. e. cummings is reading his work."

I take a deep breath. "I guess the listing in this morning's paper was wrong."

"Wrong? How can it be wrong? It says right here, 10:45 A.M. *Under Milk Wood*. Something funny's going on. That's the second time this month."

"It's just an error," I say. I explain to her that a line must have been dropped, by either the clerk who typed the listing or the linotype operator who set it.

"There's something fishy," she insists and I hurriedly suggest she call the station. I hang up before she can ask me for the station's telephone number. The Paper has a long-standing policy that every caller must be treated with the utmost respect and courtesy and all requests for information, within the bounds of good taste, of course, must be answered. Most of the time I don't mind, really. It breaks up the day and it is often interesting, searching through musical encyclopedias for the answer to some argument or checking the clips in the morgue for the date of death of some legendary actress or Pulitzer Prize playwright. But this is the fourth call about an inaccurate radio listing in the last two weeks. This woman thinks it's the end of Western Civilization as we know it if there's an error in The Paper. She should only know that what in all probability it really means is that the old-time linotype operator who did the listings for years just retired and the young fellow who took his place is not as proficient in his craft. No big deal.

Sharipp. Sharipp. It's almost eleven. At five minutes after, as if by signal, a stream of reporters in white shirts and dark ties will file through the swinging door of the men's locker room and take their places in the Cultural News Department at the gunmetal-gray desks that are grouped around stout pillars marked DRAMA, MUSIC, DANCE, ART, RADIO-TV, and MOTION PICTURES. On the other side of the cavernous men's locker room streams of other reporters are seeping through the city room and beyond, to the various tributaries of SPORTS and BUSINESS-FINANCIAL and REAL ESTATE NEWS. Upstairs, the ladies of the Women's Page are already on their midmorning break.

Back here in "culture alley," Ashley Franks, the Cultural News Director ("Cultural Director, whatever happened to editors?" one of the old-timers whispers into my ear every Friday before the weekly Cultural Conference), and the chief critics will arrive at their desks a bit later, all in jackets. Randolph Thoburn, the Drama Critic, is the one exception. He is always in his cubicle by ten o'clock. Of course he's hardly around after lunch.

The copyboys have set out the paste and stacks of copy paper and books of carbon sets and the early editions of the afternoon newspapers; the clerks are busy proofreading the listings of tomorrow's radio and television and concert and theater events; the secretaries have opened and sorted and distributed the morning mail. The day begins anew, each dawn a new day, each day a new beginning. *Sharipp.*

3

Luis is late with the coffee wagon again. Where is he? It's almost twenty minutes after four.

The afternoon's dictation was heavier than usual. That full-page layout on *Psycho* the other Sunday with those graphic shots of Janet Leigh in the shower really raised some hackles. Ashley has been bombarded with mail from irate readers all week and Damon Crewes, the motion picture critic, hasn't gotten so many letters since he found *Black Orpheus* trivial.

At first both Damon and Ashley were delighted with the *Psycho* mail. "Controversy is the lifeblood of a newspaper," Ashley told me.

"When you get letters like these, Arlyn," Damon said, "you know you're being read. What do I care what they say as long as they spell my name right?"

The letters to Damon Crewes tell him he's either a genius or a movie moron but those to Ashley are different. They are of a more philosophical nature. Ashley answers all his mail graciously and tersely, but the letters written on very fine vellum with embossed letterhead cause him real anguish:

"In view of your large influence, particularly with the many youths who are introduced to your hallowed newspaper in their classrooms through your special school rate plan, can you at all justify giving precious space and moral approval to this degenerate opportunism that masquerades as art?"

Or, my favorite: "I expect when I open my paper each morning, as my father did before me, to be able to read it and consume my breakfast without being confronted with nauseating details from a motion picture I would never choose to see."

When the letters kept coming, into the second week, Damon Crewes and Ashley began to have some doubts. Perhaps the layout was in poor taste, I heard Ashley say. More serious than the letters was the offhand remark of the Publisher's niece who works on the Women's Page and is famous around the paper for delivering each of her numerous babies on the weekend and returning to work the following Monday morning. This isn't true at all, of course. It's just one of those often repeated, unchecked, totally inaccurate stories that circulate in the city room. For each birth she has taken two months off before and six after.

I know for a fact that the Publisher's niece does not have the power to control stories the way her late father, the Publisher's brother, did. Still, her comment, repeated throughout the newsroom, that "Daddy would never have permitted that disgusting movie to be so glorified in The Paper," sent shivers through Ashley. Was she speaking for herself or had she been talking to her uncle? Did other members of the Family feel as she did? Perhaps the layout *had* been too bold. How should this be handled in the future? There would be more films of this nature. How should daring films be treated henceforth? Should they be played down, just reported as news and not featured? Perhaps that would be safest. Ashley and Damon were discussing this at my desk when I returned from lunch the other day. They didn't bother to move away when I sat down, but continued to talk right over my head. That's how I know about their concern.

A shadow falls across my typewriter. I look up. Moe Greenside's big belly is jutting over my desk. Standing next to him is an even bigger man, taller and broader, but this man's large chest tapers into a lean waist and narrow hips.

"Arlyn, this is W. B. Hallam," Greenside is saying. "He's going to be joining the Washington Bureau and he'll be up here for a while getting the hang of how we operate. He'll be doing city stories and working on the City Desk and he may need some help from you people back here. Arlyn is Ashley Franks' right-hand gal," Greenside tells Hallam, "and, as you can see, one of the better lookers around."

"I'm going to need all the help I can get," W. B. Hallam says to me with a soft, barely perceptible Southern slur. "And the name is Bill." His large, well-shaped hand is enclosing mine. His extraordinary yellow eyes are enveloping me. My stomach flips.

"Hi," I manage from a tightening throat before the two men are gone, stopping now at Jean Blake's desk. Was that a wedding ring on his finger? I squeeze my eyes shut to recall his left hand resting on top of our joined right hands. I hear Greenside introduce Gil Gilchrist as our Ace, the Bane of Broadway, and Tony Weather as our human shovel —a scoop a day. Tony acquired his last name years ago when he was a clerk and it was his job to run to the Weather Bureau for up-to-the-minute maps.

"And here's John Campbell," Greenside is saying, "a very able, soon-to-be City Desk assistant. Congratulations, John, I just heard." John stands up and extends his hand. "Pleased to meet you, sir," he says to W. B. Hallam. I guess Hallam is important or John would never be so polite to him. John told me the other day that it shouldn't be too long before he makes reporter.

"The City Desk is a good showcase," he said, talking

about his impending promotion. "And if I don't mess up I should sail through in record time, all those old farts out there."

When I asked him if he was going to keep the secret job he has with that theatrical producer, he just shrugged. I wonder if he'll be able to hold both jobs when he goes out front to the City Desk.

I asked Ashley if I could replace John as the clerk in the Cultural News Department and he thought I was being funny. "Is that your way of asking for a raise, Arlyn?" he had said. "You want his job so you can bug out on me for half the day too?" When I explained to him that that wasn't the reason, that as a matter of fact the clerk's job paid less than mine but that I would be willing to take the cut in pay if it meant I could get to do other things, Ashley said he understood. "But you're my secretary, Arlyn," he added. "You have had ample opportunity to meet people and no one would ever call your job routine. And you can't say we slave-drive you around here, can you?"

The stack of mail gets smaller. Another half sheet of letterhead into the typewriter. I type Ashley's four-line, thank-you-for-your-interest, you-keep-us-on-our-toes answer smoothly and automatically. Now the envelope to address and another half sheet into the typewriter.

What a farce the rigmarole of testing was that they put me through in Personnel when I was hired. After working for the government the typing I have had to do here is a piece of cake. When I was the Junior Secretary in the Publisher's Suite I did have a fair amount of typing to do, it's true, but there was no pressure. I had more than enough time to do it in. Actually, time often dragged unbearably, there were so many of us up there.

My main function in the Publisher's Suite, it seemed, was to be available for any service or chore no matter how large or how small that the Publisher, his wife, his daughters, his niece, his nephew, and their sundry children, poodles, and spouses might want done.

When I returned from Europe, vowing not to be a secretary ever again, I took my time looking for just the right job —one that would be a stepping-stone to a career, was how I phrased it. After six weeks of steady, methodical searching, I was finally convinced that holding out against secretarial work was as foolish as everyone said. I *was* cutting off my nose to spite my face, as the impatient counselor at Careers, Inc. told me before sending me here. With my skills and appearance, she said, I could command top dollar as an Executive Secretary or Administrative Assistant. I *was* wasting my time looking for those rock-bottom starting jobs that never led where they promised anyway. And I *was* overqualified for those jobs. They were for girls just out of college.

The instant I entered the lobby of The Paper I knew this was it. Whatever it is, I'll take it, I thought as I rode the elevator to the eleventh-floor Personnel Department. Later I realized that it was this initial feeling that kept me from walking out of the Personnel Department several times during that long, humiliating afternoon. I hadn't taken so many tests in one day since college and been subjected to such intense grilling about every aspect of my private life. Even the government job, as I recall, didn't require all those personal questions. And weren't my credentials impeccable? The Paper makes its own judgments, I was told. Finally, I was judged suitable to be a Junior Secretary in the Publisher's Suite. By the end of the day when I was informed of this I was, to say the least, grateful.

I wasn't certain if Maggie would try to block my move down to the news floor, but everyone in the Publisher's Suite seemed genuinely delighted for me when my transfer came through. "You'll be happier down there, Arlyn," Maggie had said as she presented me with the Bonwit's gift certificate. We were in an upstairs room of the Theater Bar where the entire Publisher's office staff surprised me with a goodbye lunch. Ironically it had been hearing Maggie talk so much about her friend Prudence De Witt's dissatisfaction with the new arrangement in the recently reorganized Cultural News Department and Prudence's heart-wrenching decision to take early retirement that had sent me scurrying for the job, first to Personnel and then to Mr. Purledge.

Purledge indicated right off his doubts about my being suitable for the job. But he did interrogate me at length. He began by carefully arranging a yellow legal-sized pad on the tiny table between us in one of the airless little interview rooms off the city room lobby.

"Now," he said, "I want to find out all about you."

"It's on file in the Personnel Department," I answered.

"I know," Purledge replied, clearing his throat and coughing that dry cough of his, "but just between you and I, I do things my way. Now, let's start at the beginning. What is your father's full name, age, country of birth, and what does he do?"

Incredible! Every year of my life accounted for, every member of my family pinned to Albert B. Purledge's yellow pad. I hated myself for not correcting his grammar and telling him to stuff the job and walking out even if it meant not getting back into the Publisher's Suite and having to leave The Paper. But I dutifully and meekly presented my life to this man who held my ticket into the city room. The few times I had been in the city room on errands it had excited me wildly and now, knowing it was so close, just beyond those double doors in the lobby outside this room, made it difficult for me to concentrate on Purledge's questions.

"So, let me get this right, your father is a supervisor in the Allegheny County Treasurer's office."

"Yes. That's correct." His rimless glasses aimed right at me, reflecting beams from the overhead light directly in my eyes.

"So, in 1959, January, you returned to this country and began working as a Junior Secretary in the Publisher's Suite."

"Yes, sir."

After almost an hour of this kind of questioning and

dozens of sheets of paper turned back on his pad, Purledge put down his pencil and leaned back, aiming the light from his glasses back to the ceiling. I was dying for a cigarette. But since Purledge had ceremoniously removed the ashtray from the center of the tiny desk and placed it behind his right elbow, forcing him to make grueling contortions when he flicked ash from one of his chain-smoked Camels, I decided to forego a cigarette. I wasn't entirely certain if he was gallantly keeping the smoke away from me or playing some weird game.

Some people say Purledge's circumspection is the result of the McCarthy scare The Paper had when a number of reporters and editors were called to testify at the hearings. There's no way a Communist could be hired now, they say. But me! Really! I've never even signed a petition. After all I *was* cleared to work for the government.

". . . and so," he was saying, "I think I'll take a chance on you. Ashley Franks really should have a graduate of an Ivy League college for his secretary, but you are highly spoken of upstairs. Of course it's different here on the news floor. You were just the Junior Secretary in the Publisher's Suite, but here you will be secretary to the Cultural News Director, the head secretary, so to speak. You will be representing Ashley Franks. He needs a secretary with finesse. Of course, where you went to college isn't always that important. Take my own secretary, for example. She never even went to college but she looks and acts like an Ivy League girl. Dresses right and speaks right, if you know what I mean. We've been together for almost five years now and I have never been embarrassed by her. I'm going to take a chance that you're like that. I'm going to give you a trial as secretary to the Cultural News Director, Ashley Franks."

I spin another half sheet of letterhead into the typewriter and glance over in Ashley's direction. All is well. He is slumped in his chair, staring off into space, picking his nose. So much for finesse.

"Say, uh, Arlyn," he calls, stirring from his reverie, "has the coffee boy been around yet?"

"Not yet."

"He's getting later and later. What do you think it is?"

I shrug and spin around on my swivel chair, surveying the Cultural News Department. All around me secretaries and assistants and reporters are slumped at their desks or hunched over their typewriters. In little partitioned cubicles critics are leaning back in their posture chairs, their feet on their desks. All are shifting their eyes from their typewriters to the big wall clock on each pillar, to the narrow corridor where the coffee wagon should have appeared long ago.

"I'll take a walk and see what's holding him up," I tell Ashley. "I could use a walk, in fact, everyone could use a walk. It's all this hot air back here. We're being asphyxiated."

"You're probably right," Ashley agrees. "It's those damn windows nailed shut."

The city room is beginning to jump now, to vibrate with that late afternoon electricity. Rows of reporters feverishly attack their typewriters, shirtsleeved editors conspiratorily huddle in impromptu conferences, and a low buzz accompanies the hundred jangling telephones that ring repeatedly. The City Editor stalks the rows of desks peering over hunched shoulders to make sure that the stories he and his staff had planned that morning are bearing fruit.

"COP-EEE." It is Harvey Kassell roaring for a copyboy to pick up the book of carbon sets he has just ripped out of his typewriter. Harvey once ran for copy himself, perhaps answering summonses as loud. A boy rushes up to his desk to snatch the book and rush it to Jackie O'Keefe's station in the middle of the room. There it will be separated, sorted, routed, and started on its journey into tomorrow's paper.

There are times I wish that I could be a copyboy. The pay is lousy and all the guys complain interminably about having to fill pastepots and fetch coffee, but they move through the nerve centers of the news operation and are practically assured of automatic promotions to clerk and assistant and reporter just by showing up clean-shaven every day. During the War, I've heard, women did all these jobs and some of them are still on the local city staff.

The myth is that the copyboys now are all Ivy League PhD's who speak six languages but I know for a fact that this is nonsense. Actually there are always a couple of really bright copyboys but most are just very nice young fellows who are graduates of all kinds of colleges and even some who have not been graduated from any college at all. Some are outgoing and aggressive but just as many are shy about speaking up and asking questions. Some are downright idiots and how they manage to get promoted is what amazes me.

Purledge made it perfectly clear to me that I should not expect to be promoted to a writing position. That was definite. Purledge was the sole arbiter of who was and who wasn't recommended for any job in the news operation. I accepted his dictum then. I write on my own time, when I do, for myself. Since my horrendous experience at Gladstone where I had taken the secretarial job with the promise that I could write copy and then had what I wrote literally stolen from me I had put aside the idea of earning my living writing.

After the breakup with Allan and my impulsive dash to Europe I concentrated on writing short stories and a novel. Of course, no matter how much I tried to control my material and build the tightly plotted, intricate, razor-crisp work I admired so in others, my stories always ended up as crypto-autobiographical emotional outpourings. What I wrote in that period after the engagement was broken was helpful to me, I'm sure, but of little interest to anyone else. Who would want to read those searing pages and pages that tried to tell my side? It embarrasses me to think about them. And I still burn with shame at the memory of sitting in that college short story course and reading my work out loud. There was supposed to be some humor in it but I hadn't expected the class to laugh so hilariously, and at all the wrong places. I guess I'll never be able to erase the image from my mind of Dr. Baldwin's shaking jowls or the amusing critique from that long, lean Korean Vet who was the star of the class with his long, lean prose.

The gin rummy game in the middle of the city room is in full swing and as I walk past the double row of players I am ready.

"Isn't that right, Arlyn honey? There are no virgins anymore are there? I had to go back and find a seventeen-year-old to marry to make sure she was a virgin." It is amiable Sid Schwartz, the only one of the card players and kibbitzers who doesn't look like a refugee from a road company of *The Front Page*. He is still under thirty and his belly hasn't potted yet. He has been a favorite of the City Editor's ever since his copyboy days. He is known for being able to work wonders at City Hall, where he has the record for getting traffic, drunk driving, or any other kind of ticket fixed with the maximum of speed and the minimum of notoriety to The Paper and the particular editor or reporter involved. A man after my father's heart.

"To each his own," I answer as airily as I can. He had addressed himself to me and the card players and anyone else in earshot. The exchange is actually a continuation of a conversation I had had with him and a few other reporters at Peter Simon's desk a few days before. Simon's desk is the gathering place for the younger, sharper noncardplaying reporters, Schwartz's generation of copyboy. When I first came down to the news floor they had showered me with attention and I had gone out to the Theater Bar for a drink with a few once or twice. But when I learned that they were all married, I retreated. That kind of aggravation I don't need anymore. Another relationship with a married man is not on my agenda. That's why Bob Mann seemed so attractive last week. He is one of the few halfway decent eligible men around The Paper—or anywhere else in the city for that matter.

There he is now, lounging on Peter Simon's desk. For the reporters whose assignments didn't turn out to be much in the way of stories and for those who are kept on tap all day waiting for that catastrophe, the late afternoon is a time to lounge or hide, hoping that nothing breaks now and the early good-night will come as expected.

I turn quickly to retrace my steps. How can I face Bob Mann after last night's fiasco? Perhaps it was a bit impulsive throwing him out that way. Was it rude? How was he to know how I would react, how I loathe it when a guy buys me dinner and thinks that gives him the right to pounce on me.

My eyes are drawn across the city room. W. B. Hallam is staring at me. Over dozens of heads and slouched bodies I feel his hot eyes. My eyes find his. Then he inclines his head slightly to unlock the gaze.

"What's up, Arlyn?" It is Paddy O'Connell, the City Desk secretary. As he greets me his eyes roam over the rows of desks in front of him.

I stop. "Hi, Paddy." A chat with Paddy will give Hallam a chance to wander over toward me. "What's that?"

"What? Oh this. This is my sermon roster. I have to fill it in for the weekend. It's coming to that time of year when the fellows aren't so eager. I have to go look for them. That's what I'm doing now."

"Sermon roster?"

"Yeah, you know, the list of copyboys and clerks and the sermons they cover." He holds the clipboard filled with sheets of copy paper toward me. "I have to assign them and see to it that they're paid. Used to be they only got paid for what was published. Nowadays we pay them just for going."

Paddy starts to walk among the rows of desks and I follow.

"Copyboys? Paid for sermons? Published?"

"Yeah, you know, the kids cover the sermons, come back and write them up, and they run in Monday's paper. They get five dollars but no one does it for the money. It's kind of expected of you if you want to move up. Shows initiative. What you can do. It's one way of writing something that gets printed." His eyes scan the room.

"It's rough now," he says. "A lot of the regulars drop off during the summer. Somehow they would rather be on the beach on a sunny Saturday or Sunday, especially during a big weekend like the one coming up." He looks at me and raises his eyebrows quizzically. "I can't understand why." We both laugh at his joke.

"Can I do one? I'll be in town this weekend." It is out of my mouth before I know I am saying it. Suddenly I have found a sweetness in the adversity of having no plans for the Fourth of July weekend coming up.

"You? Well, gee, I don't know. I guess so. But I'd better check it with the boss."

I see Paddy O'Connell scrawl my name on his sermon roster. "I'll let you know no later than Friday noon."

"Thanks," I manage as I leave him, my head spinning. I was resigned to having nothing exciting to do for the three-day holiday, just some shopping for Nantucket, cleaning closets if I felt like it, and perhaps going out to Jones Beach with Kit Rockwell. Now my stomach is churning and my nostrils are twitching. I might have a chance to do a sermon.

I would be covering something for The Paper. I would go somewhere, come back and write about it, and then see what I wrote in print. It would be only a couple of paragraphs, of course, and unsigned, but I would know it was mine. And Mr. Purledge would be as impressed with me as he is with the copyboys who cover sermons to show him what they can do.

In the corridor that leads from the city room back to the Cultural News Department, Bob Mann blocks my path.

"I've been looking for you," he says. "Come on, I'll buy you a drink."

My face is burning. Is it turning red? Mann is acting as

though last night never happened. I'm confused. And his blue eyes look so friendly.

"You were looking for me? You must want to kill me or something, the way I acted last night." Even as I say it I hate myself, but I'm not surprised at my words. In the long run, really, what would be the point in making a big deal out of what happened?

"Forget it," says Mann. "We'll try again. What about that drink?"

"I'd love to but I have to get back, I . . ."

"Okay, listen," he says, plunging on without waiting for me to finish my sentence, "can you come out to Fire Island this weekend? You mentioned the other night that you had no plans. Peter and Mimi Simon have a great place there, lots of room, and they're inviting me and you. They're having another couple too so it should be fun. And we can have a chance to talk. How about it?" He takes a quick breath and adds with a sly grin, "And pouncing is definitely verboten. You see, I am interested in more than one thing."

How can I resist when he puts it like that? The Simons are known for their very "in" parties. Mimi is a fashion writer for *Harper's Bazaar* and they are said to know just about everybody. Spending a weekend at their place sounds very exciting.

Paddy O'Connell and his clipboard flash into my mind. What if the City Editor says okay? What if Paddy can put me on the sermon roster? But it may never come up. Paddy didn't seem too encouraging. Not for this weekend anyway. And what about Bob? Can I back off at the last minute, leave him without a date for the weekend? Why worry now, it may never come up.

"It sounds like great fun, I'd love to, but there's one thing . . ."

"Lovely," Bob says, "here's the plan."

"I'm awfully sorry." The soft voice seems to flow down on us. Bob and I both look up at the presence standing next to us. It is W. B. Hallam. "I'm trying to find the morgue without a roadmap. I guess that's a mistake around here."

"Sure is"—Bob laughs, pointing toward the morgue—"but you were headed in the right direction. Just don't be led down the path to culture."

"The primrose path to the everlasting bonfire," Hallam calls out, chuckling as he continues toward the morgue.

"One of those," Bob Mann mutters.

"One of what?"

He looks at me and rolls his eyes. "Some Bible-quoting Southerner. Just what we need around here."

"That's not the Bible, that's—"

"Well, no matter. Here's the plan. I'm going out there tonight, right now, as a matter of fact, since you won't have a drink with me. I have time coming to me and I love lazing on the beach alone." His chuckle disturbs me but I let it pass. "Mimi and Peter are driving out Friday directly after work, as soon as he gets his good-night. You can drive out with them. You be all packed and ready to leave from here when Mimi picks him up at six-thirty. Keep your fingers crossed that he's not on a late-breaking story."

"I'll be ready."

He takes my hand and squeezes it. "Terrific." He starts back toward the city room and I continue on the other way, down the hall leading to the Cultural News Department. Luis is entering from the other end with the coffee wagon.

4

Folded up in the back of the Peugeot, my weekender suitcase on the seat beside me, I watch Peter Simon negotiate the turn from the Grand Central Parkway onto the Long Island Expressway. Mimi and I were told to be absolutely quiet. She is leafing through a copy of *The New Yorker*.

"I have to have absolute quiet," he had explained as we approached the turnoff, "otherwise we end up in Corona or Rego Park or some other godforsaken outpost of Queens."

"Stranded in Middle Village," Mimi had said ominously, "never to be heard from again."

"Ye gods, I'd rather perish here and now," Peter added, a monocle in his voice. The husband and wife then looked at each other, pleased with their repartee.

"It's no joke, m'dear, once I—" Mimi began, but Peter cut her off: "Okay, guys, this is it. First person who talks gets it in the heart. I need ze purrfuct quiet, mitt not a sound. YOU HEAR ME!"

Mimi had snickered and swiveled slightly in her seat to wink at me. I lifted my eyebrows in return. Actually I was happy for the enforced silence. From the time I got into the car until Peter had to have quiet to get on the Expressway, there had been a barrage of questions directed at me, followed, often before my answers, with jokes and puns in various dialects and expletives in several languages. At first I had enjoyed the questioning, but I began to get a bit weary of having my answers repeatedly stepped on.

Peter wanted to know where I was from and where I had lived and Mimi wanted to know where I had gone to school and where I had worked. Mimi seemed to lose interest when she learned I was a secretary. "I thought," she said, "that Bob said you were some kind of editorial assistant." That was the last thing said before we all had to be quiet so Peter could make the turnoff.

"Did it again," Peter says with an overblown sigh, taking his right hand off the wheel and wiping imaginary sweat off his brow. "There's no end to my talent."

"Or talent to your end," says his wife. Her words come out from between her teeth. She turns again to face me. "Peter's an excellent driver on straight lines, it's these curves that get him, you know."

A funny bit, but I wonder if Mimi is serious about Peter's driving. From where I sit he seems hesitant and a bit tense, especially when he changes lanes. His driving is making me tense. "The traffic really is terrible tonight," I say. "I'm not sure I'd even attempt to drive when it's like this. It's been so long since I've driven regularly. It was too mad in Europe, and I don't have much reason to here."

"Whatever made you go to work for the government?" Mimi asks, pulling down the sunshade and checking her makeup in the clip-on mirror. "That's the last thing I'd ever want to do." She sucks her lower lip into the upper and rubs them both together, back and forth in quick strokes.

I pull out my standard answer. "I wasn't going anywhere in this advertising agency that I was working for and I just wanted to get completely away from New York and the country and work somewhere else for a while."

It is usually a very successful answer. It leads to questions about the advertising agency and I am full of wonderful tales about that place.

"What was the name . . . ?" Mimi begins but Peter does not allow her to finish the question. Instead he breaks in with a question of his own.

"An affair of the heart gone sour?" he asks, catching my eye in the rearview mirror.

"Yes, that too," I answer, my sad tone telling these kind people that it's still too painful to talk about, this love to end all love, dead now these three years.

But Peter misses the nuance of my tone, or perhaps he is not really kind. He keeps pressing. "Is it something you talk about, was it a really serious thing that you ended with a flight to Europe?"

"Peter!" It is Mimi. "What kind of saccharine drivel is that? It's beneath you to pry information out of Arlyn. It just might be possible that the poor girl doesn't want to talk about it with strangers."

"We're not strangers. She's been sharing our sacred Gigi for almost two hours now. How intimate can you get? Besides, maybe she wants to answer. Let her speak for herself. Speak for yourself, Arlyn," Peter commands.

The back-and-forth between Peter and Mimi has given me some time to decide how much I'll tell them. Peter's question threw me and Mimi's intervention surprised me. I'm still not sure of Mimi's motivation. Is she genuinely concerned about my feelings or is she just using me to attack her husband?

My words are true, my tone is false. I am very flip. "It wasn't very melodramatic, I'm afraid. I broke up with a boyfriend and at about the same time I got passed over for a promotion at the advertising agency. They went bananas over what they thought was a brilliant Yalie, who was actually stealing my stuff. Nobody wanted to believe me—he looked so right—so I got disgusted and quit. Then I heard about government jobs overseas. I knew a girl who was applying and I did too. Sometimes I'm very impulsive."

"What's it like working over there?" Peter asks. "Row on row of cornfed, silken-tressed examples of wholesome American pulchritude turning into tantalizing temptresses of the evening, maidens on the Rhine driving the poor protectors of the free world mad with their wild abandon. You don't seem the type."

"How would you know the type?" Mimi asks sharply before turning to ask me the same question herself. "Seriously, you really don't seem like someone who would go off and work for the government in a job like that."

How many times have I heard this before, from everyone at home to Isabelle. Nice work for a Jewish girl! *Come home. New York, that's one thing. But Europe! Come home. There are plenty of jobs in Pittsburgh. I know I could get you right on at the Court House till you find what you want.* Dad was super positive. *I'm sure you could find something exciting right here. Downtown is booming now.* And Mom was super worked up. *What if something happens to Grandma? So far away. We haven't told her yet. She could never understand. Why would you want to go back there —and to Germany!*

"The job was nothing, an ordinary secretarial job," I tell Mimi and Peter, "but it wasn't draining, if you know what I mean, and the money was good, especially with the exchange rate. I traveled a lot, every chance I could get. It was fun."

A strange look passes over Mimi's face. She's about my age and she and Peter have been married since they were in college. I know girls at home like that, girls who have never gone anywhere alone, every trip and vacation with their husband. Maybe Mimi's the same. I remember the countless times I took off for some exotic place; the tingle of expectancy; the exhilaration on arrival; the crushing loneliness, or the heightened pleasure of meeting someone. I know what Mimi's next question will be.

"Weren't you ever lonely? I can't imagine traveling alone."

"How do you know she traveled alone?"

Peter is right, how is she so sure I traveled alone.

"Sometimes I was alone, sometimes I was with a girl-friend, and sometimes I was with a man," I say quickly, in one matter-of-fact breath.

"Isn't it depressing when you travel alone or with just a girlfriend? Don't you need to be with a man to get into the really good places?"

"Sad but true," I answer. "There are a lot of restaurants and clubs that don't want you if you're not with a man. And in some cities you have to be careful where you walk at night. But it's a lot better than not traveling."

"Do the Italian men really pinch?"

I am shocked at the low level of their questioning.

"You haven't been to Italy?"

"Only London and Paris," Peter says. "Rome is next. If the Italian men really pinch, that is." He grins at Mimi, who playfully slaps his thigh.

"Some pinch and some don't," I answer in my most world-weary voice, debating whether to tell them about Aldo. I decide not to. The last person I told was Kit Rockwell. "Arlyn," she had snorted, "not you too. It's like seeing the Sistine Chapel and throwing a coin in the fountain. The obligatory Italian lover."

"Well, no dago Don Juan is going to pinch my wife," Peter is saying in his toughest Robert Mitchum voice, paus-ing a beat for effect, "or she'll turn around and let him have what-for."

The laughter subsides and the car grows quiet. Gigi, as they call the little Peugeot, is making good time but the traffic is heavier now. Peter hunches into the steering wheel, concentrating on the driving, and Mimi slides over and leans lightly on his right shoulder, her hand on his thigh. Every so often she runs her fingers languorously up and down the length of it, squeezing his knee, scratching a long polished fingernail along the grain of the cord trousers. When I see couples like this I envy their intimacy. When you come down to it, for all the bickering jokes, they do seem to be good for each other.

Allan and I were good for each other too. Or so I thought then. This is what the expression "I must pinch myself to make sure I'm awake" means, I used to think when we would lie together. Here is the answer to all my dreams lying right here next to me. Even near the end I felt that.

Sometimes it's hard to remember the good part of it, the early days of that miraculous first summer, the long full Sundays at Jones Beach, the magical nights at Lewisohn Stadium, discovering those Czech and Hungarian restaurants, cuddling in his room in that old lady's apartment on 110th Street. Mostly now all I remember is the end, my terrible outbursts and tears, an endless supply it seems, and his stony silences except those words, spoken and repeated in that carefully rehearsed tone: "Arlyn, this has nothing to do with you. But I have to get away, to sort out my thoughts, to be alone. I want you to keep the ring and if you want to I would like you to wait. I'll keep in touch. I think I'll only need a few months. If we marry now I'll always regret not getting away for a while."

Mom was the worst part of it. Friends, people at the office, they were easy to handle. "I broke my engagement. It's over. Allan and I decided not to get married. He wanted me to keep the ring but I gave it back." But Mom. That was something else. *You'll be alone. You're already the only one in your whole high school class and practically the only one of your college friends without children or a husband. It's not good. To be alone.*

Dad was better and once he got used to the idea of Europe he began to see it as a good idea: *See the world, it's a good idea. Then after a year you come back and I'll find you a nice job right here.* Poor Daddy. He never did understand me, my need to leave the city he loved so much, the city where he always delivered practically the whole ward to the Democrats, even in 1952.

My head smacks against the inside of the car door. Bright lights flood a huge parking lot. Peter moves the car into a space and Mimi turns smiling to watch me straighten out. I am stiff, a tall girl doubled over in a small car.

"You slept," she says. "I dozed a little too. Poor Peter, he wasn't able to sleep much. He had to wake himself every so often to make sure he was still on the Expressway."

"A fitful sleep," Peter intones, now an old man with a wizened voice.

I wonder how long I slept and if Allan's presence would be hovering over me the entire weekend. Go away, Allan, it's not fair. It's not fair that every time I'm with a happily married young couple I ache to be married to you.

The next minutes are spent in the rush for the ferry, arms loaded with suitcases, garment bags and packages of meat on ice. Peter disappears and returns to the ferry with a carton of carefully packed groceries. Mimi looks into the box and raises her eyes to meet Peter's, which have been waiting expectantly. She nods approval. Everything he had ordered is as it should be.

5

Following Bob Mann across the large, airy living room onto the wooden deck, I see only his stick legs. He is wearing a white tunic that reaches to his knees, a tunic of the finest cotton, he told me, that he bought in Indonesia.

The sky is brilliant, a dazzling blue this morning, and the sea is calm. Mimi is stretched on a chaise pointed in the direction of the rising sun. She is facing us. As we approach, a couple sitting at a large, white pedestal table laughs at something Mimi has just said as they turn to watch us. It is Ed Hart and Janet Dugan. He is a compact, fiftyish little man. I sit down between them.

Next to me Janet Dugan is magnificent in brief white shorts and an orange halter. Suddenly I am aware of women being younger than I am. Both Mimi and I are over twenty-five and here's Janet only twenty-one, if that. Her bursting ripeness rudely confronts us. How did it happen so fast?

Yesterday Janet was introduced to me as Ed Hart's good friend. Edmund Hidley Hart had been a Foreign Correspondent for The Paper until he was lured away, in Bob's words, by the filthy lucre of N. P. Nyes, the giant public relations firm, an octopus whose arms, in the form of ex-reporters, reached into every newspaper office in town. I had heard the Ed Hart story differently. According to Lowell Abbott, who had worked with him on cityside before the War, Hart's pride was hurt when he was brought home and beached, dumped back into the pool of cityside reporters after years of glamorous posts in the Far East. It was pride and not the money that drove poor Ed into public relations, Lowell told me, adding that though Hart had done a terrible job overseas that was beside the point. "Why did it take them nine years to find out?" Lowell reasoned. "Is that fair to a man?" Perhaps it was this sentiment that made Lowell and the others so receptive to Ed's pitches from his clients no matter how out of left field they were.

Peter enters the deck from a galley kitchen and sets a tray with orange juice, coffee, cream, and fresh strawberries on the table. "Comes ze revolution . . ." he begins, but no one is paying any attention to him.

"Where are the Sunday papers?" I ask, looking around the bare deck.

"Peter has to go for them," Janet says.

"Isn't it time?" Bob asks. "I'm anxious to read the details of that Truman story. Old Harry really lashed out at Kennedy."

"Yes, Peter," Mimi says, "you could go pick up the papers now."

"Yassum, Miz Scarlett, I'se goin'," he answers, shuffling and scratching his head.

"You want company, I feel like a walk," Janet says, standing up and tugging her shorts down over the vagrant curly blond hairs escaping from her crotch.

Ed Hart watches Janet and Peter leave the deck.

"The chassis's still good," he says to Bob in a stage whisper, "but it's almost a hundred thousand miles now, time for a trade-in."

Mimi, to my surprise, remains quiet. I would have expected her to have something to add to Ed's remark.

Bob Mann leaves the table and arranges two lounge chairs so that they face the sun. He plumps the foam-filled pad on one and signals to me to come over and sit next to him. Ed Hart is already face and stomach down on a turquoise air mattress which he has positioned close to Mimi so he can point directly at the sun. Mimi has turned several inches in the last fifteen minutes so that no part of her is in shadow. I stretch out in the chair next to Bob and he winks at me before opening the copy of *Advise and Consent* that he had left under his chair yesterday.

"Bain du Soleil, who's got it?" Ed Hart shouts, jumping up, shattering the now peaceful deck. We all follow Ed's lead and grease up. The deck grows quiet again. The sun is pushing toward eleven o'clock, the easy morning will soon be giving way to midday harshness.

The only sounds I hear are the gulls and the lapping of the waves as they gently wash over the beach below. Mimi and Ed had been talking and laughing in low whispers, but now they are quiet. Surely there's nothing between Ed Hart and Mimi. Just because a man and a woman laugh and joke together, for goodness' sake, doesn't mean they're having an affair. I laugh and joke with married men all the time and I know that most of the time it doesn't mean a thing. Sometimes, of course, the spark is there, but even then usually nothing happens. In my case, at least. Lately. That is my one rule now: No married men. When I do go for dinner or drinks I try to steer the conversation so I can learn his marital status. If he is married, I stop seeing him immediately, no matter how attractive he is. Some girls, I know, think I'm crazy. Married men are the only men around who aren't babies or queer, they say. It's only for laughs. You have to have some fun. And if more comes of it, one friend told me, so be it, that's *her* problem. If she can't hold on to her man, why should you worry? No one ever broke up a happy home, she said, believe me.

No, not them. Not Ed and Mimi. It's too obvious. They're very old friends, Bob said. Ed helped her when she was starting out, got her an assignment for a piece that was a sensation in *Vogue*. At the time, Bob told me yesterday, the word was that either Ed or Peter wrote the piece. "Ridiculous malicious envy," Bob said. "Peter does have a certain style, but between you and me," Bob added, "Peter's features are overrated. He writes like a quiff at times, don't you think?" I didn't know what to answer. I could only imagine what Bob meant by saying Peter wrote like a quiff and I wasn't sure that was all that bad. I thought of Oscar Wilde. As for Ed, Bob said he couldn't write his way out of a paper bag. All his stuff was pasted together on the Foreign Desk. Mimi, Bob assured me, was perfectly capable of writing for the market she reaches. She has that nice light touch, he said, and, as you can see, she lives and breathes fashion.

Mimi and Bob Mann? My heart begins to thump. Is it showing? Am I getting red? Is that it? Is it Mimi and Bob with me as the beard? Friday night only the four of us were in the house. After we fell heavily to sleep, logy from those delicious wurst sandwiches and lulled by the beer and the sea, did Bob awake and steal out of our twin-bedded room to Mimi? But this is silly. I've been seeing too many new-wave films. Pure fantasy.

Bob is dozing. His finely chiseled features look quite handsome in repose. His blond hair glistens in the sunlight as it must have when he was a child. What will today's nap bring?

Yesterday, after a lovely walk on the beach and cocktails and giggles with the others on the deck, we finally made love. I was surprised at the thinness of his legs and arms, spindly really. He looks much better in clothes. He was careful not to pounce, as he put it. But I was so groggy from the sun and sea air that it really didn't matter much. Last night, though, was another story.

After enormous quantities of wine and steak and laughs at dinner—that Mort Sahl routine of Peter's is really very

funny—and dancing to those funky blues records with Ed
Hart, I was extremely excited, fully awake and alive with
anticipation. Wet and wide open, I tried very hard, relaxing
as the books say to do, really trying to lead and guide him
past the barrier reefs to my heaving, lapping shore, to use
an apt metaphor of my own. But it didn't work.

Laughing voices and the rattle of a wagon on the deck's
bare floors startle me. Peter and Janet and another couple
are standing in front of Mimi, a red wagon between them
piled high with Sunday newspapers.

Am I seeing right? What on earth is Teddy Lowe doing
here with his arm around that blond creature? Does he recognize me? I stand up and join the others as we form a semicircle around the newcomers, the Publisher's nephew and,
some say, heir to the entire empire, and his stunning companion.

"Teddy, this is Arlyn . . ."

"Hello, Mr. Lowe."

"Why hello, Arlyn. Arlyn this is Miss Rogers." He pulls
her slightly toward me. "Miss Rogers," he says to her, "this
is Miss . . . uh . . ." His cheeks are very red. Sunburn? Embarrassment? Anger?

"Crane," I answer, "Arlyn Crane." I extend my hand to
Miss Rogers. "Hi," I say, "haven't we met somewhere before? You look familiar."

Miss Rogers' neck seems to tighten as she answers. "I
don't think so," she says as she smiles stiffly and shakes her
head from side to side.

I suppose she's right. How could you not remember
where you met someone as ravishing as this. I probably saw
her in a movie or play or advertisement. She must be a
Hollywood starlet.

There is a lot of loud chatter on the deck. Theodore
Henry Lowe looks terribly uncomfortable. It is definitely
embarrassment that has made his cheeks so red. After a few
strained pleasantries he announces that they have to be on
their way.

"But you can't leave now," Peter says, emerging from the kitchen with a large pitcher of martinis. "You must sample my secret recipe." Peter raises his eyebrows and lowers his voice. "I got it from a sailor in Singapore. It is guaranteed to put hair on your chest." He leans close to Miss Rogers and leers. "You bet your life it will."

Teddy Lowe, as he is known throughout The Paper by one and all, makes an effort to laugh and appear relaxed but he seems tense. "Really sorry," he says, "but we have to run. Miss Rogers is the cousin of an old school friend, you know, and he asked me to pick her up on my way over to his place for lunch."

Miss Rogers has struck a carefree pose, trying, it seems, to avoid, at whatever cost, eye contact with me. No matter how I maneuver around the deck she is always one step ahead of me, averting her big, blue eyes. She looks as though she's hanging on Teddy Lowe's every word, but when he crooks his elbow toward her it takes her a couple of seconds to figure out what he's doing and for her to slip her arm through his and follow him off the deck. Teddy Lowe has refused Peter's offer to be led back to the dock. "We'll find it," he calls as they hurry through the living room.

As I watch them I am positive that I have met Miss Rogers before. Logic tells me that it was at some party or other, some similar situation where we were each with dates who spoke and introduced us briefly. Yet somehow I have a nagging feeling that it was more than that, that I know Miss Rogers better than that and, more puzzling, that she knows me.

As soon as it is determined that Teddy Lowe is out of earshot everyone begins talking at once.

"He really gets the crème de la crème, doesn't he," says Bob Mann. "Nothing but the best for Teddy Lowe."

"Wonder how much something like that costs?" Peter muses.

"Did you see that body?" asks Ed Hart. "Prime. Absolutely top-dollar prime." I look at Janet but she doesn't seem to have heard Ed's remark.

"Those gold thongs," she is saying, "are thirty dollars at Saks. I saw them there the other day."

"And did you see how those pants fit her? It looked like she had nothing on underneath. She must have been poured into them. One fluid white line to her ankles," Mimi says before turning abruptly to her husband.

"Peter, how did you ever get him to come back here with you? He seemed sorry the minute he got here."

"I tried to get him to come for dinner but he couldn't. They're off a boat and meeting another one about three. I thought he'd stay for lunch but something made him change his mind."

"Where did you meet him? Tell us about it." Bob Mann is sitting on the arm of the chaise. He pours himself a martini before passing the pitcher around.

"They were in front of the store. They seemed to be at loose ends, waiting for another boat. I suspect they left the first one on impulse. Apparently there's a three-day blast on one of those big corporate yachts and they're joining it."

"I heard the Rheingold Yacht is in the water around here," Janet says.

Peter continues. "At first he seemed a bit uneasy, but after we made a few jokes he seemed to relax a bit. Right, Janet?"

Janet nods. "They were just killing time until the next boat came. They had their gear at the dock. He seemed delighted to be invited to lunch."

"Maybe when he saw me he changed his mind," I say.

"You? Why you?"

"Aha, holding back on us, Arlyn?" It is Mimi looking at me with renewed interest.

"A spot of intrigue?" Peter asks, arching his eyebrows.

"I knew him when I worked in the Publisher's Suite. I knew the whole family." I say it in such a way that it is clear I am perfectly willing to tell all the Teddy Lowe stories I know. But there are no takers. They must know as much, if not more, office gossip as I do. Or so they think. The discussion about Teddy Lowe has ended. There is a mad scramble for the papers.

"Gawd, can this Eugenia Sheppard woman write!" Mimi announces to no one in particular. I am amused. Bob had told me that Mimi is being spoken of as the new Eugenia Sheppard.

The papers are all very skimpy today, as they usually are on the day before a holiday when all business is shut down. The newshole shrinks to almost nothing on days when the big department stores don't advertise.

"Shit," says Peter, his head deep into the main news section of The Paper. "They really cut me to shreds." He had been eager to see how they played a feature he had written on Friday about the wedding of two dancers from *Bye Bye Birdie*. Rock 'n' Roll replaced Mendelssohn in the ceremony.

"They must have needed the space for the Gene Fowler obit," Bob says, looking over Peter's shoulder. "Runs almost two columns. But you read fine, everything's there, you're just sensitive about your precious prose."

"Poor judgment on the desk's part," Peter continues. "There's plenty of fat they could have cut out of this paper before touching my story. Here, look at this, a whole half column . . ."

Peter is not as annoyed as he would have us believe. He is, after all, talking about a story of his in The Paper today. He is affecting a particular kind of newsman's crybaby style. Would that I had such problems, to be complaining about a couple of paragraphs cut here or there. As he talks I have pangs of regret. All Thursday night I could hardly sleep thinking about doing a sermon, going to a church today then returning to the office to write it, and late tonight waiting at the newsstand on Eighty-sixth Street and Third Avenue for the City Edition and, right there, doing what Peter has just done: ignoring everything else and searching The Paper for my story.

When Paddy O'Connell had told me on Friday morning that he had no sermon assignment for me this weekend I had mixed feelings. It solved the problem of what to do about Bob Mann's invitation, but after the high of Thursday's fantasizing, it was a letdown.

The Boss, as Paddy calls the City Editor, had said I could be used only if none of the fellows was available. Paddy shrugged and held out little hope for me. When I think about it I feel saddened. It was such a lovely fantasy.

Ed Hart is telling Peter about the Floyd Patterson–Ingemar Johansson fight last week. "Were you at the Polo Grounds?" Peter asks.

"No," Hart answers, "but I know Floyd's problem. If he hesitates, the jig is up."

Everyone laughs but me. I hate remarks like that no matter how clever they are. Like all the jokes about the new President of the Congo and potboilers and Eichmann.

Bob Mann begins to read aloud from Walt Walton's column about why Kennedy invited those Negro leaders to lunch last week. Walton has some particularly pungent things to say about it and Walt's windy words of wisdom are always good for a laugh. But Peter breaks in.

"That's the lunch that Ernestine Herbert was bitching so much about," he says and everyone wants to hear why Ernestine Herbert was bitching.

"She had it all set up to spend the day at home with Kennedy, Jackie, and the kid," Peter tells us, reaching over for the almost empty martini pitcher. "She even had that new hotshot photographer Corso relieved from some special assignment to go along to do the pictures. She had to pull a lot of strings for that, more than her usual amount of whining and nagging until the picture desk finally gave in. And then she got bumped when Kennedy decided to invite the spooks to lunch. She was really having a fit. Didn't you hear her ranting all over the city room?" He looks at Bob Mann, who doesn't seem to register the incident. "That new guy,

Hallam? Weren't you there? He finally took her out for a drink. He practically had to lasso her."

I am not surprised by the squishy warmth that floods through me at the mention of Hallam's name. I feel again his eyes on me from the other side of the city room. How could that have been my imagination?

"A Southern gentleman to the hilt," Bob is saying, "either that or he wanted to pump her."

"It must have been to pump her," Peter says. "Who would want to hilt Ernestine Herbert? Or pump her, for that matter." His leer is expected and unfunny. "But seriously," Peter continues, "why would he want to pump her? He's supposed to have tight connections with the Senator and the whole Kennedy camp. Isn't that why they hired him?"

"With Senator Kennedy? I never heard that." Bob Mann looks crushed. "I heard he was hired because of his Southern perspective, his know-how about the sit-ins and all that."

"Well, whatever," Peter says. "He seems to have the brass snowed."

"Whoever are you talking about?" Mimi asks.

"Just another new star hired to glitter in the firmament of the Washington Bureau," her husband answers. "Up here for orientation. He hasn't actually started yet, he was just in the office chewing the fat the other day when Queen Bitch Ernestine blew her fuse. Time will tell if he's really first class but my own suspicions are they've been had again." He looks at Bob Mann.

"I can understand Ernestine's being upset," Bob says pointedly, ignoring Peter's comment about W. B. Hallam, "but she should be enough of a newspaperman to take it without carrying on like that. Besides, what did she expect? She may do that luncheon-at-home drivel better than anyone else, but it's still drivel. It's okay in its place but it should never take the place of hard news."

"How the hell does she ever get herself off the Women's

Page anyway?" Peter asks. "That's where that stuff belongs. It burns me up when I see one of her soufflés in the news columns. It's a dangerous trend."

"Why does she upset you so?" Ed Hart asks slyly.

"She doesn't upset me, for Christ's sake, I feel sorry for her. She pushes so much because she's got nothing else. You know what she needs."

"I wonder," Bob grins. "Did you ever think she could be a les?"

"That's right," Janet Dugan says. "I heard you can't tell by looking. Some of the most feminine girls are like that." She giggles and the others join in.

The first time I heard remarks about Ernestine Herbert being a lesbian who didn't like men I was shocked. She certainly didn't look or seem like one of those women to me.

Janet sails the Real Estate section onto Peter's lap, where it lands with a thud. "No digs of interest this week," she says. "Enough of this shoptalk. Who's for a dip before lunch?" She jumps up and leads the way down the ladder to the beach, dropping her white shorts and revealing an orange bathing suit bottom to match the halter.

If I were a man I would choose Janet's healthy exuberance over the China doll perfection of a Miss Rogers any day. Miss Rogers looks as if she would break. It's possible I think this because I identify my own looks more with Janet's than with Miss Rogers'. Not that I think I'm as spectacular-looking as Janet Dugan. But I do hold my own. Janet, of course, has a great body, but my long legs and height mask the rest of my imperfections and though I don't have her tawny golden color I do tan nicely in a way that complements my brown hair and highlights, I think, my straight white teeth. At least I don't peel.

6

Gil Gilchrist is humming and I am banging my typewriter keys as hard as I can to drown him out. Da de, da dum, da de da dum da dum. Can a hum be smug? In goes another set of copybooks. Clack-clack. Clack-clack. His two stubby fingers stab at the keys of the big, black machine. When the offices were redecorated, as the story is told, and the wooden desks with the green linoleum tops and pre-War typewriters were replaced with the gunmetal-gray steel desks and lightweight pastel typewriters like the one I can only raise a rickety tinny sound on, Gil Gilchrist had kept his Underwood.

"What a brouhaha," Jean Blake told me. "He went right to the Publisher himself."

Jean had been around The Paper forever herself and probably had a story, but it was Gil's that was a favorite. He had come to work for The Paper in the business department when he was fifteen years old at a time when The Paper filled its ranks of office boys with the best and brightest from the neighboring slums. One muggy night in the summer of 1937, the story goes, the Old Publisher's limousine, en route to a shipboard bon voyage party, broke down just on the other side of Tenth Avenue. When the chauffeur went for help, a crowd gathered around the long, black automobile. Young Gilchrist, lounging on a stoop, sized up the situation immediately and rushed to the stalled Packard, where he posted himself, keeping his friends and neighbors back beyond an invisible line. "It's the Boss," he had said, "I don't want you should crowd him."

Young Gil, as he tells it now, respectfully refrained from looking at the comely, chiffoned blonde sitting next to the Old Publisher. Gil had heard that what's-her-name, Julietta something-or-other, that dame who sang high on the "Sunday Coffee Hour," was playing footsie with the old man on the q.t. "I knew," he says now, "that an incident, no matter how trifling, might have made the other papers and been an embarrassment to the Old Publisher, who was known for his high standards of morality." That's true. I have heard many times how all first drafts of editorials dealing with public and private virtues that appeared in The Paper so frequently then were written by him.

Gil, as he says, did yeoman service that night and held the crowd at bay. The chauffeur soon arrived with a taxi and a mechanic and the Old Publisher was on his way with his tootsie undisclosed. So, it turned out, was Gil Gilchrist. Such foresight, no matter how intuitive, did not go unrewarded. Of course Gil had not been so self-effacing as to refrain from identifying himself to the Old Publisher, while carefully averting his eyes from the singer. The next day, when he was personally thanked in the Old Publisher's oak-paneled office, he was asked if he was happy on The Paper.

"Well, to tell you the truth," said young Joseph Timothy Gilchrist, "I always wanted to try my hand at reporting."

"Excellent choice," said the Old Publisher, and that afternoon Gilchrist was at the East Side Police Shack learning the ropes. So was J. T. Gilchrist, the Bane of Broadway, born.

Da de, da dum, da de da dum da dum. Gilchrist has a story he loves and he is at one with his typewriter. He has read me his lead and I disagree with him that it definitely is a front-page story: "The musical *Camelot* is reported to be coming to Broadway next season with the largest budget and projected gross in theater history."

"Who cares?"

Gil was all aquiver. "Exclusive. I got it exclusive. No one has it yet."

"I'm sure I read it before."

"Not about *Camelot*," he hissed.

Now Ashley is badgering him for a summary. Gil resents this, all this newfangled gimmickry. "Let them read the story," he says. "If you let me alone for five minutes, you could have the whole story for the four o'clock conference, Ash, and you wouldn't need a cockamamie summary in your hot little hand."

"Gil," Ashley says wearily, "they need it for the syndicate, too. It could go out on the wires. It would be in papers all over the country."

J. T. Gilchrist throws Ashley his most withering look and continues typing. He couldn't care less about the syndicate or the rest of the country. Since becoming a Broadway reporter in 1941 he wrote for a constituency that was bordered by Fifty-seventh Street on the north, Thirty-fourth Street on the south, Ninth Avenue to the west, and Sutton Place to the east. What happened beyond those borders was of no interest to him or his readers, he thought. Their world and his revolved around the Broadway theaters and the actors, writers, producers, directors, and occasional lighting genius or costume wizard who make it all work.

Ashley picks up the typed copy piling up next to Gil. He scans it and then throws the top book of paper and carbon to me. "Do me a favor, Arlyn. Type it up as a summary. Fast. I'm already late." He walks away toward the men's locker room.

I copy the first three paragraphs of Gil's story, editing as I go. I am not as surprised at the loose grammar and careless syntax in the raw copy of most of the old-timers, and not a few of the younger reporters, as I used to be. Somehow I had had this crazy notion that everyone who wrote for The Paper was well educated and familiar with the minimum standards of good grammar. In the same way I had also thought that everything in The Paper was true and that any errors of fact were inadvertent.

But a reporter for The Paper does not have to have perfect grammar any more, say, than he has to be scrupulously accurate about his facts. A lot of people would argue with me about the latter saying that was the one thing The Paper insisted on: absolute honesty. That may be true but I happen to know that it doesn't always work that way. And I'm not talking about the so-called gray areas where truth is difficult to determine and often is viewed as a matter of opinion. I'm talking about out-and-out deceit.

I was only in this job a short time when a junior drama reporter came to me late one afternoon, his red hair flying, his freckled face glistening as he waved sheets of paper at me. The Drama Department secretary, he told me, had gone home early and he needed my help. He was on his way to the weekly cultural meeting with a feature he had just written about a man named Sparky, who, it was said, had changed more light bulbs on Broadway marquees than any other light-bulb changer on the Great White Way. The lead of the story announced an award to this man for his yeoman service to the theater.

"I can't get Lew James on the phone," the junior drama reporter said to me, tossing a sheaf of papers on my typewriter. "Do me a favor and keep trying till you get him. Tell him they wouldn't buy the story as it was, that the only way we can make it news is if this guy gets an award. Read him my lead and tell him to set up an award and get a press release out to back up my story."

The story not only ran, it ran on the much-sought-after

Second Front Page, with three pictures and a splashy feature headline. Two of the pictures showed very clearly the marquee of a big musical that was beginning to lose business. This surely would pump some new life into it. What a coup for Lew James, truly the Press Agent's Press Agent. And, in addition to obliging Lew James, the junior drama reporter added a feather to his own cap. He won a Feature of the Month Award.

Some people, of course, were outraged by the story, especially those who knew the background. When Moe Greenside found out about it, he blew his stack. But it was too late. He had already gone home when the piece was sent to the copyreader, where it was edited for the next day's paper.

A whole army of copyreaders sits at the ready to render unto The Paper's style those things that are suitable for The Paper to publish and The Paper's readers to read. At this very moment Moe Greenside is hanging over Lowell Abbott's desk trying to negotiate the most delicate way to tell the readers about rumors of a scandal brewing in the art world over the possibility that outsized penises on the terracotta Etruscan warriors at the Museum may be a reflection of some turn-of-the-century archeologist's own wit, mistake, deception, or outright envy. Needless to say, a lot of important people are shaken and there is much consternation. The Museum, like The Paper, has a reputation for infallibility.

Greenside was a copyreader before he was singled out and elevated like so many other copyreaders before him, men who can be seen each day at the beginning of their shift staking out their allotted space on the horseshoe-shaped copy desks with their precisely sharpened pencils and their cigarettes and/or Life Savers (many are trying not to smoke) and their chewing gum and antacid tablets. All copy will flow through their hands and under their rigorous scrutiny on its way from the reporter's typewriters to the composing room upstairs where it will be set into type.

Greenside symbolizes one of the complaints many people have against The Paper's dogged insistence on uniformity and on its refusal to move with the times and fill its columns with lighter, brighter, more individualized stories. This may well be true, but personally I fall into the large camp around here of those who swear allegiance to Moe Greenside. He is warm and friendly and fair-minded and he has been nice to me. And when you come down to it, that's what really counts.

I yank the summary I have just typed out of the typewriter and toss it on Ashley's desk. Then I pick up my purse and head for the Ladies Lounge. Bob Mann had called earlier and asked me to have a drink with him at the Theater Bar. Yesterday, the first day back after the weekend, he was out on a story most of the day and I didn't see him. He phoned me last night and we chatted briefly. Apparently I passed his test. Mimi and Peter approve of me. They like my style. They want us out again this coming weekend. There's a big party at a house up the beach. I told him I wasn't sure.

I'm still hoping that Paddy O'Connell will have a sermon for me this Sunday. I checked around and a lot of the fellows are itchy to bug out of doing sermons for the summer. "Kills the whole weekend," one guy told me.

Also, I've been thinking and I really must end it with Bob once and for all. My first instincts, as usual, were right. Driving back from the weekend I realized that he really was a bore. But what killed me was the way I had acted; because I didn't want to make trouble or spoil the weekend I held my tongue and then afterward I felt soiled. How could I have let him make all those jokes about Negroes and Africans and Helen Keller and not say anything?

And if that wasn't enough, there really isn't any chemistry between us anyway. When you get down to it, he just doesn't appeal to me. He's one of those guys who looks good as long as he's dressed. In his case, clothes do make the man. I made up a little joke about this: Tripped up again by

F. R. Tripler. But the joke's on me, winning that old battle again.

Ernestine Herbert is standing with her back to the full-length mirror in the Ladies Lounge, pulling on white kid opera-length gloves and surveying her rear image in the mirror. Her dark, mahogany-tinted hair is fashioned in an elegant upsweep, revealing her patrician brow and strong profile. A pale green, off-the-shoulder tulle cocktail dress falls gracefully over her long body. She is twisting around to check the back of her dyed-to-match pale green opera pumps. Everything passes muster and she gingerly removes the gloves and slides them into a long, skinny plastic bag. They fit perfectly. She removes the silk shoes and slides each one into its own plastic bag. All the plastic bags fit neatly into a small round model's case.

"Big do tonight?"

"Yaw," Ernestine answers while working at the zipper of the model's case. It is stuck midway. "Late in the season for the real people," she continues, finally getting the zipper to move, "but everything goes haywire in an election year. It's a Kennedy fund-raiser, way out on the Island."

"One of those hundred-dollar-a-plate things?"

"Something like that. Twenty-five, I think." Ernestine slips into her black leather I. Miller pumps. "This one is for contributors of over five thousand dollars and workers. It's not really for the money, you know, but it gives the workers a chance to rub with glamour and it gets them charged up for the fight. Much like the ancient practice of rubbing sacrificial blood on the warriors. Only this is caviar—red, I'm sure."

I laugh at the image. She is really quite clever.

"Well, once more into the breach," Ernestine says, throwing a dirty raincoat over the tulle dress, picking up her purse and suitcase and notebook, and leaving the Ladies Lounge.

Walking through the city room toward the back door I sense the eyes on me. It is true what they say about eyes burning into one's back. I can feel it now. And I can feel who the person is. I turn and see W. B. Hallam, as I knew I would. He is talking to Harvey Kassell but his eyes are on me.

As I approach the rear of the city room Bob Mann leaves his desk and walks to the aisle, falling in step with me. At the northeast corner we turn and push through the fire door and start down the back stairs. Immediately he pushes me up against the wall and presses his body to mine. "Not here," I say, pushing him away and hating myself for even continuing down the stairs with him. I must tell him that I can't see him again. But not now. Why make a scene? It would be foolish.

In the Theater Bar his hand slides up my thigh, pushing away the slippery nylon pleated skirt of my dress. Is he crazy? I shift my leg. His hand moves into my lap. I gently lift it back to his lap. This has happened to me before. Just because I go to bed with someone they act as though they own me, that any time and any place they can paw and maul me.

I nurse my whiskey sour, sucking on the orange wedge and planning the words I will use to tell him I will not go away with him. He is rattling on about some story he just heard about this former newspaperman at N. P. Nyes who found a whore who does backbends from a barstool. He had her put on as a temporary secretary for one of the most straitlaced old bastards left at Nyes. To everyone's surprise she could type and spell and perform all the secretarial functions quite well and stayed for the entire three-week period.

When he finishes I begin abruptly. "I won't be able to go with you this weekend," I say. "I have my name on the sermon roster and I hope to be called." Why go into any other reason? That would be too hurtful to him and unnecessary.

I can't believe his response. He leans back against the fake zebra banquette and laughs. Then he reaches out and runs the outside of his index finger down the side of my face to my throat. "Sermons. You? You have other talents, m'dear. You should spend Sunday morning in bed with someone who cares."

Shit! Why did I tell him about the sermons before I got to do one? Ever since I spoke to Paddy O'Connell my mind has been leapfrogging from sermons to other, better and bigger stories, some features, a promotion to reporter, awards. It makes the Lexington IRT almost pleasant in the mornings. And now Mr. Wrong here has brought me back to reality. A waste of my time, he is saying. "It's a long way, Arlyn, from sermons to cityside."

Thank God, Lennie Morse walks over to us. Tears are welling in my eyes, a combination of hurt and anger. But that would be silly, to cry over a remark like that no matter what the reason. Morse nods hello to me though we've never met. He's new on The Paper.

"Bob," he says, "do you have the private number of Senator Humphrey's man? Someone said you two hit it off when the Senator was on that fact-finding tour of Asia last year."

"My book's locked in my desk," Bob says, standing up and throwing some money on the table. "Come on, I'll get it for you." He looks at me, indicating I should rise.

The three of us leave the Theater Bar and cross the street to walk around to the front of the building. We can go down the back stairs but we will have to go up the front elevators. I feel squeezed by the two men talking across my face.

In the elevator I'm pressed against Lennie Morse. He's really very attractive, tall and balding in a sexy way, and I'm enjoying the feel of his hard muscular body against mine. I look up and find his eyes on me. Somewhere in midair, floating above that long, fraught-with-yearning look between us, the words "too bad," encircled by a neon wedding band, flash a warning. His wife, I heard, is expecting again, for the third time, and they have just bought a house in New Rochelle.

Inside the city room I peel off to walk up the narrow corridor that leads to the Cultural News Department. I turn the corner, and before my eyes can focus, on anything I know something big has happened. I can feel it: the noisy, clacking, late-afternoon rhythms have been replaced by an eerie silence; clumps of people stand talking to each other in hushed tones. I move quickly toward my desk.

"*Arlyn!* For Christ's sake, where the hell have you been?" It is Ashley, his jacket off, his tie loosened, his shirtsleeves rolled up. He is standing with the telephone in his hand. He covers the mouthpiece and calls out to me: "Randolph had a heart attack. We're trying to locate Betty." He returns to his telephone conversation.

Randolph Thoburn? I turn to Gil Gilchrist for an explanation. His blue eyes are merry.

"He's over at the Astor. Our esteemed Drama Critic is caught in the last act, so to speak."

"What?"

Tony Weather walks over to stand in front of me. He strums an imaginary guitar on his chest. He croons, "He's dying in the saddle at the Astor Hotel."

"Tony!" Gil snaps.

"What a way to go," says Tony. "Old Hotpants, himself. Damon and Lowell just ran over with Broadway Maxie."

I am confused. Tony lowers his voice and mutters to Gil, "He died with his hard on."

I ignore the remark. My head is spinning. Broadway Maxie, the seedy little aging wire room telegrapher. What does he have to do with elegant, refined Thomas Randolph Thoburn?

Ashley slams the telephone receiver back into its cradle and calls out, "The ambulance is on its way. I sent John Campbell over to the precinct so he could cover from there if it gets sticky, if there was any foul play or anything that makes it more than a routine police matter. Did you reach Betty yet, Arlyn?"

"No, I was just finding out what happened to Randolph. Shouldn't I wait to call her? What can she do from Nyack anyway, and with her poor health, you know, shouldn't we wait until he gets to the hospital and see what the doctors say?"

"Good thinking," Ashley says. "Whatever happens, she'll be a mess."

"Should I go over to the hospital and talk to the doctors? Then I can give Betty a firsthand report."

"It's more than that," Ashley says. "You know where he was?"

"Yes."

"Well, aside from Betty's feelings, it will be difficult if this gets talked about around town. You know how the Publisher hates scandal. Better have the ambulance doctor call me as soon as they arrive at the hospital. I told Lowell and Damon to take care of the driver and the attendant, but I want to talk to the doctor myself."

I pick up the phone.

"Wait, here's Lowell," Ashley says, "let's see what he has to say."

Lowell is breathless and coughing hard. A crowd gathers around him.

"Lordy, that was a mess. She's only a little birdlike woman and he was sprawled across her, all two hundred pounds of him. Good thing we took Maxie with us. He'll get them to keep it quiet." Lowell looks at Ashley.

"Did you talk to the ambulance attendant and doctors?" There is an impatient tone to Ashley's question.

"Eh, what? I don't know. It all happened so fast." Lowell stops to light a cigarette with shaking fingers. "They got him off her and onto a stretcher and the doctor said minutes were precious, that it all hung on a thread, if Randolph would live, that is. Damon and Maxie went along to the hospital. Maxie said he knew the admitting clerk. I helped that poor woman sit up, she was stiff, and I waited until she got dressed."

"Who was she?" Gilchrist asks.

James Lowell Abbott III looks down his long, patrician nose at Gil. "I wouldn't know."

"He juggles two or three," Gilchrist says. "One comes in from Iowa every year for her vacation and he clears the decks for her. He met her through that 'You Can Write Prose for Money Correspondence School' he's connected with. One of his students. I wonder if it was her. It's about the right time of year."

"Poor Betty," Lowell says, "what about her? Anybody call her?"

"Poor Betty, my foot," says Tony Weather with unusual venom in his voice. "You do have to sympathize with him, having a wife like that. A bitch on wheels, except when she's on one of her benders. It hasn't been easy for him, even I got to admit that."

"She was a real beauty, too," says Gilchrist. "Didn't seem like such a nut case then, but you never know. She was crazy about him, I tell you. And he was crazy about her, too."

Ashley had left the group to go back to his desk to answer his phone. He returns now, wiping perspiration from his face with a large handkerchief. In the midst of all the excitement I realize that Ashley is more alive than I have ever seen him, his long face, usually dry and scaly, is glowing now. It somehow makes him seem younger and more attractive than I would ever have imagined. For the first time all the stories I have heard about how great he was on the City Desk make sense.

"Arlyn," he barks, "when you locate Betty tell her to get to the hospital as soon as possible. The next few hours are crucial and they want her there."

I pick up the phone and dial. There is no answer in either Nyack or their city apartment. "She must be on her way in," I say. "Was she coming in to go to that off-Broadway opening with him tonight?"

"She loathes off-Broadway," Gil says. "She's probably coming in to see one of her doctors."

Ashley gets my attention. "I'm going out front. Keep trying her. Boy, he really complicated things this time."

What is Ashley talking about? I turn to face the others just in time to catch the look that passes between Lowell and Gil. I recognize that look. Something not too clean is in the works. In my brief time on the news floor I have learned to recognize the look that two people exchange when they are going to talk about the dirty deal a third just got.

Tony Weather, lounging in his chair, drumming his fingers on his desk, is the one to blurt it out.

"The bastards! Can't wait until the body's cold to talk about it."

"I thought you hated Randolph."

"Hate him? That's childish, Arlyn. We have had our differences, but let bygones be bygones. He's a human being, for Christ's sake, hanging on for dear life, and all these vultures care about is their own Machiavellian plots."

"I don't understand."

"You tell her," Tony says to Gil. "I'm afraid if I do I'll lose control."

"I don't know nothin' but what I read in the papers," says Gil, rolling his chair back to his desk and picking up his telephone.

Gil's ability to keep his nose clean and stay out of the way of each new power group that forms and reforms on The Paper earns him a grudging respect. Everybody talks to him, nobody trusts him.

Lowell rides his chair over close to me and leans forward.

"I guess you didn't hear yet, I only heard late yesterday. The poop is that Randolph was to be axed at the end of next season. His heart attack is exactly one year too early. Roger Glickston won't be available until the beginning of next summer when his teaching year at Oxford is up. The plan was for Glickston to do the European scene during the summer and take up the job officially in September. Randolph's poor timing throws everything off."

Am I hearing things? Is this for real? What's going on

here? "I guess this is what brought on his heart attack," I say, my anger mounting.

"I doubt if he knows," Lowell answers.

"You doubt if he knows?" I can feel my face heating up. "If you know and Gil knows and Tony knows and now I know, how can he not know?"

"Take it easy, Arlyn," Lowell says touching my arm. "For one thing, he doesn't want to know. And it's still only a rumor."

"That's right," Tony says. "Nothing is for sure until it happens. Until you read it in the papers. Look at Ashley. Slated for City Editor all those years and then when the time came they did this whole reorganization thing, squeezing him away from the City Desk completely and dumping him back here."

"How can you call it dumping, it's such an important part of The Paper," I say, "and if it's true, what you say, why did he agree to come?"

Lowell has gotten up and walked back to his desk, saying, "Is that my phone?" as he goes. Phones are ringing all over the department. One may be his.

"You don't know about Lowell either, do you?" asks Tony, rolling his chair to the spot beside me that Lowell has just vacated.

"What about Lowell?

Gil interrupts, calling from his desk, where, though holding a telephone receiver to his ear, he has obviously been tuned in to my conversations with Lowell and Tony.

"How could they make a man like Lowell a Cultural Director?" he asks. "How would it look?"

"You know he's a fagola, don't you?" Tony says to me, lowering his voice.

"So?"

"So," Tony continues, "be that as it may, he happens to be a damn good newspaperman, one of the best. You know that."

I agree.

"And he's respected up and down the art and museum world, the way he built up that beat. When they reorganized and threw us all together here in, you should excuse the expression, Culture"—Tony spits out the word with distaste—"Lowell was the logical choice to be top man, except for Gil, who didn't want it. Lowell was next in line in senority. Only, how can you make a fairy your top editor, even if it's culture?"

"What's that got to do with Ashley?" I ask, though I am beginning to see the connection.

"They were looking for a place to put Ashley away and they came up with the perfect solution," Tony says, shifting his eyes toward the corridor that leads to the City Desk. "They wanted to make room out front for Harry Hotshot."

Now I am confused. I know that Harry Hotshot, so called, is on the rise outside as Editor in Charge of Special Projects while waiting in the wings, everyone says, but I never connected him with Ashley's being Cultural News Director. Machiavellian indeed! It's positively Byzantine.

Tony Weather looks at the clock. It is almost six-thirty. He gets up and strolls to the men's locker room. I pick up the phone again to try Betty's numbers. No answer at either place. I close up my desk and reach for the *Journal-American*. What's Dorothy Kilgallen up to now? A lot of people make fun of her. Bob Mann calls her the chinless wonder, but I kind of like her. The tough way she goes after a story and damn the consequences. She's the closest thing around to Brenda Starr.

Sometimes I fantasize that I'm the only one around when a big story breaks. Every once in a while *Overset* runs a piece about this or that wire room employee or night rewrite man heroically getting a story into the paper that might otherwise not be printed until the next edition or next day.

Tony returns wearing his jacket. A short, round man, he's another one who looks better in a suit of clothes. His summer-weight cocoa-colored straw hat is tipped back on his head, giving a roguish look to his usual flabby demeanor. But Tony is quiet now. It's as though he checked his ever-flapping tongue in his locker when he reclaimed his jacket. It's quitting time and his eye is on the clock. His bus for Montclair, New Jersey, leaves Port Authority on the hour but he must wait for a good-night from Ashley before he goes. It is only a courtesy now, but one that is observed. There are hardly ever any late-breaking stories in the Cultural News Department that would necessitate all hands remaining on deck until dismissed.

Ashley returns from out front and nods to Tony and Gil, then begins to walk around the Cultural Department saying good-night to reporters sitting at closed, cleaned desks like students in school waiting to be let go. That's what I thought when I first saw this ritual being enacted.

Except for someone here or there typing a story, poring over yellowing newspaper clips from the morgue or talking on the telephone, the Cultural News Department quickly empties in Ashley's wake. My phone rings.

"Bill Hallam here." The voice slides over me. "I'd be most pleased if you'd have dinner with me tonight. Is that possible?"

So soon! Talk about moving fast!

"I can't leave until I complete a phone call. I'm trying now."

"I'll call again in ten minutes." He clicks off.

My hand is shaking as I try Randolph's city number. I am almost sorry when Betty answers. I want to think about what just happened.

"Betty," I say, gathering myself together, "don't be alarmed, but Randolph has been taken to St. Clare's Hospital. He had a heart attack and they want you there. Damon is with him now. Can you get there yourself, or do you want me to come be with you?"

Up until a minute ago I wished I would be needed to accompany Betty to the hospital. Now I dread that Betty will accept my offer.

"Bless you, child," Betty says, "that's very kind of you, but I can take a cab the few blocks myself. I guess it's bad."

"I'm not sure," I lied. "The clerk at the front desk will be waiting for you. Ashley will meet you there. He'll be over soon."

"Thank you, dear." Betty's voice is clear and childlike. "I'm on my way."

I hang up and sit waiting for the call. I look at my bare arm and see the familiar red splotches. The phone rings.

"How about that dinner?"

"Love it."

"What time?"

"Fifteen minutes in the lobby?"

"Perfect."

Ashley is closing up his desk. "Betty's on her way," I call to him. "I told her you'd be there."

"Good. Thanks. See you tomorrow." He turns and disappears into the men's locker room.

7

Lights from the big apartment buildings shine through the trees as the cab curls along the park drive toward the East Side. I am leaning back against the Checker's patched seat, both at ease and excited. I haven't felt this way in a long time. And it hasn't let up all evening, ever since I stepped into the lobby and saw Bill waiting for me, nonchalantly leaning against a marble column, dragging on a cigarette, his eyes tracking the troops of ten-to-sixers filing out of the elevators.

His brief intimate nod and quick turn to guide me out of the crowd and into step with him through the double doors and into a cruising cab were, I thought, just perfect. Even in my most detailed fantasy, I couldn't have planned it better. From that first moment on, as they say in the song, I had been both strangely calm and at the same time never unaware of the intense agitation centered in my crotch.

A moist breeze blowing through the cab's open window is ruffling Bill's thick hair, standing the short, neatly parted sandy-gray hairs on end. What is he thinking as he looks out of the window in this cab that we are sharing as if it were a bed we had just made love in? Instead of physical sparring, though, there has been one long, lusty session of intellectual nudgings and verbal pokings, satisfying in itself and offering a delicious foretaste of possibilities: my job, his job, his likes, my likes, back and forth, all evening, the first, preliminary superficial information lightly stroked back and forth without strain or pretense. Now we are at rest, coming down.

But I am too excited to be totally relaxed. Is this really what I think it is? Is he all that I think he is? So physically attractive that the mere thought of him turns me to jelly. But that's not all. There's the other, too. He seems so good at what he does and so sure of himself. He's a winner. And he's not nasty like so many men. He has sensitivity. A sensitive winner, the magic combination. Or am I reading too much into this? I've done it before.

"When I saw those kids," he had told me, twirling his wineglass, "and realized the full implications of what they were doing, I knew that no matter what this or that Senate Committee recommended, sooner or later they would have to listen. The whole country would have to listen to those kids. And I want to be there."

We were sitting in a noisy Italian restaurant on Forty-sixth Street and he was talking about how covering the sit-ins of those Negro college students last winter had profoundly changed him.

"But I thought you said you would be covering the Senate for The Paper."

"Not exclusively. That's why I wanted to leave the *Journal*. They had me at the Senate and chafed when I roamed afield, doing stories about those kids. They didn't much want that kind of story, especially from one of their Washington people. I gave it too much credence, you see. Anyhow, it was time for me to leave. Ten years and you should push on in this business. I was sliding into a comfortable niche. It was like having an old pair of slippers on my brain.

I was approaching middle age without a fight, almost in my sleep."

"And those student sit-ins woke you up."

"That they did. Even now people don't realize the brilliance and audacity of what they are doing. It's not just lunch counters, Arlyn. It's a way of life. A whole tradition of attitudes is about to be ripped away in the South. And when it happens, I want to be on the scene. They talk about registering all the nigras to vote."

He quickly corrected himself. "I mean Negroes. I personally don't mean any slight by the word, but I know it doesn't sit well up North so I am consciously erasing it from my vocabulary. I'm surprised it slipped back now. You must make me feel down home."

Bill doesn't seem to have the same problem supporting Kennedy that a lot of the reporters around the office have. "Why should the sins of the father be visited on the son?" he had said when I brought up what people were saying about Joseph Kennedy's refusal to come to the aid of Jewish refugees in 1939. As far as I was concerned it wasn't only the sins of the father. What really got me mad was all the steamrolling, all that money and power and buying of elections. And there's where his father came in. Look at what they did to poor Hubert Humphrey in West Virginia, I said. Just look at what Harry Truman said the other day. The Kennedy machine is even too much for him.

Bill agreed there was a lot of dirty stuff there, but politics is a dirty business, he said (he's telling me!), and it would be hard to find a politician as advanced as Humphrey, not to say old Harry himself, who wasn't pretty well sullied by the time he won his first local election.

"That's just the point," I had said. "We all know this, then why do we pretend that these men are saints motivated by altruistic visions of leadership? Why don't we just say what it's all about?"

Bill had tipped his wineglass to me then and said, his eyes dancing over me, "How could someone so beautiful be so cynical?" I felt like exploding. The waiter appeared to again rearrange the plate holding the check and we realized that it was almost eleven o'clock.

We are moving quickly up Fifth Avenue in the Seventies now, while Ella Fitzgerald is Hooraying for Love on the driver's FM radio propped between the meter and the dashboard. I turn to Bill just as he turns to me. We both speak, almost simultaneously. I go first. "Would you like to come up for a drink?"

"I was just going to ask you the same thing," he says. "My hotel's at Eighty-sixth and Madison."

"My place," I say, and Bill agrees.

My place is a renovated studio apartment in Yorkville, a third-floor walk-up.

Once inside the apartment I am surprised to see Bill sit down on the black-cushioned Danish-Modern armchair. With only that chair and the couch to choose from, almost all my dates choose the couch, eager for me to join them there, to begin the wrestling match as soon as politely possible. Every once in a while I am surprised by a Bob Mann pouncing immediately or someone like Bill who takes the chair.

"How about a drink?"

"If you have bourbon, that would be fine and dandy," he says, "with a glass of water, please." He winks. "Got to clean that Eye-talian wine out of my system." I had noticed that except for an occasional folksy or colloquial expression, his speech is pretty much standard American. He seems to play that silky soft twang at will, stretching it to caress, raising it for humorous emphasis, swallowing it for a tough effect.

In the kitchenette I rummage in the cluttered cabinets. "Will Scotch do?"

"Use your bathroom?" he calls. I wonder if he will look in the medicine cabinet. John Campbell was saying the other day that all good reporters do. I hear the toilet flush and the water run and am embarrassed for my thought.

His huge frame fills the tiny opening into the kitchenette.

"I might have expected you didn't know many bourbon drinkers," he laughs, returning to sit on the chair.

"Should I?" I ask, walking toward him with a tray of glasses, a bottle of Scotch, and a bowl of peanuts. "Most of my friends drink Scotch."

Leaning over him I set the tray down on the end table. I look into his eyes, which now are a smoky topaz. "Anyway," I say, surprisingly nervous as I sit down on the couch, "why should I have bourbon? I don't know a lot of Southerners."

His big handsome face breaks into a broad smile. He stretches a long leg out, shoving an enormous cordovan shoe between my pointed patent leather pumps.

"That's a myth that must be destroyed," he says, taking the Scotch and swigging down a big gulp. "Ugh!" He reaches for the water. "Southerners aren't the only bourbon drinkers, it's very popular all over now. Sales are skyrocketing every year. 'Course 'taint the one hundred proof, but what is these days?"

"If I do buy bourbon, what should I buy? Is the proof important?"

Am I talking about bourbon?

"Please don't buy it for me." My stomach crashes. "But if you do," he says after a beat, "I favor one hundred proof, bottled-in-bond Kentucky bourbon, Old Grand-Dad or Old Crow."

Our eyes meet in an electric moment. My groin is tingling, my crotch is wet.

"I knew you'd know." I lift my glass to him. He returns the gesture, winking slowly. Then he changes the pace.

"I had better know, my first job was in the dee-stillery. A mere lad of sixteen, I was."

"A distillery! That must have been fun. What did you do?"

"Ran barefoot over the hops. That's real sour mash." He is laughing.

"I deserved that." My face is burning. "Why should working in a distillery be any more fun than anything else."

"Actually it was fun. I was a summer guide. Starting with the Derby in May, visitors to the area turn up for tours of the distilleries."

He raises his glass to me. "How about you? What were you doing at sixteen?"

"At sixteen I hadn't done anything but baby-sit for the two brats next door. But at seventeen I spent the summer in the County Jail." I wait for his response.

"I do declare." Now his eyes are sparkling and bright. He didn't bite.

"Well, it wasn't exactly the jail, it was the County Treasurer's office"—I say it fast—"in the Court House, right next to the jail. But to me it was like a prison. My father insisted I go on as summer help. It was excruciatingly boring. I had to sit at a big desk in a large room with other people sitting at big desks and except for a few old-timers who kept the books and knew the combinations to the safe no one had more than an hour's worth of work to do every day."

Bill is nodding his head with understanding.

"You know what I'm talking about?" I ask.

"I know," he answers.

"Most people don't. At least those I've talked to about this. 'What's the complaint?' they would say. 'A cushy job, good pay. What do you want?' But I was on the verge of screaming the whole time. I could only take so many cigarette breaks and hear so many weird dreams and heartbreaking tales of near-hits and almost-had-its of the daily number before I thought I'd lose my mind."

"You sound bitter. Didn't you get anything out of it?"

"Funny you should ask that. I did, to a point. But a week or two was all I needed for any material for stories or anything like that. As a matter of fact, I wrote some stories in college about some of the people I worked with and what playing the numbers, not necessarily hitting, meant to them. But at seventeen, to be spending the whole summer in that place . . . Ugh. I had terrible fights with my father about it. He felt he had it coming to him, the pay was the best I could get anywhere, of course, and he just insisted that I work there. He had put so many people on the city and county payroll and now here was his own daughter acting too good for it, refusing what he had to dispense, disdaining what so many others were eternally grateful to him for. He couldn't understand how I could want so badly to go away to be a waitress."

Bill is looking at me oddly. "That's wonderful," he says. "He's handing you a plum of a job and you want to go away and work beneath your station, so to speak."

We both laugh at the line. "That's about it," I say. "I guess I've made my peace now, but for years I was ashamed of his court-house connection. I haven't told too many people what my father really does. But of course you know."

"I know. He delivers the vote."

"He sure does. That's why what you say about those kids at the lunch counters is so exciting to me. If Negroes wait for the politicians they might just as well forget it. Their politicians are just as bad as ours."

"But they're theirs."

"That's true. My father says he's for Stevenson now but he knows he doesn't have a chance and he doesn't even like him."

"I'm sure he'll have no trouble getting behind the candidate when the time comes."

"No trouble at all," I say, laughing but feeling sad for my father or for myself for being the daughter of a man without convictions, I'm not sure which.

Bill has refilled his glass and is looking at me now with all his might. It is a look that sets me on fire.

"I ask again, how can a woman as desirable as you be so cynical?"

Desirable now instead of just beautiful. It's coming. I can feel it. I must do it now. Now or never. I must ask *the* question, the question I've been avoiding all night.

"Do you have a lot of family in Kentucky?" There! He doesn't show a sign but answers as calmly as you please.

"My old man's gone now and my mother lives across the river outside Cincinnati with my sister, but I got some kin around I see now and then. Mostly at funerals."

"How about your wife? Where are her . . . kin?"

The glass poised at his lips hangs in the air. He doesn't take the drink. Abruptly he brings his hand down to the little table and slams the glass harder than he must have anticipated. Water sloshes onto the table. He reaches for his handkerchief to wipe it up. "Sorry," he mumbles, not looking up. I don't take my eyes off him.

"You've been waiting to spring that one all evening. It's the first thing about you that hasn't been aboveboard." His words sting. He's probably not married and now I've ruined it with my nasty suspicious nature. But how could a man like this be single in 1960? It is impossible. A miracle. Perhaps he's divorced, a widower, maybe . . .

"How can I tell *you* that my wife doesn't understand me? It would be an insult to you. And yet, that's about what it is." He is sunk deep into the chair now, his weight has forced the webbing to sag beneath. As he talks he loosens his tie, wrinkles appear on his once-smooth shirt. His eyes search mine. "I guess you've heard it all before."

"Not recently."

He looks hurt. My answer sounds much flipper than it really is. I try to soften my words.

"I didn't mean that as harshly as it sounds. It's true, though. Lately I've been much more alert and on my guard. You said I was waiting to ask that question all evening. I should have forced the issue much earlier, at the restaurant, and then the evening would have been just a casual dinner with a friend."

He sits up, his back erect. "Shall I stay or go?" he asks softly.

My insides are loop-the-looping with amazing velocity during the long silence that follows. I begin to pick at a loose thread in my skirt. "I wonder how Randolph is," I say, proving that it is still a casual dinner between friends even though we are sitting in my apartment ready for the next step. Earlier, when I had called the hospital from the restaurant, Randolph's condition was listed as stabilizing and Bill had said that was a good sign. Now he ignores my remark about Randolph for the ruse it is.

"Do you want me to leave?" he asks again, his voice coated with a natural husk. He is tightening his tie. I know if I sit quietly he will stand up, brush off his jacket, and be gone and we will never go beyond this moment, never . . . If that's what I want to happen I will just sit here and pull at this thread, I will . . .

I am off the couch and standing over him. He smiles as he reaches out and gently pulls me to him, easing me onto his knees.

8

I wish the old windbag would leave. Up until a few minutes ago I had been having such a pleasant time opening the mail and thinking about Bill and me, warm and watery thoughts that cascaded over me, showering my skin with tingling prickles as heated images splashed through my mind: his thighs spreading to encompass me; my fingers traveling down his long tapered back to the base of his spine; his lips encircling my nipple; our laughter as we lay nude last night throwing strawberries into each other's mouth.

Then C. R. Price waddled into the almost empty Cultural News Department and rolled John Campbell's chair up alongside my desk. Plopping down, he began: "I never got to finish that about the time Monty . . ."

Tuesday. Wednesday. Thursday. Three glorious, magical nights. Right after work yesterday we picked up delicatessen and went straight to the apartment to have more time to spend together. As soon as he is free tonight he must rush for the shuttle to Washington. I won't see him until . . .

"You know how that expression got started, 'Battle of the Bulge'?"

"Huh?" Price is leaning very close to me, peering up at me.

"'The Battle of the Bulge.' You know the origin of the expression?"

I nod yes but Price proceeds to tell me anyway. Price has been visiting me ever since I made the mistake of going to the Overseas Press Club with him a few months ago. It seemed harmless enough then, that sparkling April lunch hour when I was rushing out of Lord & Taylor and he blocked my way. One quick drink and a chance to see the inside of the place with such a glamorous name. Why not?

At the bar I couldn't believe it. This kindly looking old man, this cherubic grandfather complete with bifocals, a gleaming bald head and smooth chins, was actually rubbing his stubby knee against mine. If it hadn't been so ludicrous I would have been annoyed. It was a pain, though. It took away from my pleasure at being in the famous bar and studying the murals and the other patrons. Pointedly I moved my leg away from his and gathered my purse and gloves. "I really ought to be getting back," I said as I jumped off the stool. "Thanks so much."

I had thought that would be the end of it, but it was only the beginning. Since then Chet Price appeared every so often, pulling up a chair to sit beside me and spill his storehouse of anecdotes on me while I opened the mail. The first few times I did find it amusing to listen to his intimate gossip about the greatest names of the age, Ike this and Monty that, but soon I found him to be a crashing bore. He had been a correspondent in Europe during and right after the War and now he is filling the time until his retirement, updating the advance obituaries of the world's leaders.

Ike is a favorite. Ike the General, however, not Ike the President. "A terrible disappointment to me," Price admitted. Bill was just saying last night how Washington is coming to life now that people realize that the President will be gone. Even with Nixon, he said, at least it will be interesting. Washington is a very in town, almost a small town; everything revolves around the social life where deals are really made. I remember reading something in *Overset* about how the wives keep it going, the wives of the Senators and Congressmen and the wives of the journalists. Bill doesn't like to talk much about his wife, JoAnn. He did say, though, when I asked, that she had really done her best to keep up her end of the social obligations. But, he added, and I wondered about this, sometimes she was really out of her class. There was only so much he could expect from her, he knew.

I could do better, I was sure. JoAnn had never gone to college or traveled. From what Bill said, she was a simple girl who lacked the sophistication he needed now. They say as men advance they need more advanced wives.

Price has left the "Battle of the Bulge" and has returned again to the Court of St. James's and that Joe Kennedy anecdote he was telling me at the Overseas Press Club Bar just before I left that day. Here comes John Campbell to the rescue, thank goodness.

Campbell is juggling an armload of newspapers and a container of coffee. He slams the papers on his desk and walks over to stand rudely behind the chair Price is sitting on. There are at least thirty empty chairs in the Cultural News Department at this moment, but John makes it clear that he wants his, the one with CAMPBELL scotch-taped on it in 120 pt catastrophe headline type.

Campbell addresses me over Price's head. "You see what the Idiot wrote about the new Bergman?" John Campbell always called Damon Crewes the Idiot. John reads *Cahiers du Cinéma* and makes a point of hardly ever agreeing with Damon. In this morning's paper Damon questioned "the veracity of women like those in Bergman films" in general and "pondered the impotent conclusion" of the particular film under review, *Dreams*.

Chet Price is standing now, waiting to get my attention.

"I'll finish that about Joe Kennedy and Winnie some other time," he says when I finally look at him. He waves and leaves the Cultural News Department.

Campbell watches Price leave. He puts down the coffee he is sipping and picks up an enormous pair of scissors. He begins to turn the pages of The Paper, cutting as he talks.

"Do you know that every time one of those A.K.'s makes a speech or gets a cold, that old fart pulls out the obit and adds inserts?"

"I thought that each year they lived out of the public eye he cut a couple of paragraphs out of their obits. He was practically in tears last month when MacArthur was so sick. I think space was tight that day and he had orders to cut a column."

"He does that too," Campbell says, "but not with the real biggies. He creams when they get sick. Ever see him adding the medical reports? Especially Adenauer and Eisenhower. They're his heroes. Did you ever notice how lovingly he crawls over the proofs of their obits, penciling in the inserts?"

"Especially Eisenhower, though he has been a terrible disappointment as president." I say this in Price's fatuous tone and John Campbell and I both have a good laugh. Presley the porter walks by pushing his trash can on wheels. He puts a fresh package of silicone-treated yellow dust cloths on my desk, winks, and continues on. I haven't decided yet whether he's doing me a big favor, as his wink implies, or he's conning me. After all, shouldn't *he* dust my desk? Still, I'm happy to have the cloths. My clothes would be filthy if I didn't dust my desk and chair regularly. Newspaper offices are very dirty places. Some of the secretaries dust their boss's desk but I couldn't do that. And Ashley hasn't asked. When it gets too bad for him he calls Presley over to do what needs to be done. Presley is busy most of the time with the executive bullpen. How does Ashley get him when he needs him? Does he tip him? Slip him a ticket? What would Presley Pendergast, the Deacon of his church in Queens, want to see on Broadway? *Toys in the Attic? The Tenth Man?*

"I'll miss you," Campbell is saying, talking of his promotion to the City Desk, "but I shall return." His dream is to one day unseat Damon Crewes and be The Paper's motion picture critic.

"I wonder who my replacement will be," he adds, "as though anyone could replace *me*."

"Don't you know, it's Mike Diamond."

"Mike Diamond. You got to be kidding. They were going to fire him last week."

"I hadn't heard that, but I'm not surprised. He seems like a real nothing. I tried to talk with him a few times when he first started and gave up. It took him two weeks to learn how to fill the pastepots. Finally one morning I had to tell him he ought to get a new can and I was only down here a few days myself. It took them long enough to find out about him."

John Campbell looks at me with disgust. "But that's not why he was almost fired, for God's sake! A guy needs a chance to learn. They were up the wall on the National Desk last week because he dropped the AP wires on the Suburban Desk. They were marked National Siegel and he thought it was for Nat Siegel on the Suburban Desk instead of Abe Siegel on the National Desk. That's when Abe Siegel said he never wanted to see that boy's face again."

"So why wasn't he fired?"

"Well, who the hell is Abe Siegel to say who should be fired? There's a lot of resentment that he's been getting too big for his breeches ever since he was moved into the slot. A slotman runs his desk, not the whole damn floor."

"So they dump Diamond on us. Typical. There are a lot of new people out front aren't there?" I ask casually, picking up another piece of mail.

"You mean that guy you're running around with?"

I keep my voice steady as I ask, "Is that the latest bit of

inaccurate information making the rounds of the city room?" *Sharipp*.

"Don't worry. It's not all over the place yet. Your roving reporter was walking up Forty-sixth Street the other night when I saw you stagger out of that intimate little restaurant and steal into a cab. Pretty chummy."

Sharipp. "It was nothing. I bumped into him and went for a drink. He knew my cousin in the Army. And besides, it was a noisy, well-lit restaurant and we weren't staggering."

Campbell takes a sip of coffee before he speaks. "My lips are sealed. I won't even mention it to Eileen. You know her big mouth."

This is his idea of a joke. Eileen is his wife and she is so quiet people often forget she is around. Once in a while when she can get her mother to sit with her two babies she comes down to the office and waits for John to finish and they go to the opera or a play or a concert. I wonder what they would do for entertainment if he wasn't the clerk in the Cultural News Department and able to get free tickets. They do not seem to be able to live on his clerk's salary with much left over. His two white shirts are fraying badly at the collar and he lets his heels run down to the end before getting new lifts.

I was invited to dinner in their Upper West Side apartment once. The three of us ate while the two little girls played in the next room. It was all very warm and cozy, the sparsely furnished apartment, the spaghetti dinner, the wine, and the talk of the future. Plastic toys were everywhere. Eileen laughed a lot as John and I talked about the office. She seemed to know about everyone we mentioned.

John is reading the morning headlines to me and I am making the appropriate comments but my mind is on Bill again, and the past three days, or, more accurately, nights. Evenings would be more exact, for he insists on going back to his hotel room no matter how late it is. The last guy I went with was a lawyer who never wanted to come to my place. He insisted on this because he lived in deathly fear of missing telephone calls. He was a Deputy Commissioner in a city housing agency.

Tony Weather and Lowell Abbott come out of the men's locker room talking excitedly. "Did you hear?" Tony calls to me, "Randolph just died. They just got word at the City Desk."

I am stunned. On Wednesday the prognosis was still good and yesterday Ashley had talked to him briefly on the phone.

"He threw another clot last night," Lowell is telling us. Ashley pushes briskly through the door of the men's locker room and heads straight for my desk.

"You do drive, don't you, Arlyn?" he asks.

"Yes, but it's been a long time, I don't . . ."

"Good. Would you take Betty back to Nyack? I'd ask someone else but we have that damn policy meeting this afternoon with the Sunday Department and we need everybody's input about the reorganization of the television pages. And besides, I'm sure Betty could use a woman's touch now. She's a wreck. She wants to bury him from up there." Ashley shrugs. "What can you do? It makes it hard for us. She's having the funeral on Monday. We'll have to get a memorial going down here at a convenient time."

My head throbs. Small clusters have gathered and people are talking in low voices. Occasionally there is a loud chuckle or a burst of laughter. They are honoring Randolph, telling stories about him, some recent, some from way back, some tales out of school, as they say. They are talking with affection and cynicism. Damn. I would like to be part of the group. Instead, I am caught here while Ashley methodically discusses policy meetings and convenient memorial services.

Ashley continues, his voice matter-of-fact. "She'll be expecting you at her place about noon. She wants to give you lunch first. You know how punctilious she is." He returns to his desk.

The groups are splitting up. I must get ready to go to Betty. Betty, the widow. Randolph is dead, his wife is now a widow. I try to remember his last words to me. Was it something clever he tossed over his shoulder on his way to the Astor on Tuesday afternoon? It probably was, but on a busy Tuesday who remembers a clever remark lightly given, never suspecting it represents the last words one will ever hear from that person. And Randolph. What did he think trotting off to his tryst at the Astor on Tuesday? Did he love the woman? Was she indeed the student of his correspondence course, the woman from Iowa? Did Betty know about his other women?

My stomach tightens. Lunch? How will I ever get through it, sitting there in poor Randolph's apartment surrounded by his things? I turn to look at Randolph's partitioned cubicle against the wall behind me. Someone has shut the door. How weird. That door is never shut and now it is. Who did it . . . and so fast?

I'd better get going. "You know how punctilious she is." Why should she bother, today of all days? Why don't I just grab us something fast at the deli? It's eleven-fifteen now, I suppose she's already started to fix the lunch. Maybe it's helping her, giving her something to do.

In the Ladies Lounge I decide that I will walk to Betty's. It's only twenty-five short blocks downtown and two east. I can easily make that by noon. And I can have time to think about Bill. I really haven't had a moment to sort out my thoughts since Tuesday when I got off the elevator and he was leaning against the pillar, waiting for me. Just a short time after Randolph arrived at the hospital.

9

In the soft evening I am in no hurry to return to Manhattan. Missing the parkway entrance near Nyack I drove down winding country roads into New Jersey, drinking in the musky smell of honeysuckle that drifted into the rental car.

Nyack had delighted me, even though my mission there had been a grim one. It did not take much fantasizing for me to see myself and those children I will have someday in that setting, transferred without a thought from their usual habitat on Madison Avenue in the neighborhood of Public School 6 to Betty and Randolph's charmingly rustic home and that honking yellow school bus.

What a great way to live, I thought, when I first walked up the brick path to the handsome Victorian house set on the hill overlooking the Hudson River. Once inside I was convinced. Worn velvet settees, a parlor organ of ancient vintage, marble-topped, carved mahogany tables, plants in hand-painted porcelain cache pots, herbs growing in the kitchen window.

Despite her grief, Betty proudly showed me the house,

the monument to her life with Randolph: his study in the turret, a small round room filled with his rolltop desk and the pictures of theater greats lining the walls; her potting shed and studio. Randolph had often told me about his wife's green thumb and what a talented craftsman she was. Betty dismissed the studio with a wave of her hand. "I fool around," she said, "nothing serious." I noticed that cobwebs were growing from the loom. The potter's wheel was covered with a thick layer of dust.

It was when I was glancing at the books in the living room bookcase (an old habit of mine) that I came upon Randolph's *Rockland Adventure,* a book of his I had never heard of. Betty was in the kitchen at the time talking on the telephone, arranging for the woman who helped her with the housecleaning to come and be with her over the weekend. Family and friends would be coming and going, Betty had said, but Martha would stay. "She's really closer to me than any member of my family now," Betty told me on the drive up.

I still can't get the photo on the dust jacket of *Rockland Adventure* out of my mind. It is a picture of Randolph and Betty standing in front of their house, the house that is the "subject of this humorous and affectionate account of a year in the life of a city couple in the country." The year was 1937 and the look of the thirty-two-year-old Randolph would not change much in the next twenty-three years. The large frame, heavy chest, and sparse, longish hair were set for life. But Betty! When Betty returned to the living room I strained to find beneath the pads of fat the sweetheart face and luminous eyes of the twenty-two-year-old actress.

She sat down on a faded green velvet couch opposite me and I held up the book, still in my hand.

"I never knew you were an actress." Her face seemed to sag more. I was sorry immediately. What a blunder!

But she pulled herself together. "Oh, I never think of myself as an actress. Why should you? A Broadway play at twenty-two hardly makes one an actress. When the book was published I hadn't even looked for work for almost a year. I kept planning to get back to it after the house was finished and the book was finished, et cetera, et cetera. And then after my illness . . . but enough of that."

Betty's illness was talked about around the office in whispers and with raised eyebrows. At various times I had the impression that Betty was a madwoman, an alcoholic, a drug addict, a hypochondriac, or all four. There was talk of electroshock therapy. There was also a child somewhere, I knew, but I wasn't sure if the child was dead or institutionalized.

"Randolph has certainly written a lot of books," I said as I returned the book to the bookcase. Another blunder, referring to Randolph in the present tense. But Betty didn't seem to notice.

"Oh, my, yes," she answered. She seemed to be taking his death better than anyone had expected she would. Perhaps it is because she has so many arrangements to make and details to think about. The grief will come, I could almost hear my mother saying. When she is alone again and has nothing to do, the grief will come.

"When Randolph landed that contract for the Choice Plays series we were so deliriously happy," Betty was saying. "We didn't have to choose between a European vacation and a new roof. We were able to do both, in the same year. *Rockland Adventure* was a labor of love for us, but it never made any money."

My eyes fell on a studio photograph of a cherubic boy of about two set in a heavy silver frame. The boy was posed on a polished library table with a ball between his chubby legs.

"That's my sister's boy," Betty said to my unasked question. "He's a physicist. Only twenty-one. Teaches at Cal Tech. A brilliant boy—we're all so proud of him. My favorite nephew. I hope he gets here for the funeral. He spent his summers here with us. Our son, Randy, was born the same year Billy was, you know. I only had him home until he was two." As she talked she looked out through the bay window to the river beyond. "I suppose you know all about it."

"Not really."

Betty continued, telling the story, I realized, for herself as much as for me. "I just thought he was the most beautiful thing in the world." She reaches for a cut-glass decanter from the long table behind the couch. "How about a drink?"

"No, thank you," I said, thinking of the long drive back, but when I saw Betty's face I changed my mind. "On second thought, I'll have one."

"Good." Betty seemed pleased. She took a deep breath and sighed, then gulped her drink. I sipped the brandy slowly, feeling its warmth spread through me.

"Poor Randolph, I guess he never got over it. After it happened he just threw himself into his work. It was a blessing that he had all those books to do. It took him even longer to acknowledge it than it took me. What a year that was, once we started taking Randy to specialists. You see, for months I refused to listen to anybody. 'He's all right,' I would say, 'just taking him longer to develop.' We all read Gesell in those days, but I still wouldn't admit the unthinkable. My mother visited from Oklahoma when he was seven months old and, cruel as it seemed at the time, it was she who finally convinced me. I hated her for it. And hated her double when she told me something I had never known. That her mother had had a sister who was 'different.' Poor Aunt Sara, my mother called her. When I was growing up I never knew about her. Never knew that Sara had spent her days drooling from a daybed in the dining room until her mother died and she had to be put away because my grandmother and her brother and sisters couldn't take care of poor Sara."

Betty poured herself more brandy. "'Do it now,' my mother urged. 'I know from what my own mother told me, it's not fair to the other children and it's no life for you. He will never develop the way other children do. What you do for him now as a baby you will have to do his whole life,' she told me. I fought and screamed at my mother, accusing her of loving my sister more. I was so jealous. My sister's boy, two months younger than Randy, was doing everything he was supposed to be doing ahead of time."

Betty had finished a second glass of brandy in one gulp and was pouring a third. I wondered if I should try to stop her, divert her. But why? It must make her feel good. Her voice, husky and low, droned on in a monotone: "Randolph was stunned but he was so wise. He said we shouldn't do anything rash. We went all over after the doctor confirmed what my mother said. The Mayo, Johns Hopkins, someone we heard about in Boston. Finally, just after his second birthday, we did it. It wasn't a bad place. It was pretty, with lots of trees and gardens, not far from here. We visited him every week when we weren't traveling. But he didn't survive, you know. We lost him just before his eleventh birthday. I'm not sure he ever knew who we were."

Tears began to stream down Betty's cheeks and her hand shook as she poured the brandy. I felt awkward as I got off the settee and crossed the room to sit beside her on the couch. I touched her shoulder to comfort her, tentatively at first, then more firmly. She fell sobbing against me and I held her in my arms. "Maybe if I had kept him I could have done something for him—you know, they do marvelous things now. We were always afraid to have another child anyway. Randolph was so good to stick with me. It was a great disappointment to him, not having a son. He came from good old New England stock, you know, loads of prominent lawyers and judges and not a few fairly well-known teachers. My original ancestors were from New Hampshire, too."

The thought of her own good stock must have given Betty strength. She sat up and blew her nose and sighed deeply several times. Then she stood up and adjusted the combs in her upswept hennaed hair. I sensed that she was finished talking about her child and I was certainly relieved. It was the worst thing I had ever heard, a mother talking about her defective, dead child with such anguish and regret. And it all happened so long ago! When I thought about having children I never thought that they wouldn't be beautiful and healthy and super-intelligent.

Poor Betty. And poor Randolph. But what a shit he was. How could he do that to her, didn't she have enough trouble? All afternoon Betty talked about him as though he were some God, this August Personage, this Respected Critic and Wise Husband. I almost forgot that he spent so much time rolling in the hay, as they were fond of saying around the office, with a number of chippies. It turned out that in addition to that poor birdlike woman at the Astor, Randolph had other regulars. At the office they said he had to, Betty made his life so miserable.

Did she? Was she really so unsuspecting? Isn't it supposed to be true that when one spouse in a long-standing marriage doesn't know the other is cheating it's because that person doesn't want to know?

And what of Mrs. William Burton Hallam? What of her? What does she know, going about her business all week in Washington, taking care of her home, shopping in the supermarket, driving her daughters to school and not aware that her husband has fallen deeply in love with another woman. But is he? So deeply in love? And if he is, what kind of man would deceive his wife like that? And if he's not deeply in love, what kind of man would deceive his wife and girlfriend as well? Is William Burton Hallam a shit, too?

No, it would never have happened between us if he and JoAnn had had such a good marriage. Didn't he say it had been deteriorating for a long time? I had nothing to do with it. And of course he will not continue to stay with her, to live a duplicitous life. This weekend while he is home he will surely tell her what has happened, how he met a woman he cannot live without, how they must begin to dismantle their marriage. Hey, he never really said it like that. Watch it. Perhaps it's just a three-day miracle. Perhaps we won't see each other that way again. Perhaps it was just the madness of the moment, a meteorite streaking across the summer sky, blazing for three nights and then dying out. Like those shooting stars up there now, in the inky summer sky over Manhattan.

Too bad Paddy O'Connell didn't have a sermon for me to do on Sunday. It would certainly give me something to look forward to this weekend. But keep trying, he had said; any week now, who knows, one of the regular guys is sure to bug out on me.

10

A soft breeze blows through the open church door and ripples the arch of heraldic banners above my head. I am transfixed. Something dark and unpleasant is stirred deep inside me by the double row of banners that hangs beneath the high ribbed supports of the Gothic ceiling.

It is my third Sunday sermon and my first in a church so grand and imposing. The brick Presbyterian Church, though parish to some of the richest and most powerful people in the world, is the very opposite of grand in its understated simplicity, and the Unitarian Church on Lexington Avenue is what I had expected it to be. But here, smack in the middle of Wall Street, in the hallowed Trinity Church, with Alexander Hamilton's bones just a few feet away, I sit, twenty minutes early for the service, filled with wonder and awe at the sight of lions both rampant and couchant visible still on the faded and threadbare standards that do look for all the world as if they had led holy crusades a thousand years ago.

The banners make me feel uncomfortable. I feel like an

interloper here in this bastion of Militant Christianity. "Smite the heathen," it says in the hymnal I am flipping through. Is that who I am? No, I'm not the heathen. Am I the heretic? Or just the plain Jew? What is my role in all of this?

See. Look. This is what you did to Our Lord. Like this. Up the street, Mommy, Victoria, she stretched out my arms like this and held them against the wall. Right there in Josie's vestibule. Look, like this. This is what you did to Our Lord.

I don't think I was more than six, but honestly, Bill, it's like it happened yesterday. I can almost feel her hands on my arms. I don't know why I'm telling you about it now. I just feel so free with you, I guess. It's always there, just beneath the surface, yet I never talk about it, or even think about it consciously.

I'm honored, indeed, that you choose to tell me. I can't know enough about you. I can't get enough of you or know enough about you. You sure do fascinate me, my hot-blooded Jewess. Let me melt in the warmth of your arms, your breasts, your belly, your loins. The Bible comes to life when I'm fucking you. Comfort me with apples, with pears, the plums of your tits. Time rolls backward and we are in a tent in Bashabeer, we are . . .

Please, Bill, I really don't enjoy this.

What?

All this Biblical stuff.

You're offended?

I'm not offended, I just don't like it.

Sorry, it gets me excited thinking about it, that's all. I've never been with a Jewess before and, believe me, everything I've heard is right.

When I think of being Jewish I think more about sitting with my grandmother upstairs in her shule on the High Holy Days and trading one of her dill pickles for a piece of my friend's mother's sausage than I do about David and Bathsheba. I think about being called a Dirty Jew by some kids when I was little and being restricted at certain resorts now.

Like this. This is what you did to Our Lord.

What are you doing here in His house anyway, Their Lord's? But this is silly. I represent the Press, the Free Press, and I am the objective reporter who can go anywhere and report on anything. I am the eyes and ears of the public, the conduit to them of what happens here today.

I open my notebook to read again the information Paddy O'Connell had given me on Friday: The Reverend Ralph Sutherland Fletcher of the Protestant Episcopal Church of Baltimore will talk about the need to build bridges to the Negro community through the establishment of slum parishes.

A steady trickle of worshippers has begun to move quickly down the aisles and into the pews, taking what seem to be regular seats. I had sat down in the front of the church on the right side of the middle aisle, just where I would have had I been a critic for The Paper covering the opera or ballet or a Broadway show. In my anxiety not to be late I had arrived before the ushers. I hope I'm not sitting in some family's traditional pew. I was careful to sit where there is no brass plaque.

My notebook is turned back to a clean page and my pen is jammed into the spiral binding just the way I have seen Ernestine Herbert jam her pen into her notebook. I am ready. I am not as nervous as I was the first time, or the second, but I am not completely relaxed either. This is good. Though sermons are really a snap, I must not allow myself to get sloppy. I must pay careful attention and make sure there are no deviations from the prepared text. I won't be able to get a text until after the service. Last week I picked up a copy of the minister's text in advance, but Friday, when I called the rectory, I was told that the Reverend Fletcher would not be arriving from Baltimore until late Saturday night.

The voice from the pulpit startles me. A slim young man in a dark suit is making an announcement: "The Reverend Fletcher's plane was delayed last night," he is saying, "because of hurricane winds sweeping up the coast. This morning Reverend Fletcher was still unable to leave Baltimore by air and he took the train. That broke down outside of Philadelphia and he hired a car that was sideswiped and forced off the road by speeding hot rodders on the New Jersey Turnpike." The slim young man pauses a beat. "The Reverend Fletcher just telephoned. 'There comes a time' he says, 'when one must listen to Providence,' and we concur." There is a rustling in the church and I think I hear a few titters. I am straining to hear the young man's words. "The Reverend Fletcher," he continued, "will, by the Grace of God, be here next Sunday. Dr. Maxwell will deliver this morning's sermon."

The titter rises to a crescendo and explodes in laughter. By God, it is funny. I jump up and rush toward the church office. It is eleven forty-five. Not as good a story as a baritone dropping dead in mid-aria at the Met, but it *is* something different. Perhaps I can make a light piece out of it.

The Religious News Editor, Ken Bancroft, a real gem, is off today and his snotty assistant, Franklyn Rawlings, answers the phone.

"Fletcher didn't make it, he had a series of mishaps, and Maxwell's doing the sermon. I have a really funny quote about Fletcher's delay."

I know instantly it is a mistake to have called, but it's what I'm supposed to do.

"Nah," Franklyn is saying, through his nose, "we don't need Maxwell again. Thanks for calling, Arlyn, I can use the space."

"But can't I do something? Did you ever see the old

banners they have here? Have we ever done anything on them? I don't remember ever having read about them and they are fascinating. I could find out about them and—"

"Banners? Why would we write about old banners? We cover religious news."

"Is there anything else I can do today, another sermon?"

"Nah. We got everything else covered. Go have some fun."

"But I really wanted to cover a sermon today." Am I whining? "Can I come in and rewrite something for you? Just for practice."

"Nah, Arlyn, I got Ned Potter coming in with a sermon. He can do that, clean up the odds and ends. Why don't you go home and bake a cake or something? Bring us in a piece tomorrow."

Ned Potter. That creep! Ken Bancroft had to practically write his whole sermon last week. I was waiting to show mine to Ken and it took forever while Ken redid almost every line. And he's been doing them at least two months now. It's bad enough he can't write, he can't even learn the basic rules of attribution. He just sticks quotes in his story without hanging them on anyone!

When I see jerks like Ned Potter moving ahead it really burns me up. I know it's no skin off my back, but still it makes me mad. I think it will eventually hurt The Paper. I said this to John Campbell once and he only laughed.

"Institutions are always manned by armies of assholes, Arlyn," he said. "A few high priests direct the activities of the multitude. It's the nature of the animal. That's how you keep the institution strong. The trick is to get to be a high priest."

Good old John. Perhaps he's right. I take one last look at the banners, shiver, and leave the church.

11

The morning's bright sun doesn't reach into the narrow canyons of the financial district. Wall Street is deserted and dank this Sunday morning. I sense the presence in front of me before I hear the words.

"Hello there, what brings you down here?" The accent is Spanish. I look up to see Luis, the coffee boy, standing in front of me smiling broadly. Or is it Luis? Where is the stiff white cafeteria jacket, the slicked-back patent leather hair? Who is this person, this double of the coffee boy standing here so relaxed in that loose Italian knit jersey and the paint-splotched dungarees? A lock of hair falls on his forehead.

"I could ask the same of you."

"I'm taking my Sunday stroll. I live just a couple of blocks away from here."

"You live down here?" I am surprised. He grins, delighted with my reaction. "I didn't think anyone lived down here," I add.

"Oh, there are many of us," he says. "Only we're supposed

to be invisible. Technically nobody lives down here. I'm in a loft."

"A loft! You?" He's not really a coffee boy at all, he's a painter or a poet.

"Come," he says, placing his hand on my elbow, "I'll show you. And my paintings, too."

"Then you are a painter. I was wondering." What a break to meet him like this. And to be invited to his loft. A friend of Allan's was a painter but he didn't live in a downtown loft. He had a large studio on West Sixty-seventh Street and made a lot of money doing illustrations for magazine advertisements.

"Wondering?" He looks at me quizzically. "What were you wondering?"

"Oh, nothing." I'm ashamed for having been surprised that he is a painter. I know that the city is full of people in menial work, waiters and waitresses and janitors and stock clerks who are really actors and actresses and painters and poets and novelists. But somehow I never could imagine Luis as an artist. It's awful, but you do tend to think of Puerto Rican coffee boys without any other identity.

We are moving quickly now, turning corners, walking on streets whose names I had never heard. Gold. Platt. John. And Slips. What are these Slips? Is this really Manhattan? Luis turns and smiles at me. We are on a block of dingy and decrepit factory buildings now. "My street," he says proudly.

"But where?" I ask. It doesn't look as though anyone lives here.

"Come." He takes my hand and pulls me forward. A loft! I am excited. John Campbell has been talking about taking me and Eileen to a loft happening as soon as the fellow who runs them gets back from the West Coast. I told Bill about it and he got very upset. "You'd best stay away from that kind of thing," he said, frowning. When I questioned him I was sure he wasn't even clear in his mind exactly what a loft happening was. I was dying to find out. Well, at least now I was going to see a real loft.

"Here we are," Luis says. We are standing in the middle of the block in front of a dirty glass-paneled double door marked No. 45–47. He pulls me into the vestibule and releases my hand to take a key from his dungaree pocket. I watch in fascination as he opens the heavy inner door.

"What was this?" I ask, as we enter the hallway whose green-painted walls are streaked with what looks like a hundred years of grime.

"Was? Is," he corrects me. "There are still some factory tenants in the building, but, you know, they are not engaged in very lucrative businesses. A bunch of old guys on the third floor turn out metal fittings of some kind for ships and two other old guys with about thirty people working for them make leather straps on the fourth and fifth. Don't ask me what the leather straps are for. A few months ago they had a birthday. Their grandfather started the business in 1860, they told me. Sold to the Union Army during the Civil War. Their cousin, they said, is one of the last old-time coopers left in Manhattan. You know what that is, a cooper?" I think I know but I'm not positive. "A cooper," he continues, "is a barrel maker. Their cousin is one of the last, a dying breed, they said."

There must be a lot of good feature stories here. The loft itself, the factories and the artists who live here illegally. The last cooper. He would be a separate story.

The only light is what shines through the dirt-encrusted windows on each stairwell. Luis looks at me impishly. I am taken aback. Usually his eyes are hooded and unexpressive.

"Are you a mountain climber?" he asks me.

"A what?"

"Can you climb a lot of stairs? Are you in good shape?"

"Of course." I rush ahead, taking two steps at a time.

"Not so fast," he calls, "better slow down and pace yourself. You don't know what's ahead." He is laughing.

"I've climbed bell towers all over Europe," I shout from

the first landing. "This is nothing to me. Are you sure *you're* not out of shape?"

I hear his laughter echoing up the stairwell after me. He is right, I should pace myself, but I cannot stop now. I run up another flight. The pain in my chest is excruciating and a bit frightening. I must stop. Let him have the last laugh. Who cares? I collapse on the metal stairs in the middle of the third flight. What am I doing here anyway? Bill will be furious when he finds out. Shall I tell him?

Luis' thonged sandals flop rhythmically on the metal stairs as he approaches. When his feet turn the corner and come into my view I am disturbed by the sight of his toes. The long, pointed toenails somehow repulse me. Perhaps I ought not to continue up.

"So," he says, extending a hand to help me up, "you met your match on this staircase." His laugh is easy. I like his warmth and friendliness. I feel comfortable with him and push the image of the toenails out of my mind.

"Who else lives in this building besides you?" I ask.

"No one. I'm the only one who lives here. I only rent, you know, theoretically, as a studio. I'm not supposed to sleep here. Fire and all that. But the landlord, as long as he gets his money, what does he care? There are no commercial takers for this area anymore so the few dollars he gets from me is better than nothing. It is easy for him to turn his head, you know. He has so many violations. I'm just one more. He gets away with it because no one cares about artists in this city, just real estate."

"You're not afraid of fire?"

"I don't think about it."

"Why aren't there more artists here? Why not on the second floor?"

"There is no toilet on the second floor."

"Oh." When he says it, it sounds so logical. I want to ask him why toilets can't be put in but I don't.

"Isn't there an elevator?"

"Yes, but I can only use it when I'm allowed to be visible. During business hours. It is locked on weekends."

I see a huge 5 on the wall in front of me. We continue on. Another flight. What if there is a fire? Will I be trapped? I lean over the banister and look at the long drop below me.

We come to 6 and stop. "Here we are," Luis says, pulling another key from deep inside his dungaree pockets. He opens a padlock and pushes a heavy metal door. Bowing slightly he ushers me inside. "Entrée." He is mocking himself, I am sure. Or is he?

Inside he takes my hand again to lead me toward light. I cannot get my bearings. We are in an enormous room. No. Room is too inadequate a word for this tremendous area of floor and ceiling and pipes dimly lit by a row of dirty windows. I hear the sound of rushing water.

"What's that?"

"Don't mind it," he tells me. "It's the toilet. It thinks it is Niagara Falls." We laugh as he pulls me along. I almost trip over a large mattress to the left of the door. It is covered with a blue India print cloth exactly like the kind my mother uses as a summer throw on the living room couch. It makes me feel very strange to see it here now.

"Come," he says, and I follow him across the vast space toward the windows. A large easel stands on a pine platform. Next to it a long wooden plank table on sawhorses holds dozens of coffee cans whose sides are covered with dried drippings of bright-colored paint. Brushes are everywhere, long-handled artist brushes and the short stubby brushes that you buy in hardware stores and use to paint the windowsills. Spatters of bright colors dot the splintery floor.

Luis pulls a string that turns on a large light bulb in a steel lamp attached to a pillar behind the easel. There are a number of pillars spaced at intervals throughout the area. Leaning against them are huge abstract canvases thickly painted and dripped on, mostly in whitened gray-blues and pale greens. I wonder where all the color that was in the coffee cans has gone. Slashing diagonally across each canvas is a silver bar, sometimes blunt, sometimes swordlike.

The paintings do not look much different from hundreds of other abstract paintings that I have seen in little galleries around the Village, weak, washed-out imitations of Hoffmann, Pollock, de Kooning, and Kline.

"They're nice," I say. "I like the way you apply the paint."

"Thank you," he answers, obviously pleased. "They are all part of a series I am working on, you know. The title is 'Lancelot's Journey.' They represent the quest in each man for perfection."

I am dumbstruck. Does he really think those whitened swirls and swoops and bars of paint on canvas say all that? I wonder if it's me and my own preconceived notion. I must confess that I kind of expected his paintings to be warm and earthy. I am shamed by my prejudgment, my prejudices.

"How long have you been painting?" I stroll as in a gallery, from painting to painting. They are everywhere, on the walls, flat on the floor, and leaning in stacks against the large pillars.

"I started last year," he answers, padding behind me, his thongs flopping against the bare wooden floor.

"One year! Just one year?" I am shocked. I would have thought it took longer than one year to become a painter, and when did he find the time to do all this work?

"I was studying medicine but I hated it and quit to take classes at the art school. My parents were very unhappy. They have, you know, disowned me. In other words, they give me no money, hoping that the day will soon come when I will give up all this foolishness and go home to take up where I left off."

"Where is home?"

"San José." When he sees my puzzled look he continues. "I am from Costa Rica. San José is the capital city."

"Oh, I thought . . ."

"I know," he interrupts, his tone weary and hurt. "You thought I was Puerto Rican." I am surprised at the bitterness in his voice. "We are all the same to you, no matter where we are from. We are all spics to you."

"Will you ever go home to take up where you left off?"

"Never. I am doing fine since I came here. I paint in the daylight. I don't have to be at work until three-thirty. And I get my dinner on the job. That helps me to swallow the other."

Luis is leaning against a pillar. The thundering toilet is behind him and next to it a small sink. Both are disgusting, their white porcelain bodies hardly visible under the accumulation of dirt and grime and dark stains of spattered paint.

"Luis, what do you think of a feature story about lofts, the artists who live in them, that kind of thing?"

"Who would be interested?"

"A lot of people. It's interesting to me, it would be interesting to others. Most people have no idea that these lofts exist and that artists live in them. Maybe if people knew, the landlords couldn't take such advantage of you."

He walks toward me slowly. "You are much too beautiful to be concerned about such things."

Damn! Not him too. I press on anyway.

"I think it would be an interesting feature. You know, I'm trying to write stories for The Paper to get promoted to the writing staff. As a matter of fact, that's where I was today, I was . . ."

He is standing very close to me now, breathing heavily. "No, I did not know that," he murmurs into my hair. "It is not natural for a beautiful woman like you to be worried about promotions."

That's it. "I'd better be going now," I say. "I just remembered I have an appointment with a friend. She'll be calling me, she'll be wondering where I am." I take a step forward but he moves in to block my way, putting his hands on the pillar above my head. I am caught. Trapped. He is nuzzling my ear as he talks.

"I watch you all the time when you are not aware." He takes one hand from the pillar and begins to stroke my hair.

I put my hands on his shoulders. "Luis, I really must leave now." I start to walk but he grabs my wrists and holds me back.

"I have longed for you from afar, let me show you how I can adore you and make you happy up close." He kisses both of my hands. "I can see you are a woman who needs a real man. I get the feeling you are not always satisfied, that you do not know what real love between a man and a woman can be, that . . ."

"Let go of me, please," I say in my firmest voice. "I am leaving now." His answer is to tighten his grip. Now I am angry. I was being civil and now he's acting like this. It's not fair. He speaks and his tone is harsh. "Why did you come here, leading me on? It's not fair. You throw yourself at me and now you want to run away. You are just like all the others." He hisses his last words. "American virgin. I thought you were different."

Leading him on! I want to kick him in the shins with my pointed pump but I am afraid, afraid of angering him. He is about my height, but he is wiry and strong. I know I am no match for him physically.

I lean against him and he loosens his grip on my wrist. My purse is still on my arm. He pulls me to him and covers my face with wet kisses. Did he lock the door? Can I get to it and open it and down the stairs? Will he become violent? Is it worth it?

I am tickling Luis' neck now. "Let's go over to the mattress," I whisper, my voice as sultry as I can make it. It's a chance, maybe it will work. We move toward the mattress and I get on the side near the door. I pretend to reach for the zipper down the back of my dress while he begins to unbutton his dungarees. Now. I rush for the door, pull it open, and start down the six flights of stairs. My heart is jumping to my throat.

I don't stop to look up. He is not following me. He is hanging over the banister screaming like a fishwife. Daylight never looked so great.

12

The sun roof is crowded with Business Department employees but Isabelle and I manage to find two empty chairs.

"So," she says, without a break in the story she had started in the Ladies Lounge and continued on the cafeteria line, "it was unmitigated disaster all around. I'll never waste another Sunday at my cousin Seena's Beach Club again." She bites into the ham salad sandwich she has just unwrapped. "Yuck! Why do I ever set foot in Ptomaine City?"

I ignore her comment about the sandwich. Complaints about the company-run cafeteria are a reflexive staple of conversation around The Paper. I personally find the cafeteria convenient and reasonable and would save my complaints for other areas.

"But it was such a great day for the beach," I say. "Didn't you enjoy yourself at all?"

"No." Her answer is emphatic. "They were all slobs. There was one guy who actually said 'dese' and 'dose' and he kept asking me where I was from and I said the city and he kept saying, 'Yeah, but where in da city? Brooklyn? Queens? Da Bronx?' I don't think he ever met anyone from Manhattan before."

"But Isabelle, you don't live in Manhattan. You live in Brooklyn."

"Just to sleep. I spend all my time in Manhattan and I'm definitely considering taking an apartment in the city at the end of the summer. How about you? Did you have a better than lousy weekend?"

"It was okay. I went to do a sermon but the guest minister never showed up. I called Rawlings but the snot wouldn't let me come in and write anything. He said to go home." As I answer Isabelle's offhand question I realize that I had conveniently buried the events of yesterday. During the cab ride home from Luis' I had felt so dirty and ashamed. How do I get myself into these things, I kept thinking. Even after a hot bath, a nap, and a walk I was still agitated and during the night I tossed and got up and listened to the radio and smoked, unable to sleep for hours. But today dawned new and fresh and Luis was far from my thoughts.

Now I see his toenails and the paint-encrusted toilet bowl and the dark stairs as I race down them into the street.

"No," I tell Isabelle, "I went home and slept. It was kind of a wasted day."

"If you ask me, those sermons are a waste of time altogether. I can't see why you knock yourself out on your day off. Nothing will come of it. You're just wasting precious weekend time that you could be using to better advantage."

"You're great. You just got finished telling me how you wasted your day yesterday, how you spent *your* Sunday."

Isabelle is undaunted. "At least I'm trying. Someday it will happen."

"And with all your running around," I say, "it will probably happen right here under your nose. Someday your prince will come and take you away from all of this, some white knight reporter or up-and-coming editor."

"Not on your life." I'm surprised by the sharpness of her reply. "Not one of them," she continues. "I've come to the conclusion that to be married to a newspaperman is for the birds. I see it from this end and, believe me, it's not a pretty sight. The calls to hold dinner, and not always, you can be sure, because of a pressing story; the out-of-town travel, and you know what happens on the road. No, not for me."

Isabelle seems to be on a new tack. But, of course, she changes all the time. One day The Paper is sacred and reporters are gods beyond her grasp, another time she seems to aspire to snagging one and then she comes up with something like this. Is she making an innuendo about me and Bill? No, Isabelle wouldn't be subtle. It's probably just that some guy in the newsroom is giving her a hard time. Probably married and telling his wife to hold dinner.

"Well, if you don't want the guys here why don't you go to work in some other place, some company where you'd meet the kind of man you're interested in? Doesn't that make sense?"

"Arlyn, I'm amazed at you. You, of all people. Always talking about how important it is to like your job. You know how I feel about mine. Judd may not be the busiest person in the world these days, but it's still great, just to be sitting out there, in the hub of everything. As long as I have to work I can't imagine working anywhere else."

"Sorry. I didn't mean to get you so upset."

"I'm not upset. And I didn't say I wasn't interested in any man in the entire building. I was talking specifically about the men in the News Department." She leans close to me. "Don't turn around," she whispers, "but behind your left shoulder there's a guy reading *The Wall Street Journal*." I wait until Isabelle turns her head and squints her face to the sun before I look. He is a tanned, handsome man who is absorbed in his paper. His Glen plaid summer-weight jacket is carefully hung on the chair behind him and the cuffs of his immaculate white shirt are neatly turned back. There is definitely an air of success and confidence about him.

"Who is he?" I ask.

"He's one of the new ad salesmen they're hiring. You know, they went recruiting for some young, aggressive types. Don't you think he's great-looking?"

"And this is why you drag me up here?"

"You hate it here?"

"No, as a matter of fact it's very pleasant."

"He's not here often, only when he doesn't have a business lunch, I figure. I think he's trying to keep his California tan from fading. He's not married."

"You know him?"

"Just to nod and smile." Isabelle takes her lipstick and compact out of her purse and carefully replenishes the lipstick she has just eaten off. Does it look as silly when I do it? "You know my friend Ruth," she says after blotting a perfect imprint of her lips onto a tissue, "you know who I mean, the Advertising Manager's secretary? She told me."

"How come he's not married? What's the catch?"

"Then you admit he's cute?" She snaps her compact shut.

"He's more than cute. He's sensational-looking, if you like the type."

"Oh sure, if you like the type." She is mocking my tone.

I clarify. "I mean, everything about him seems perfect, almost too perfect, like an Arrow shirt ad. He looks like a model."

"His roommate is handsome too. I saw them at the theater the other night."

"How do you know he has a roommate?"

"Ruth told me. They have this fabulous apartment in the East Sixties. They had a housewarming brunch a couple of weeks ago and Ruth and her husband went. Ruth got friendly with him, took him under her wing. You know she's been secretary in Advertising for a million years and knows everything there is to know about the place. She thinks he'll really make it big as a salesman."

"Why doesn't Ruth introduce you? Lunch or something. Couldn't you meet accidentally on purpose?"

"She's going to have this little party in early September."

"September?" I can't resist teasing Isabelle a bit. "A guy like that could be taken by September."

"True. You think I ought to hint that she should do something sooner? But there's not much time. We'll be away. I can't wait to go now. What about you?"

Isabelle looks at me slyly. When we made our vacation plans it was true that I was just as eager as she is to meet a man on Nantucket, especially after she convinced me that I should try it, that it wasn't really so bad, not like the regular resorts which I absolutely refused to go to with her. Now, of course, since Bill, I find the notion of going away to a singles scene a bit unnerving. I'm not even sure why I'm going except Bill keeps insisting that I keep to my vacation schedule. I don't think he realizes quite what Nantucket is.

"I'm looking forward to it," I tell Isabelle. "It should be nice to swim and cycle and see something different. A vacation is important even if you don't meet a man."

"Bite your tongue." I look at her face. She is not kidding. There is a look in her eyes that tells me she is uneasy, wondering whether she made a mistake urging me to come away with her. I am not even sure just how much she knows about Bill and me. For some reason I don't offer information, and so far she hasn't asked. When she does I will talk about him.

I laugh at her concerns and reassure her. "Oh, Isabelle, don't worry. I won't be a party pooper."

She seems relieved. "My girlfriend Roz told me we're going at absolutely the right week. She just came back and said the ratio last week was almost three to one. She came home early. Why waste the money? I told her I had heard that August was a better month. Who are you waving to?" Isabelle asks as she turns to see Maggie Moran wave back to me. We both watch as Maggie walks over to join a group on the other side of the sun roof.

"Thank God for small favors," Isabelle says. "I can't stand her."

"Maggie's all right," I say. "What do you have against her?"

"The Publisher this and the Mrs. that. The way she runs on about the Family, as though she's one of them. You like her?"

"When I was working in the Publisher's Suite I never thought I'd see the day that I would say this, but I guess if you're not working for her she's okay. She used to get on my nerves. She wanted me to do everything her way. It would stand my teeth on edge the way she'd say, 'I have found that if you do it this way it seems to work better.' I guess it was her tone. But sometimes when she just sat and talked she wasn't so bad. Her stories about the Family were always interesting if you edited out her blind adoration. Oh, that reminds me. Remember I told you about Teddy Lowe showing up at Fire Island?"

"No, you never told me. What are you talking about?"

"I must have. At the Simons'. Didn't I mention that he appeared on their deck one morning with this absolutely gorgeous creature and—"

"You were so busy telling me how you decided that Bob Mann isn't for you. Do you still feel that way? Anything new there?"

"No. Yes. I mean, I still feel that way."

"So what about Teddy Lowe? He's always with some gorgeous dish or other, or so they say. What's news about that?"

Isabelle's cynicism doesn't surprise me. All over The Paper opinion about Teddy Lowe is divided. Some see him as an amiable playboy and are admiring and slightly envious of his way of life while others have nothing but contempt for the sniveling weakness inherent in his inability to assume his responsibilities and take his rightful place on The Paper, if not for himself, then out of gratitude and feeling for the Poor Pub. I once heard Gil Gilchrist phrase it in exactly those words.

When the Publisher adopted Teddy he was known as a

wild one. Even Teddy's own father, the Publisher's brother, had given up on him and died a disappointed man. The Publisher, of course, was living with his own disappointment. His only son had been killed in a jeep accident in England during World War II and people say he never got over it. His daughters, it is said, all married ineffectual men. At any rate, the Publisher seems to think so. When a power grab began to brew on the Board of Directors, the Publisher outmaneuvered everyone and adopted Teddy, thus assuring no outsiders could push in. I learned all this from Maggie in many installments, but that about sums it up.

The adoption was almost ten years ago and although Teddy married a Vassar girl who produced three children for him, he never did manage to settle down. He is supposed to have some function as liaison to the Business and Editorial departments and though his father's office was redone for him in a modern style and he has a fleet of secretaries he doesn't spend much time at his job.

"Actually, it's not Teddy Lowe who interests me," I tell Isabelle, who is waiting, despite her professed lack of interest in the subject, to hear yet more gossip about him. "It's the girl he was with," I say, wondering if Isabelle will understand. "I had this feeling that I knew her, that I had met her somewhere."

"You probably did. That happens all the time," Isabelle answers.

"I know, but this is different. Something about her haunts me. I keep seeing her face. It's funny, but I'll be walking along the street on my way to the subway and suddenly her face will pop into my mind. I only saw her for a few minutes and yet I seem to recall her perfectly, her doll-like features and this mass of soft white-gold hair. Just this morning before I was fully awake . . ."

"She must really be gorgeous to have you go on about her like this."

"In a way gorgeous seems too weak a word. She is truly

breathtaking, like painted porcelain, and her figure is sensational. But there's something else. She's not just a blond sexpot, not like all these other would-be Marilyn Monroes you see all over the place. There's something—how can I explain it—something almost ethereal about her. Her hair kind of cascades around her face. It has to be set to the teeth but for some reason it doesn't look it."

"Well, you certainly are engrossed with her," Isabelle says. "Who is she? What does she do? Did you get to talk to her?"

"No. That's just it. Every time I tried to look at her she seemed to turn her head. They were only on the deck with us for a few minutes. I keep playing the scene over in my mind and I'm sure I'm not imagining it. She was definitely avoiding me. After they left, everyone was saying how high-priced she is, some kind of fancy call girl or something."

"Ecch. How can they do that, those girls, sell their bodies? I don't see any difference between them and ordinary prostitutes, do you? In fact, I have heard they're even worse. I've heard the really high-priced ones do any damn weird thing the John wants. I mean anything."

I try to visualize what Isabelle means but it's hard to imagine. Does Teddy Lowe like to whip that lovely creature while her hands are tied to the bedpost and her bosom bursts out of a Merry Widow like those lurid covers on the books in Times Square?

"What weird things?" I ask.

"Oh, you know." Isabelle's face flushes. I think she's blushing. She bends over to pick up her purse from the floor. I wonder if she's blushing because she's thinking of the weird things or because she doesn't know.

"We'd better get back," she says.

"Right." I turn and see that the ad salesman is no longer on the sun roof. Too bad. I would have liked another look at this Adonis.

13

That stupid song. Why can't I get it out of my head? This isn't even a bikini anyway. A bikini has to be below the belly button.

"Hello, Arlyn, gallery hopping?" It is Ernestine Herbert standing in front of me, cool and crisp in a brown plaid dress with an enormous white piqué collar. Her gloves are neatly tucked into the outer pocket of her bag. Behind the gloves I see her notebook with a ballpoint pen jammed into the wire spiral. Why on this steamy Saturday in midsummer does she look so self-possessed when even in this little sundress I feel like a wet rag?

"No, I'm doing some shopping for my vacation," I say. "I'm going up to Nantucket. Are you gallery hopping?"

"In a sense. Some background research, that kind of thing. But I'm about ready for a cup of coffee and a cigarette now. Will you join me?"

"Love to."

"I know a fairly decent place over on Madison about

three blocks north," she says. "How's that? Will you have time to finish your shopping?"

"Yes. I have almost everything I need now. I just bought this bathing suit." Ernestine peeks into the bag I hold open.

"La-di! Less is more."

"It's not really an official bikini. At least I don't think it is. It covers my belly button and it has a bit of a bra. See."

"And it's not yellow, polka-dot," Ernestine says, laughing as we start to walk over to Madison.

"That stupid song. I heard it on the radio this morning and can't get it out of my mind."

"So you came right out and bought a bathing suit."

"I really do need it and anyway it's not that itsy bitsy, teenie weenie."

Ernestine stops and walks closer to a little gallery a few doors from Madison. She stands scrutinizing it and takes out her notebook.

"Do you want to go in?" I say. "I don't mind waiting here." I add that to be polite. I would love to go inside with her and watch her work.

"Won't be necessary now," she answers. "I can come back later. I'm particularly interested because of those little still lifes there. That kind of thing seems to be cropping up in some of the best places these days. I wonder if it's a trend or what it means."

"But the sign here says the gallery closes at noon today. It's almost that now."

"Good catch," Ernestine says as she bends closer to the discreet sign in the corner of the window and squints to read it for herself. "If you don't mind, I would like to go in now. I won't be that long. If it's really something I have to pursue at length I'll return. Come on."

After a momentary blindness, my eyes adjust to the long narrow ground-floor room. Each painting on the soft gray walls is lit with its own light. Everything else, the deep plush carpet, the upholstered couches placed about, the thin man who greets us and his suit are all that same soft gray.

I turn toward the right and begin to amble in front of the paintings, studying each one as I go. Most are larger than the one in the window that Ernestine pointed out but none is nearly as large as the canvases you see in the better-known galleries where the big-name abstract expressionists show, the galleries that have those wild openings. I once had a date with a guy who took me to one. He claimed he never bought dinner on Tuesday night, just made the big openings. I think he met girls there, too. He wasn't invited or on any press list or anything like that. He just crashed. He said it was easy. He bragged about it quite a bit, said he got in practice crashing weddings when he was younger. "As long as you look right," he told me, "you can usually talk your way in. And at weddings," he added, "a single man is an asset, there are always a few girlfriends of the bride who don't have dates."

Ernestine and the thin gray man are strolling behind me talking about the pictures on the wall. "Our patrons," he is telling her, "know what they like. They cannot be badgered. Why should one have to redo a whole room to accommodate what's being passed off as art today? Our patrons prefer to have a painting that fits *their* taste."

I was surprised at Ernestine's next question. "Do your customers make final judgment on the paintings they buy or do they leave it to the decorator?" How could he answer that? It makes his customers seem less than cultivated patrons of the arts. It makes it seem as though they are buying paintings as decor and that when they change the decor they will change the art that surrounds them. But I am more surprised by his answer.

"Some people of course leave it entirely to the decorator but increasingly today there are those who like to spot and get in on the ground floor with an unknown artist by themselves. That sense of the gambler, you know. We do have people who come right in and see something they like and buy quickly, but of course once the price has begun to rise and an artist's stock is climbing it's wise to have the advice of an expert. Art can be a pretty steep investment, as you know."

Ernestine nods as she writes in her notebook. I suppose you can ask any question. Ernestine starts toward the door and as she walks she puts her notebook back in her bag. I follow, assuming that she is finished. At the door she turns and asks another question.

"Those little still lifes that you have in the window, I've heard it said that paintings like those and some of these in here are knocked off in assembly-line fashion and then merchandised as the work of individual artists, signed and with false biographical information; that the differences in each painting, which are attributed to the painter's talent or individuality, are really predetermined by what is asked for by customers and their decorators, so many orange highlights, so many with mauve, and so forth, depending on what's in vogue at the moment."

Even in the subdued light I can see the thin gray man turning slightly red. Or is it orange or mauve? But he pulls himself together, rebuttoning his jacket and gallantly answering Ernestine in what must be the most imperious tone he can muster at the moment.

"Our paintings *and* our patrons speak for themselves, I think. We know what we like and we don't, you know, have to answer to anybody."

Ernestine thanks him warmly, says she thinks she has everything she needs but if not will call him again, and we leave.

On the street she removes her notebook from her bag and writes in it as we walk. I am silent. When she is finished I turn to her.

"I never knew that, what you were asking him, about the assembly-line paintings. Were you disappointed in his denial?"

Ernestine takes my elbow to guide me across Madison Avenue.

"I'm not sure it was a denial, Arlyn, and I have no way of

knowing if what I asked him is true. I'm just asking, right? I suspect there's some truth in it but the point is to ask it of enough people and to weigh their responses while taking into consideration what particular ax they are grinding. The fact itself is not as interesting to me as the idea that some of our more illustrious citizens may be letting their wives buy art this way. When I talk to an important man's wife I always look around to find his influence, or lack of it, in the overall taste of their home. I think this kind of detail tells us a great deal about a person, especially an elected official."

I understand what Ernestine is saying, I think, but I'm still struck by her question. When I hear the guys in the office on the telephone I don't hear questions like that.

"Weren't you afraid he would think of that as an impertinent question and not talk to you? I hear reporters say you always have to be able to go back to your source."

"To a point that's true," Ernestine says, "but I have to take that chance. To me there are no impertinent questions. Anything I want to know I ask. The only decision is when. A question like that I generally save for the end. I remember when I was first starting out and my editor at the time wanted me to ask some famous hat designer, whose name escapes me at the moment, if *she* would wear that silly hat with a snood that she contrived for the women in war plants. I just thought it was the most impertinent, impolite question. Not only did she answer me, she said of course if she were working around machinery and had to keep her hair from bollixing up the works she would wear it. And then she reminded me that no matter what anyone else might think she thought everything she designed was pretty. It really was a great quote, I can't remember the whole thing. It made my story. Years later when I interviewed Coco Chanel I had no trouble at all asking her about the criticism that she had been too friendly with the Nazis during the occupation. One should always try, you know, to go beyond the obvious, the piece that every other reporter will be writing."

This is really exciting stuff. I want to keep talking to Ernestine, hear what she says about her methods of reporting, but we have reached the coffee shop. In the office she is friendly enough but she is always on the go, as my mother would say. In the halls or in the Ladies Lounge she never seems to have time for more than a quick greeting and perhaps some patter. Nothing like this.

The waitress appears at our booth immediately and I order a sandwich. Ernestine studies the menu very carefully before asking for a side order of cottage cheese, a side order of cole slaw, and a cup of coffee.

The waitress raises her eyebrows. "There's a minimum after 11 A.M.," she says, tapping her pencil on the menu to indicate the statement about the minimum.

"That's all right," Ernestine assures her with a wave of her hand.

"Dieting?" I ask, feeling guilty about the two slices of Jewish rye surrounding the thick roast beef that is coming to me.

"I am," Ernestine answers without coyness. "I was up a pound on the scale this morning so I'm cutting out starches till it drops."

I marvel at her discipline. Five pounds, maybe, or three. But to begin to watch at one pound! Ernestine is so tall and slim you'd never think she watched her weight at all.

"You must have to eat a lot of rich foods at those luncheons and dinners you attend," I say.

"Oh, not really," she answers as we light up. "I always make sure I'm not hungry. Then I don't have to worry about eating. I can concentrate on watching everybody else."

That's a good tip to remember. If I ever make it to cover a luncheon or anything like that I'll remember this.

"Do reporters usually eat before that kind of assignment?"

"Heavens, no. You ought to see some of those so-called representatives of the Fourth Estate. Like pigs at the trough. It makes me so ashamed sometimes. Can't wait to feed their faces at some freebee bash. Acting exactly the way the public relations people know they will, pushing and jostling to get to the food, thinking they've put something over on someone, getting a free meal, and if they're out of town, charging their paper for the meal."

"But don't a lot of people consider their expense account as part of their pay?" I ask.

"Wouldn't it be better though if they got it in salary?"

Ernestine Herbert, I have heard, makes a very high salary, almost as much, it is said, as some of the top men.

Our food arrives and we begin to eat.

"Are you doing a big story about the art people buy?" I ask. I don't say it but I wonder about Lowell Abbott. This is his beat.

"No," she answers, cole slaw slipping out of the corner of her mouth. Quickly and daintily she dabs it with her napkin. "As I was saying before, I think it gives a clue to character, and another thing, so many of my people, the people I write about that is, are into collecting art in a big way now. When I write about a piece of art they own, I want to be absolutely clear in my mind who the artist is, what the different galleries specialize in, that sort of thing, as well as knowing which paintings are ordered by the decorator like bolts of drapery. You'd be surprised how much my perceptions have sharpened in just two forays into the art netherworld. This is my third time out. I just woke up this morning and realized I had no deadline and so here I am. I've been so tied up with that whole Hyannis Port scene. It's a relief to be away from it for a while."

"Do you have regular days off?" I blurt this out and I'm not sure why. Is it impertinent and impolite of me to ask Ernestine this? I'm thrilled to be going out to do sermons on my day off, yet I have to admit it helps that I don't have anything better to do, that Bill isn't around to do something exciting with on Sunday mornings. And my goal is to be promoted so I can relax, so I don't have to work on my days off. Am I asking if she has nothing better to do, if she has no one exciting to spend her day off with?

Ernestine responds to my question with a low, throaty laugh. "That's a good question. You hit a nerve. There's a real philosophical split here. There are those who think they work for a corporation and can keep corporation hours, when they walk away from The Paper they walk away from their jobs until they return the next day. And there are those like me who feel we are journalists who ultimately have to answer to ourselves."

I suppose I look puzzled. Ernestine is puffing on her cigarette and smiling down at me.

"Don't you owe your allegiance to The Paper?" I ask. That's not really exactly what I wanted to say but she continues before I can expand my statement.

"If a journalist does a job to please himself," she says, "and he is a good journalist, then his paper will be well served."

"But aren't they getting away from that?" I ask, wondering if I'm really following her. "Isn't that part of the old hard-nosed-individualist-every-man-for-himself tradition that is supposed to be dying out now, all that competition among men on the same staff knifing each other to get the big stories? Isn't the excellence of The Paper the ultimate goal for everyone? I mean, given the natural instincts for a person to be the best and be recognized and all that." I am thinking of Bill. We have these kinds of discussions sometimes. He is always saying how happy he is to be on The Paper where there is this tremendous sense of pulling together for the common good. It's true that *Overset* runs a lot of stories about individual reporters but there are even more stories about the teamwork that makes The Paper what it is, the cooperation and loyalty of the troops as John Campbell calls everyone but the top editors. I know that if some of those people, those troops, knew that Ernestine Herbert was working on her day off they'd be contemptuous of her and angry to boot. "What the hell else does she have to do, Arlyn? But it makes it tough for the rest of us. We do have families, you know. And I do need that golf game. Unwinds me so I can cope with the week ahead."

"I don't know how we got on this," Ernestine says. "Perhaps it's a continuation in my mind of a conversation I was having yesterday with some of the other gals on the Women's Page. They were giving me the business for working late. I couldn't get them to see that I was working for myself as well as The Paper. It is a problem for some I know. They do have to get home to their husbands and families but since I answer to myself I don't see why it makes any difference if I stay late."

"I guess it is hard for some of them, being married and working at a demanding job."

Ernestine takes a long gulp of coffee before she answers.

"Everyone has to decide for himself," she says as she picks up the check. "I guess we'd better be going." She fishes into her bag for her wallet. I take out my wallet and lean over to look at the check. Ernestine begins to slide out of the booth.

"I do sermons, you know," I say quickly. I had been wanting to get it into the conversation for a while but it didn't come up. Ernestine moves back to the center of her side of the booth and takes her cigarettes out of her bag. "I didn't know," she says, lighting up. "That's good. How many have you done?"

"Three, and I have another tomorrow. Some people think it's a waste of time and that I should be doing feature stories instead."

"Not instead, Arlyn, *and*. If you want to move ahead, and I see you want to, do as much as you can, not as little. You have to. It won't just happen for you. You have to make it happen."

"But the sermons, I've been told, don't mean all that much. A lot of people say it's a long way—"

"It's not necessarily true that sermons aren't valuable, Arlyn. Remember, anything else you do is just more of the

same, just larger. Don't, whatever you do, slough the sermons off. Do them as if you were covering the President at
the White House or a session of Congress. You can't pay attention to the wiseacres. You have to work as hard as you
can, learn all you can, and find ways to get attention and
show off what you can do. That's where the feature stories
come in. A lot of people around the place don't like to see
hard workers but you have to do what's best for you. It's not
going to happen for you any other way. If that means working on your days off or staying until midnight to get what
you want, then you have to do it. You have to go against the
best of them, Arlyn, and the best are never lazy or medio-
cre. And you can never let up. It's all deciding what you
want."

"I suppose you're right. I've been kicking this idea I have
for a feature around but I've been lazy. I haven't done anything about it."

Ernestine's eyes narrow. "What is it?"

I feel silly telling her. She has lunch with Senator Kennedy and Jackie and here I am about to tell her of some ancient barrel maker.

She misinterprets my hesitation.

"You'd rather not tell me. Good. That's good. Who
knows? Maybe I'd steal it from you. Let me read about it in
The Paper, Arlyn. I'll be looking for it."

We laugh over this as we leave the coffee shop. But I
think she's serious. If she needed it she would use it. We
part at the corner. Ernestine wants to run over to the museum to see if she can buy a book she wants. I start to walk
east. It seems cooler now and I begin to run. There's still a
lot of time left to the day. Maybe I can get started on that
story. Maybe I can even reach the old guy on the phone or
visit him today. Who cares what Isabelle says. Who cares
what anybody says.

14

It's unreal. You can see the highway steaming outside the car and there are goosebumps on my arms from the air-conditioning. I am not accustomed to air-conditioned cars and did not think to have my sweater handy. Today the temperature outside registers ninety-three degrees. Hermetically sealed in this rented car, closed off from the noise and the dirt and the heat, it is almost like being in space, just as Bill said it would be; the two of us, all alone. I look at him now as he bears down on the steering wheel. Is he thinking about all the car trips he took with JoAnn, that honeymoon trip west that he seems to remember with both nostalgia and bitterness? "When you're on the road for hours at a time you had damn well better like each other—love is not enough—or it can be a living hell. There is definitely no exit." How do I stack up as a traveling companion, I wonder?

Remembrances of my car trips past pale in comparison with the rollicking laughter and sexual excitement of this morning. Even the trip to Capri with Aldo. How could that compare, really? The sexual excitement was present, of course, the illicit situation and the sheer derring-do of it all, and there was a lot of rollicking laughter, too. But what was it based on? Certainly it wasn't based on the fine nuances of language and thought that Bill and I share. Let's face it, despite all this talk about the language of love, Aldo and I could hardly understand each other, let alone spar with puns the way Bill and I do.

I look over at him. How handsome he looks in that navy blue knit sport shirt and those wrap-around sunglasses. Almost like a cigarette ad. If he would only let his hair grow a bit. He promised me he'd think about it. He insists he doesn't wear a crew cut, his barber has some fancy name for it, but it's as close to a crew cut as you can get. He senses my eyes on him and turns to pucker his lips. We really can't pull over again. We'll never get there. As it is, the trip is longer than we had anticipated, even taking into account Saturday morning traffic to the Cape.

But who cares? We're actually on our way! No schedules, no phone calls, no deadlines, no bosses, no wife. Nothing can intrude until Sunday night, when Bill flies back to New York. For two whole days we'll be together constantly, driving, eating, sleeping, walking on the beach. It has been difficult for me to think of anything else since he told me that JoAnn and the kids would be visiting her mother in Louisville and we could finally get out of the city together.

This happens to be the weekend that I was supposed to fly to Nantucket with Isabelle. In fact, she left last night as planned. I didn't see why Bill and I had to drive. I wanted to fly up too. But this is what Bill wanted. And I really don't know why we're going just to Hyannis. That doesn't grab me at all. I could make my way to the Nantucket ferry from any place on the Cape. Like Provincetown. I pushed hard for Provincetown. I have heard so much about it. Maybe we can still switch our plans and drive on there today.

"John Campbell talks a lot about Provincetown. Before he was married he rushed up every chance he could get."

"John Campbell? Who's John Campbell?"

"You know, the fellow who left Culture to work on the City Desk."

"The clerk?"

"He's not a clerk. He's a news assistant. Now. But he won't be for long, I can tell you. The way he moves he'll be a reporter in no time."

"Now I know who you mean. I've noticed him. He's a loser. A real flake."

"That he is, but I didn't think it showed. He's kind of careful around people he considers important to the advancement of his career."

"I can't see him being promoted. He doesn't seem like reporter material to me. Not for The Paper at any rate." I never cease to marvel at how quickly newcomers to The Paper take on the supercilious attitudes of the lifers. I was surprised to hear this kind of talk coming from Bill.

"That sounds harsh coming from you," I say. "Not everyone's the same. I thought you applauded the differences in people."

"People who do their jobs and shape up for life. But some of these kids today . . . you know." He pats my knee and smiles. I don't know why but I snap back with a subject close to his heart.

"Some people would say the same thing about those Negro kids sitting-in and causing trouble," I say.

He answers me measuredly. "Well, they'd be wrong. Those kids are out to do something important, to change things. What does this John Campbell want?"

"He wants to be a reporter. At least for starters."

"Then why doesn't he act like it?"

"What do you mean?"

"His shaggy hair and flashy shirts and superior sneer. I've noticed him and I'm not the only one. Sitting around reading that *Village Voice* and those French magazines."

"I thought journalists didn't have to be button-down corporation types. I thought that was what the attraction was for so many guys."

"It is, but to a point. A good journalist has to be able to blend in to his environment. When he's with corporation types they think of him as one of them and talk more freely. When he's with foreign service people or diplomats or politicians or generals, he must not put them off by his appearance or manner."

"What makes you think John Campbell couldn't be like that if he had the chance?"

"Because he sits out there around the City Desk and stands out, but not in a positive way. He appears to be a kook, whether he is or not. How could an editor trust him to represent The Paper with dignity?"

Poor John. To celebrate his promotion he threw away his two raggedy white shirts and bought a couple in those new pastel colors. I wonder if anyone besides Bill thinks they're flashy, that they make him stand out.

"So," I say to Bill, slapping his knee playfully, "he sits out there and stands out. Neat trick."

Bill laughs heartily. "You don't let me get away with anything, do you?"

"Why should I?"

"Why are you so concerned about this John Campbell?"

"I'm not concerned, just interested. Maybe I'm more than interested. Maybe I'm jealous. I wish I could get promoted to news assistant. I wonder if doing sermons will really help me."

Bill squeezes my knee. "Po' lil' ole secretary, doin' her lil' ole sermon."

I am stung but not all that surprised. Bill has teased me about the sermons before, but never so blatantly.

"I know you don't take them very seriously," I say, "but I love doing them."

"I take them seriously, honey. What makes you say that?"

"Well, when we talk about what I've done you're very

honest about the writing and technique and so forth, but you don't really hold out much hope that I'll get promoted."

"From a half dozen sermons?"

"Of course not. I don't mean that. I mean seeing them as a first step. I'm doing a feature story when I get back, and I may do a travel piece about Nantucket. I'm going to be on the lookout for good ideas. I have a wonderful idea for a feature story and I cleared it with the City Desk. It's about the last cooper in the city. What do you think of that? Nobody needs barrels in New York nowadays."

"That is a good one. You do come up with good ideas."

"And?"

"Aw, honey, you know I think you write very well, what I've seen anyway. It's not that. It's just that between coming up with a good idea and writing it nicely there's a lot to being a reporter in between."

"Which means?"

Bill looks out of his window briefly at the Rhode Island landscape. I know he is adjusting his features and his thoughts for what he is about to say.

"You remember what I told you a couple of weeks ago," he begins, "how one of the things I loved most about you was that I could talk to you like you were another man, how you could follow all the twists and turns of a conversation to the murky and sometimes sordid ends, how politics was not some vague abstraction to you, but a viable force and yet when we stop talking, you're all woman."

"Uh huh."

"Well, I guess when I'm not too encouraging to you it's because I know what awaits you out there. I'm not even sure you have it in you, and conversely, if you did, you'd be a different gal. Not the wonderful woman I love."

"That's so unfair."

"There. You're in a snit. No need to pout because I speak the truth."

"What makes you so positive it's the truth?" Actually, I'm not on as sure ground as I'm pretending to be. I would never, no matter what the rewards, want to be one of those women Bill is about to describe. Those types, I know, are never happy. It's not natural, it's . . .

". . . and you know it's rough out there, turns you into less than a woman. Believe me, I know. I've seen it enough." Bill has moved into the slow lane now. "We best get some coffee soon," he says.

"I'll drive for a while."

"Won't be necessary, coffee'll fix me fine. Anyway, that's the last thing you want, to become one of those poor, unfortunate, frustrated ball-breaking women who are, quote, successful in their careers but are wrecks in their personal lives. And your Ernestine Herbert is a pale imitation to some I've seen. Not that they start out that way. I have seen the sweetest, brightest young things turn into shrews in the press room. I guess you have to, to make it. I guess that's what I'm saying."

Suddenly I feel unbearably chilly. Why didn't I think to have my sweater along? Damn. I sneeze and reach for a Kleenex in the box on the dashboard. That was my idea. Never travel without a box of Kleenex handy.

"You catching cold, sweetie?" Bill looks at me tenderly.

I continue to sneeze . . . six, seven, eight. Momentarily everything stops; for an instant I am floating, I am on some faraway plane, disembodied. Then my body tingles all over and I come back.

"I don't have to be like those women," I say, but without much conviction. I am sniffling now. I sound snivelly.

"That's what they all think. That it won't happen to them. But obviously it does. In one way or another it gets to them. Sooner or later they wind up twisted, either tough alcoholics or poor, pinched, frustrated, sexless creatures. Woman was made to bear and care for children, not chase dirty facts in smoke-filled rooms."

"You seem to be forgetting our favorite newsroom drunks are all men."

Bill pulls into the truck stop. He looks at me. "You know

perfectly well that's not the same thing. You know there's nothing worse than a female alcoholic. Christ! If you could have seen what I have seen. The only thing worse than a drunken woman is a frustrated, sex-starved old hag."

Well, he has me there. There's no disputing that. The image of it terrifies me. To be a slobbering, red-faced woman running into the toilet for a nip of "special cough medicine" would be bad enough, but to be a dried-up, old, manless ball-breaker—that was too painful to even think about.

Bill steps over the ledge of the bathtub and I move under the shower head. I turn on more hot water and shift to let the full force of it cascade onto my car-weary back. Bill doesn't like the water as hot as I do, so I always finish our joint showers without him.

The motel is not my idea of Honeymooners' Heaven or even Lovers' Luxe. The white chenille bedspreads on the lumpy twin beds and the scratched maple furniture remind me too much of my mother and father's Early American Bedroom Suite. The green tweed carpet has one too many cigarette scars and liquor stains and the shower curtain is mildewed. But it was the best Bill could do at the last minute in Hyannis at this time of year. "If Kennedy makes it, some new motels have to go up here fast," I said.

"Forget the if, they've started building already," Bill answered.

I walk into the room with a towel around my shoulders. I will lie naked on the bed and air-dry. It is such a nice, sensuous feeling and a wonderful prelude to lovemaking. What's this? Bill is sitting on one of the beds with his notebook open on his bare lap. His hand is on the phone on the table between the beds. He looks up when I approach. Is he trying to find a better motel?

"We could still try some place farther from the ferry," I say. "I don't see why we have to be right here in Hyannis. I could manage to get to the ferry from almost anywhere up here on Monday morning. And if not Monday, Tuesday, that would be just as well. What would another day matter if we had a super place for our first time away?" I am stretched out on the other bed, the towel has dropped to the floor, I feel the beads of water forming as my skin begins to dry.

Bill closes his notebook and stands up. The towel he has wrapped around his waist falls to the floor. His penis, stiff and straight as a large wooden peg, comes toward me. My juices flow, mingling with the diaphragm jelly. Soon this recently soft mass of flesh which my womanliness has caused to swell into this giant fucker will be inside me, pumping, pumping, back and forth, back and forth, faster and faster and deeper and deeper and steady now, hold it, that's it, like that, keep going, keep going, steady now, yes, yes, yes o yes.

He is slowly circling my nipple with his fingertip and I am tapping my dry tongue against his cheek. We are coming down. Soon we will get out of bed and go out to explore Hyannis before dinner. I can't decide whether to put back on the white ducks I drove up in or to wear a dress. Bill shifts and sits up. His back is to me. He looks out at the closed venetian blinds as he speaks. I see the muscles tighten in his shoulders.

"Listen, sweetie, I'm going to vamoose for a while now. You just lie there and sleep. You must be exhausted, up so early. I'll be back before eight and we can go have some lobster. I'll find out the best place around."

I can't believe it. I sit up.

"What are you talking about? Where are you going?" I can feel the tension in my chest; I can hear the whine in my voice.

"I'm going over to Hyannis Port and have a look around."

"At what?"

"The Compound."

"The Compound?"

"You know. I told you."

"Told me. You told me nothing. Is that why we're here? So you can have a look at the Kennedy Compound?"

He turns around, scratching his head. The adorable dumb look. And he does look very sincere. Maybe he did mention it. God knows, we talk about Kennedy enough. Did he say he would go have a look at his home while we were in Hyannis?

He is dressing now, taking his charcoal-gray summer slacks from his suitcase. Next will come his light-blue short-sleeved shirt and his black knit tie and blue and white cord jacket.

He leans over to tweak my nipple. I feel nothing. My breasts seem empty to me now, not full and bursting as they had a few minutes ago.

"Why can't I go?"

"Let me check it out and see what it amounts to first. Maybe tomorrow you can ride over with me. He's supposed to be there this weekend and it will be a madhouse with tourists and the press. The TV people really move in. I don't know how far I'll get myself."

"Well, you know him, don't you? Won't he see you?"

"Certainly I know him. I covered him from the time he came to Washington. But it's a whole different ballgame now. I'm not assigned to cover him. Those guys and the columnists have the first crack. And you know, it's not my style to go and hang around. I can't get through to his press people now but I do think I ought to check out the scene. Maybe pick up a tidbit or two for the future. That's all."

"You're really upset that you're not covering the campaign this summer, aren't you?"

"Yep, I am. Why shouldn't I be? It's the most exciting time in the last eight years and I'm diddling around in New York City playing assistant editor to a bunch of deadbeats and callow kids, worrying about strikes on Broadway and the Long Island Railroad and . . ."

"And carrying on with a secretary."

"I didn't say that."

"That's what you mean, though."

"Don't go telling me what I mean."

"All you've been caring about is how to get in on the election coverage. You haven't even been thinking about leaving JoAnn."

The jacket is on now. The pens are going into the outer breast pocket, the notebook inside. Here comes the wallet, the car keys, the cigarettes, the matches. The words are passionate, but the voice is cold.

"You must know how I do love you, but neither you nor JoAnn would have much of a man to worry about if I wasn't rightfully concerned about my professional life, and you well know that. Before I'm a lover I must be a man."

As he talks I wrap the chenille spread around me.

"I told you that JoAnn and I have a lot to work out. You don't walk out on thirteen years like that." He snaps his fingers.

"But I also told you that I don't see how I can get along without you now and that sooner or later I would have to do something."

"I thought it would be sooner." I know how unfair I am being. It's only been seven weeks.

He walks to the bed and leans down to brush his lips against mine. "Maybe it will be," he says. He pulls the spread off me and takes his big hand and slaps me on the ass. It is playful but it hurts. I jump up and throw my arms around him and pull him to me.

"Don't you think JoAnn knows about me?"

"Why should she?"

"Well, we're not very secretive. People around the office know. Wouldn't someone who knows her have said something by now, somebody from Washington?"

He straightens up, removing my arms from around his neck.

"Men don't do things like that, honey. Get a good rest."

He pats my hair and turns to leave the motel room. Through the open door I can see the late afternoon sky. He throws a kiss and shuts the door. My ass is still smarting.

15

It was madness to come outside. What if Bill should call? He'll wonder where I am. Big choice. Where could I be, stranded in that tacky highway motel without a car? Will he be frantic.

My sandals crunch on the gravel underfoot. The sky is fast losing its bright blue color, fading to a sad, empty gray. No more long and languorous summer nights. It is August and those leisurely early summer walks up Broadway in the nine o'clock twilight are part of the past. History. Another chapter.

What gloomy thoughts! Life isn't all romantic dinners and handholding walks and whispered lovesecrets and funsex. What Bill said is true. How could I love a man who didn't take himself and his work seriously? Maybe Bill will find his way to Kennedy and get an exclusive. Wouldn't that be neat!

It must be wild over there at Hyannis Port. Here in town the narrow streets are overflowing with tourists in black knee socks and tartan plaid shorts weaving through impatient horn-honking traffic and waiting good-naturedly in long lines outside tiny fish restaurants. I feel awful. This is not where I want to be. I didn't get up in a fury and dress and defy Bill and come out for this. The Kennedy Compound. I want to see it too. All those magnificent summer houses, so-called cottages, belonging to old Joe Kennedy and his children; all those rolling, carefully tended lawns and tennis courts and that private beach; and the Kennedys themselves, all those lean, stylish women and dashing, aggressive men.

No matter how much I argue with Bill that politics is always corrupt and that the candidates look good because of high-powered public relations created with the cooperation of the press, I have to agree with him that once you accept that as a given, the Kennedy men and their women are indeed newsmakers.

"It's the image they choose to project through all this p.r. that is the phenomenon," Bill says. "For good or bad, there's no denying that Jack Kennedy is a force to be reckoned with."

I've noticed that even those on The Paper who were most against Kennedy before the convention, the Humphrey and Stevenson men, have little trouble getting behind Kennedy now, especially after the Republicans came up with Richard Nixon. Bill, of course, has always leaned toward Kennedy. As much as he could, that is, and still remain the objective reporter.

Ever since the convention, stories have been pouring out of Hyannis Port. Every day there's a picture of this or that V.I.P. or political leader standing outside the Kennedy house announcing to the world that he is behind the candidate one hundred percent. There is even talk that Truman will stump for him.

There are a lot of stories in the papers about the curious, the gawking tourists who clog the streets around the area trying to get a glimpse of something Kennedy. An eight-foot-high stockade fence has been put up partially surrounding the estates to try to afford the family some privacy, but it is still possible, they say, to see the houses from the street. Neighbors in the luxury summer resort, mostly Republicans, the papers point out, are angry at the invasion of their privacy and the trampling of their roses, but no ordinance barring citizens from the streets has yet been passed. Less is said in the papers or on television about the neighbors' complaints about reporters and camera crews always in attendance. The Kennedy family's ability to charm even the most cynical journalist is well known and it would be difficult to hear a negative comment about the press from any of them.

"Something will have to be done about the television people," Bill said after we read an account of a ruckus between an aggressive TV cameraman and one of the deans of the Washington Press Corps. "They get out of hand, storming over press conferences with their cables and cameras as though they own the place. Some of the rude guys on newspapers are bad enough, but these TV guys, they take the cake. They'd kill for a minute's air time."

The sea of Bermuda shorts and beehive hairdos stiff with salt air and Spraynet swirls around me. I imagine that it suddenly parts and I am transported to the Compound, jostling with the other reporters, snooping around, getting past the police barricades, lucking into a story. What is happening out there on this evening in early August, three months before the election? Is history being made?

I must go to the Compound. I just can't wait until tomorrow to perhaps ride out with Bill or hear his account of it. I must see the scene tonight. For myself. Smell it, feel it, taste it, touch it. It is almost six-thirty. I can get a taxi to take me out. Surely it can't take long, even with the traffic.

The black and white checked jacket dress will be perfect with the white pumps. Do I need white gloves? Those Kennedy women always wear white gloves. I'd better take them in my purse. Thank God, I threw them in. I really debated about whether to bring them along on the vacation. More and more these days I am not wearing them. But you still can never be sure when you might want them, to carry at least.

But what about Bill? Will he be furious? I'll be casual. It has nothing to do with you, I'll say. Surely I have as much right to be here as any other tourist. I won't snoop, I won't try to sneak in or anything like that. If I see Bill I will only say hello and let him take it from there. If he doesn't want to acknowledge me—as his traveling companion or whatever —that's all right with me. I understand. We can compare notes back in the room. But what if we don't see each other there and he gets back first? Maybe I'd better leave him a note in the room and also a message at the motel office. Should I say I went to the movies or just that I was out briefly and he wasn't to worry. That sounds more like it. Why lie?

What if I scoop him? What if I happen to bump into a Kennedy, one of the women or children, and get a good human-interest story? After the year of grinding campaigning for the Candidate they all put in they must have a lot to say. What about the pregnant Jacqueline? Maybe she would reveal some little something, some tidbit not yet written about her, something Ernestine Herbert and the other Women's Page reporters missed, something only I would get, something I could call into the National Desk to be inserted into the Monday morning paper, something . . .

But if I get something, shouldn't I locate the Man from The Paper who's covering up here? Don't I have that obligation, to tell him? Even if he steals it without giving me credit? Like the time I witnessed that encounter in front of the public library between Nixon and the woman with a cat on a rhinestone leash.

I should have gone to the City Desk, but I knew who was covering Nixon so I told him. His story, the only one in all the morning newspapers that mentioned the sidewalk debate, won a Feature of the Month Award. I was so angry I almost screamed right there in front of the bulletin board when I saw the award. Usually when legmen who are assigned to feed information to a reporter are involved in a prize-winning story, they are always cited, but this creep didn't see fit to give me credit. I vowed never again, but what can I do?

No one looks up when I enter the motel office. Several old people in maple rocking chairs, a broad-backed young fellow in a green and white striped seersucker jacket, and the desk clerk are all intently watching the television set perched above the stone fireplace. A commentator's cultivated voice is intoning over a fuzzy picture of Francis Gary Powers in Moscow. Bill said he really is a spy but it won't come out in the trial.

At the commercial break the desk clerk resumes talking to the fellow with the broad back. I see that he has several cameras hanging from his neck and shoulder.

"Now," says the clerk, "you want a cab to take you to the Kennedy place." She spins around to the switchboard and plugs in. She talks quickly into the mouthpiece and then looks up.

"Denny will be here in five minutes," she says. "That was his wife. He's out on a run now but he should be back soon." She looks at me.

"I want the same thing, a cab to the Kennedy place."

The cameras jiggle, the broad back tilts, the seersucker shifts, an inquiring face appears over the camera straps. Silky auburn sideburns, too long for anyone but a hood, and enormous brown eyes are all that I notice.

"Who you with?" His tone is brisk and matter-of-fact but his voice is full and rich. The desk clerk holds her speech and the phone plug in midair as she looks from this unknown man to me. She is waiting for my answer. The maple chairs have stopped rocking and I can hear my breath in quick, short bursts. Why should I be so nervous. This is ridiculous. Who am I with? I tell him I work for The Paper, but I'm not too exact about what I do. It works. My breath returns to normal.

"No kidding. That's great. You shouldn't have any trouble getting in. Why don't we ride out together?"

I agree. He moves over and holds the glass motel lobby door open for me. For once I am glad to see a wedding band on an attractive man. Really. This is strictly business.

In the cab Denny doesn't give us much chance to talk. All I have learned so far is that his name is Dan Roth and he's originally from Long Island but lives in California now and is back East to do a photo essay on the Hyannis Port scene. He has an assignment on speculation from some magazine I never heard of. He had some pictures in *Look* last January, he said.

Dan Roth lights a cigarette and offers one to me. I lean forward for the match he holds out to me. The acrid smell of tobacco burning and the stale sweat from his body mixes with the salt air blowing into the open window of the cab. I yearn for Bill. I wonder if he connected tonight. Will I? Will this Dan Roth and I be able to get near enough to the Kennedys to make this jaunt worthwhile? What kind of credentials does Roth have, anyway? He seems eager to latch on to mine. Ha! If he only knew. Will flashing my Newspaper Guild Press Card work tonight? Maybe it will, maybe it will work better here than it does at police lines in Manhattan.

Am I crazy? What am I doing, asking for trouble? Am I really going to try to push my way into another crowd? I can still feel that cop's big hand on my back from that do at Washington Mews last spring. Actually, getting in was not the problem. It was getting out. Once I had badgered my way past the guards into that charity bazaar on that darling, exclusive private street I decided the whole thing was very dull. Especially after I saw the Society Editor paying his obeisance to the thin, Ardened women manning the booths. The City Desk would tell me to talk to him and he would never be receptive to any color sidebar from me.

Slam. I can still feel it. The policeman's big hand on my

back, pushing me out of the way. I was only approaching him to ask him where the buses were rerouted. I was not part of the boisterous crowd of rubbernecks hanging over the barricade wide-eyed as each limousine rolled up to discharge this or that sleek benefactor.

When I fell forward into the crowd I began to shake. Why was I pushed so brutally? I turned and my head nearly exploded in anger: Elsa Maxwell. I was pushed out of the way for Elsa Maxwell. That cow! No one at the office was too upset. It's a scuffling business, Arlyn, you have to accept being pushed around. If you can't stand the heat stay out of the kitchen. Only Lowell had an interesting viewpoint. Would you have been so angry, Arlyn, if it had been Renata Tebaldi or Maria Tallchief? I had to think about that awhile. After all, their bodies were their instruments, instruments that gave immeasurable pleasure to the world. They had to be protected. But Elsa Maxwell!

The cab is idling in traffic. "This is Scudder now," Denny says.

"Let's get out and walk the rest of the way," Roth suggests. "We must be very near."

I take my wallet out of my purse.

"How much?" Roth asks Denny.

"Four dollars will do it, in-season rates and all," Denny says, looking out of the cab window.

I put two dollars in Dan Roth's hand. He makes a slight gesture to return it but I shake my head. He hands Denny a five-dollar bill. "Keep the change," he says; "how can we reach you if we want you again?"

Denny points to a phone number on his sun shield and I copy it into my notebook.

Once out of the cab, we drift into a crowd that is meandering along a lane where perfectly trimmed privet hedges and pink rambling roses guard carpets of green lawn. The white trim of the clapboard houses nestled close to the ground glows in the full moon now rising. The shuffling feet and raucous laughter surrounding us seem a crude intrusion on the serene beauty of the night. At least Dan Roth is silent as we walk along, scanning the area.

Suddenly we hear the noises of the crowd in front of us grow louder and more animated. Dan and I exchange looks and move faster.

"I figure if I get the lay of the land tonight, I can come back before sunrise tomorrow and know just where I want to stake out," he says. "I may be better off steering clear of the official press headquarters, at least till after I get my good stuff, you know."

"That sounds sensible."

"What I heard," Roth says, "is that the big shots get summoned in and everybody else kind of hangs around hoping to get a photo session or an impromptu press conference. They're very particular about who they let in the house, but they come outside a lot for pictures."

"Are you interested in the photo sessions?" I know his answer before he says it. Though he looks at first glance pretty much like the young fellows who work for The Paper, there is something just a bit flaky about him with those sideburns and that rumpled green striped seersucker jacket. There is an edge of hustle to him that you don't find in the guys who work for The Paper. Though they're all very competitive among themselves and perhaps recognize someone here or there on another publication as their peers, most of them exude that air of confidence that comes from knowing that they will be welcomed anywhere with open arms. Some are truthful enough to joke about it, knowing that if they should quit The Paper they might be just plain Joe Blow again. Dan Roth is just another Joe Blow.

"No," he is saying, "I want candid, exclusive stuff. That's my only shot. To get something nobody else has and better. That's why I want to prowl around. I'm as interested in the scene as I am in the candidate unless I get him really off guard. There are enough of those phony *candid shots* of him already. How about you?"

"Same. There are several people up here covering for The

Paper. I'm kind of on my own, hoping for that happy accident." I look at Roth for the usual snicker but he is shaking his head in agreement. "Anyway," I continue, "I want to see the scene, I just love to be where things are happening, where the action is. Why don't we walk this way?"

Roth's sharp eyes dart into the darkness where I have just pointed. "Terrific," he says, "it's a break in the hedges. I see you have eagle eyes, too, or whatever bird it is that sees in the dark. How could I have missed it?"

"Oops." As I approach the other end of the hedge I stumble over a thick chain slung across two overgrown bushes. There is a small wooden sign: PRIVATE KEEP OUT: DELIVERIES ONLY TRESPASSERS WILL BE PROSECUTED.

I move to let Dan Roth read the sign. He shrugs and steps over the chain, winking and extending his hand to me to follow. My heart is racing. Will we be stopped, arrested? But there's no turning back now. This is obviously the only way for us to get where we want to go.

"Can you shoot anything now?" I whisper to him.

"With my telephoto lens," he answers over his shoulder, "if there's enough light . . ." His voice drops off. We have emerged from the thicket of hedges and the dirt path. We are standing on, almost sinking into, a soft, wet lawn. Ahead we see a large house with dozens of windows, all lit up. Figures in silhouette are framed in tableaux. An informal party seems to be in progress. Groups of people, some with cameras slung over their shoulders, are sitting on a terrace, strolling on the lawn or standing at the windows. The clatter of plates and the clink of glasses mix with the sound of high animated voices and a lot of laughter. Every nerve ending in me is tingling. In a few seconds we will be in the party, circulating, talking, observing. There are so many people down there, who would question us?

"Okay. Where ya think ya'r going?" The light blinds me.

"We're just looking for Irving Avenue," I answer brightly.

"Yeah, well just turn around and go back out the way you came in. You ain't going to find Irving Avenue this way. I'll escort ya. Hey, what's this, what you doing with that camera, buddy? No pictures. Did you just take a picture? You Press? Press is supposed to register, not be sneaking around. I could have you barred permanently." Roth is up to something, but I'm not sure what.

"Oh no, we're just tourists," I say quickly. "Just wanted to have a little peek. We're from Pittsburgh. We're friends of Davey Lawrence, you know. Tell us, what's happening down there tonight? It must be exciting to be on duty here."

"Just the usual, big shots, celebrities, aides, family, Press, the important Press, the ones who were invited to supper, that is."

We are at the hedges now and I turn to have one look and to see what Dan is doing. He has straggled behind again. "Ouch, you don't have to do that," I snap to the cop. "We were leaving. You don't have to use such brute force."

"Listen, lady, don't accuse me of brute force. I ought to book you. You're on private property. See, you can read." He is pointing to the sign, clearly visible from the streetlamp behind us. He is really angry and turns to call Dan. "Hey, buddy, hurry it up." He starts to go back but Roth appears, silently joining us. As we step over the fence Roth sends an enormously sly sidelong look my way. He must have got something good.

Neither of us speaks until the cop leaves us and we are alone.

"You were great. Just great! Tourists from Pittsburgh, Davey Lawrence. Who the hell is Davey Lawrence?"

"Apparently the cop didn't know either. David L. Lawrence is the Governor of Pennsylvania, but I know him as the Mayor of Pittsburgh. He's the only Mayor I knew when I was growing up there. Haven't you read about him? The kingmaker they call him. At first he was dead set against Kennedy. The Catholic thing. Lawrence is Catholic himself and he was sure one couldn't win. Then at the last minute he threw the whole delegation to Kennedy."

"And he's a friend of yours, of course," Roth's tone is affectionately mocking. It pleases me to surprise him with my answer.

"Yes." I wait for Roth's quickened interest. He is silent. "Don't you want to know more?"

"I'm waiting," he says.

"Well, he's not really a friend of mine."

"Uh huh."

"My father's a friend of his. Actually, I'm not sure friend is the right word. My father is a crony of his."

"Crony?" Roth stops walking and looks at me directly. He narrows his eyes, studying me hard, and takes a long drag on his cigarette. His wedding ring glows in the dark. We walk on.

"That's the only word I can think of. Does crony always have to have a pejorative connotation? Maybe crony is the wrong word too. Political associate. How's that? Does that sound better?"

Roth is looking at me sideways again. "And just what does a political associate to a Mayor or Governor do?"

"He gets out the vote, that's what he does." I am surprised to hear myself saying it so casually. No talking about how Daddy is a supervisor in the Allegheny County Treasurer's office, a job he holds but rarely attends to. Just the facts. He's the lowest of the low, a ward-heeler who gets out the vote, forcing the people who are dependent on him for jobs and favors to vote the straight Democratic ticket, or else.

Isn't that your father, Arlyn, that man up on the stage sitting next to the Students for Stevenson coordinator? Why is he here? And is it true that all of us on Senatorial scholarships have to put in five hours a week minimum to organize for Stevenson or we'll lose our scholarships? And we have to wear these hugh buttons everywhere? I heard we're really being watched.

"You're ambivalent about your father's activities, aren't you?" Dan Roth and I have been walking away from the tourists through quiet streets and winding lanes. I turn to find him looking at me. The tough, hard look is gone. His warm brown eyes are open and interested.

We reach a patch of sand.

"Want to walk on the beach awhile?" Dan asks. "It's early yet."

I look at my watch. I wonder if Bill's back. "I have to get back. Someone's waiting for me."

"Oh," he says, and we begin to pick up our pace.

"Did you get what you wanted?" I ask.

"More than I expected but not everything I need," he answers. "While you were diverting the cop I spotted a couple running down the slope of grass behind us. Our commotion must have scared them. The top of her dress was off. I shot them in silhouette."

"You took their picture?"

"They won't be recognizable. I only hope there's enough to give a sense of the thing, a little hanky-panky in the splendid grass kind of thing."

"Do you think anyone will publish it?"

"Maybe not, but it will help me get other jobs. I thank you again. I did thank you before, didn't I?" He looks at me laughing. "If it does impress picture editors I'll be forever in your debt, daughter of a crony of the kingmaker, Davey Lawrence."

"Happy to have been of service," I say, curtsying slightly, keeping up the jocular tone. We are in front of the motel now. Damn. Dan made out. I'm sure Bill made out. And what about me? What did I gain from this little outing? I reach into my purse for the key to my room.

"Maybe next time I can return the favor," he says, waving goodbye.

16

"Why are all the best ones married? Married or queer?"

"That's not necessarily true," Isabelle answers. She is lying next to me, angled toward the low afternoon sun.

Am I hearing things? This from Isabelle? I sit up and let out a hoot. "You are too much," I say, looking at her frying body. "One date with your dream man and your whole tune changes."

Isabelle squints her eyes at me meaningfully. "Not one date, two, if you count Friday night."

"So two dates. But doesn't it bother you, this crass way he's alternating? *You*, Friday, Sunday, Tuesday. *Her*, Saturday, Monday, Wednesday."

"Not at all," Isabelle answers. "I think it makes perfect sense. It shows how wise he really is. Why put all your eggs in one basket? That had always been my mistake. I'd meet a guy on vacation and be available to him whenever he wanted. Sometimes I'd spend a whole week with a guy and he didn't even call once in the city. I'm glad Hal's giving me the opportunity to cast around."

"I'm all for that," I say, "but if it is as great between you as you say, how can either of you be so calculating? Don't you just want to go for broke?"

Isabelle sits up and looks at me with what can only be called contempt. "You are definitely an incurable romantic, Arlyn. That's your problem. And a dodo. I hadn't wanted to say anything to you, it's none of my business, but you really are in for a fall with that Bill. He's just fooling around and you, my friend, will end up broke or broken, with your reputation ruined to boot."

I feel myself stiffening inside, but I try to sound light as I talk. "Isabelle, you have it all wrong," I tell her. "I love him and every minute I'm with him and that's enough. I can't be bothered thinking about the future or my reputation. What will be, will be."

"Bull crap! You think about the future as much as anyone else. You still believe in miracles, that's all. But you could be more discreet, you know. You're just flaunting it in people's faces and it can't be doing either of you any good."

What can I say to that? Though we don't hide our relationship, I don't think that Bill and I flaunt it. I know that the wags around the office think it's just another quickie, cheater's thing. After the first leering looks and cracks, comment about us has subsided. Our affair is Reserve News. It has been tucked away, pigeonholed, slotted, spiked, only to be trotted out again and clucked over when a long slow afternoon has to be filled and the discussion turns, as it always does, to a rundown of office affairs, real and imagined, past and present.

I would like to tell Isabelle that it is different with Bill and me, that he will soon leave JoAnn, but much as that would give me pleasure, I hold my tongue. Isabelle's reaction when she learned about our weekend in Hyannis was so upsetting to me that I don't want to start a whole big thing with her again. And when she learned that I went out to Hyannis Port to try to crash the Kennedy houses she was almost as incredulous as Bill. Was I crazy, they both wanted to know.

When I pushed open the motel door on Saturday night he was sitting up in the nearer bed, fully dressed even to his jacket and shoes. An overflowing ashtray was balanced precariously on his thighs. When he saw me he jumped up, spewing cigarettes and ashes over the moldy carpet. But that was nothing to the sparks of angry abuse he flung over me.

"Where in God's creation have you been? I rushed back here as fast as I could. Bobby Kennedy invited me to have supper but I came back here to you. And for what? You were gone! And I wasn't going to write tonight. I checked around until I found the finest fish restaurant in the area. I just knew how much you would enjoy that. And you weren't here! I've been sitting stiff with fear, just sure that something terrible happened to you."

"I left you a note, I—"

"A note! 'Darling, have gone out for a while, back soon, love, Arlyn.' What does that mean? Out for a while. I've been here for over an hour. Do you know what you've put me through? Wondering where you could be by yourself at this time of night in this place?"

I was touched by his concern.

"I'm sorry. I wanted to go out to Hyannis Port to see the Compound."

"The Compound! You went to the Compound! Are you crazy?" He was removing his jacket now.

"Why not? I have just as much right as anyone else. The place was crawling with tourists, it's—"

"You're not exactly a tourist. You're here with me. It's tricky enough as it is, but if you got involved in some fracas it would make it most unpleasant indeed, would it not?" He took off his pants.

I began to shake as I answered. "Well, if that's what you're so worried about, it almost happened." Now I am mad. I started to undress and tell him about Dan Roth and the dirt path and the policeman escorting us off the property and I took some kind of perverse pleasure is seeing Bill's naked body sag and deflate. But it was not jealousy that caused the change in him. It was mirth. As I recounted our aborted effort to mingle with the Kennedy guests, his furious anger dissolved into an uncontrollable fit of coughing laughter.

"So that's as far as you got, you and the freelance photographer," he said, choking into a wad of tissue, tears forming in the corners of his eyes.

I stalked over to shout into his face. "And if I had been booked, what makes you think I would have involved you?"

His answer was to reach out and pull me down on him. "You're magnificent when you're angry," he said, still shaking with laughter. I watched his cock grow, and I slid up over his thigh to engulf it. But he abruptly flipped us. Suddenly I felt the nubs of the chenille bedspread pressing into my back.

"It's not funny," I protested.

"You are too much," he said, still laughing as he entered me. I was sorry that I had downplayed Dan Roth's looks, emphasizing the cameras and the seersucker jacket and ignoring the sparkle in his deep brown eyes. And I was sorry I told him that Dan Roth was married.

Isabelle is still talking about how Bill and I are taking a terrible chance. "Even Kit Rockwell asked me about it last week," Isabelle is saying. "When she asks, you know it must be a hot topic."

"What do you mean?" I think I know what Isabelle is driving at, but I'm not sure.

"Oh, you know Kit. That pinky ring, you know what that means?"

"That's her prep school ring. She told me."

"Yeah, sure. But honestly, Arlyn, don't you feel uncomfortable with her? Especially when we're talking about guys. Don't you feel like she's kind of mocking us for liking men?"

For a moment I can't answer. Isabelle has articulated what I must often have felt. But I refuse to be pulled into a character assassination of Kit.

"That's just her way. She dates. She's told me about going to the beach with her boyfriend."

"You're sure it was her boyfriend?"

"What kind of question is that? All I know is, I've heard her talk about her friend."

"And I've heard her ask you if you ever wanted to go out to the beach with her some Sunday."

"What's wrong with that?"

"So where's the boyfriend?"

"Isabelle, you're impossible. Sometimes I wonder what goes on inside your head."

But Isabelle has not heard my last statement. She is sitting up, frantically looking around. My eyes follow. All over the beach people are now standing in small groups. Isabelle and I are the only two still on blankets.

"My God," she says, jumping up. "It's past four-thirty." She tugs at her bathing suit and fluffs her hair.

I stand up beside her. "I think I'll have another swim," I say.

She glares at me. "Listen," she says, "this is no time to swim."

"Why not? The water is beautiful now."

"Don't be funny. I told you if we don't get dates for dinner before we leave here it's a mess. You can swim, but don't expect me to care if you have to eat alone tonight."

Isabelle turns and starts to stroll up the beach. "You want to see what's happening over there?" I look in the direction she has started to walk. A crowd of about fifteen has formed a circle and I hear a lot of loud talk and high-pitched laughter. There seem to be a lot more girls than guys. I know I should walk over with Isabelle but I cannot bring myself to. "I'm going for a swim," I say as I run toward the water.

The skin is tightening across the bridge of my nose. My back itches under the wired bra and strapless stiff white eyelet sheath I am wearing.

"Who can stand it?" Isabelle is saying. "No one can. It has to be done. Are you so much better than everyone else?" She is fast losing patience with me, I can see.

When I came back to the blanket after my swim Isabelle was dressed in her beachshift and waiting to leave. She hadn't connected for dinner and she was eager to get back to the room and dressed and over to the Rope Walk. There is still a chance to get a dinner date during cocktails here.

I obliged, dressing quickly, and now remaining quiet while we stand in this absurd line of girls waiting to walk a plank into the steamy bowels of this ersatz ship. How humiliating, waiting to get into a restaurant that we don't even want to eat in. It's out of our price bracket. We just want to have a drink and pick up a date for dinner. Isabelle insists it is the last shot for tonight. And she is giving it all she has, overdressed as she is in that fussy aqua lace thing.

At last. We are moving. We shuffle aboard. The scene inside is unbelievable. Layers of girls are stuffed around the bar and tables tensely eyeing the few unattached men who are roaming around looking for God knows what. We sit at two empty seats around a low, recently vacated cocktail table. Where did the former occupants go? Did they connect, or did they give up in disgust and go to buy themselves dinner? Isabelle is getting more strained by the minute. Her large friendly mouth is stretched across her face into a thin red line. She lights one cigarette after the other, taking a couple of drags and furiously tamping it out.

Time loses its meaning for me as we sit in this noisy, smoky lounge sipping our drinks, a Stinger, the Happy Hour Special, for Isabelle, two whiskey sours for me. Finally

Isabelle picks up the soggy bill, rescuing it from the puddle
it is lying in. "Yours is a dollar sixty and mine is eighty
cents, so you leave a quarter tip and I'll leave fifteen cents.
That's what you're supposed to leave."

I obey and stand up. Isabelle drops two dollars and
eighty cents on the table. It has surprised me today to see
Isabelle, who is usually so independent and positive, the
bright Manhattan secretary, revert to just another girl from
Brooklyn, automatic and unthinking in her herdlike reac-
tions.

Isabelle pushes through the crowd with me close behind
her. At the door she turns. Her face has blanched under the
sunburn. Her lips contract as she hisses in a strangled whisper, "He's here. With her. Waiting at the reservation desk."
With those words she bolts out of the restaurant.

I stall to get a good look at the wondrous Hal, Isabelle's
every other night heartthrob. He is rather nice-looking,
there is no doubt about that, tall and lean, with a fringe of
graying sandy hair and a good tan. He looks every bit his
age. Isabelle told me that it was okay that he was over forty
because he had been married once when he was younger.
Obviously, she said, he's not a fairy or afraid of women or a
momma's boy. He's just hasn't met the right one.

His date, the girl he has told Isabelle he will continue to
see every other night though he says he has fallen hard for
Isabelle, has blond hair and blue eyes and a pert nose that is
almost identical to Isabelle's. I wonder if it was done by the
same plastic surgeon. The idea that Hal is a sucker for that
surgeon's nose tickles me. Isabelle certainly brags enough
about the surgeon.

Isabelle has composed herself and is waiting for me on
the wharf. "What's so funny?" she asks, but I refrain from
telling her. We set out in search of a place to eat. It is almost eight-thirty by the time we are finally seated at a little restaurant that I would have been happy to come to at
six-thirty.

I am cranky and hungry now but the atmosphere is pleasant, the waitress is a cheerful college girl, and there are broiled scallops on the menu. Things are picking up.

This morning when I got off the ferry and found my way to the charming, gleaming white guest house I was looking forward to my stay on Nantucket with enthusiasm. I was almost relieved when Bill left for the airport last night, and I thought it was probably a good thing for us to have this separation. Sunday had been a long, wearing day for me. It started out terrifically, though. We got up late and I lazed in bed with containers of coffee and danish and the papers while he wrote his piece. What a kick it was to look up and see my man typing away at that shaky motel desk, writing an analysis of the Kennedy strategy that would be read all over the country tomorrow. And I read it first. In takes! As Bill finished each sheet he would rip it from the typewriter and toss it to me. When he finished the fourth he brought it over and dropped down to kiss my breasts while I finished reading.

The afternoon was not as much fun, however. Bill lost interest in going out. "Why don't we just stay here?" he had said. "I'll go get some sandwiches and beer and we'll just stay in bed and play and watch some television." I had turned down that invitation a time or two before in my life, but not since college. When I got dressed to go out on a date I wanted to do something, anything, not check into a motel at nine in the evening with someone I hardly knew and when I drive two hundred miles to a place I've never been, a town on Cape Cod, for God's sake, I want to get out and see it, not mooch around a moldy motel room, even if it is with the man I love.

I look up from my plate of scallops to see the guy who has the room next to ours come into the restaurant. I nudge Isabelle. "That's the guy I was telling you about, Stuart, the fellow in the room next to ours. He's alone. Shall I ask him to join us?"

Isabelle turns to size him up. "Ugh! He's more gruesome

than you described," she says, "he'll spoil my appetite." I hadn't said he was gruesome, I had just given her what I thought was an accurate description of him, tall and skinny with glasses and a large beaked nose and sad eyes. I had also told her that from what I could gather in our brief encounter outside his door when I had left our room to use the bathroom that he is shy and tense. How dare she say I called him gruesome. I stand up and wave to get his attention. At first he doesn't think I'm beckoning to him, although he is the only person standing in the front of the restaurant where I am looking. Finally he begins tentatively to walk toward us. He is carrying maps and guidebooks and a wrinkled copy of this morning's paper. Isabelle is tapping her foot under the table as I ask him to join us. What's the big deal?

"More cappuccino! I'll float away." Isabelle declines Stuart's offer of more coffee and pastry as the lanky, sour-faced waitress stands by. We are in a coffeehouse now, after having been asked to leave the restaurant at ten. The three of us have been so busy talking and laughing that we hadn't noticed the restaurant emptying out around us. Luckily the coffeehouse was nearby and open till midnight.

Isabelle is teasing Stuart about the dog-eared condition of his newspaper. "Looks like you really chewed over all the news in The Paper today," she says.

I am not prepared for his answer. In the midst of all the laughter he suddenly becomes serious as he turns to me and half-apologizes.

"I was a little disjointed this morning when we met," he explains. "The Paper wasn't available in Hyannis when I got on the ferry and I was afraid it would be sold out if I didn't hurry right down to buy it this morning. That happened to me once and I had to read the *Trib*. That's why I was kind of short with you."

What I had called shyness and tenseness he was calling needing his morning fix of The Paper.

"I was really anxious to read it this morning," he is saying. "I had heard something about Stevenson on the radio. I didn't catch the whole thing. I worked for Stevenson in fifty-two and fifty-six. W. B. Hallam has an excellent article in this morning about how Kennedy has welcomed Stevenson to the fold and will find an important post for him if elected. Did you read it?"

I can feel Isabelle's eyes on me. "You didn't tell me Bill filed," she says.

Stuart's mouth drops. "You know him?" he asks.

Isabelle and I shake our heads gleefully, familiar with the tone in Stuart's question. "Yes, we know him," Isabelle says. "And Buddy Batcholder and Damon Crewes and Hayes Harris too.

"Buddy Batcholder? You mean J. Winston Batcholder, Jr.?"

Isabelle bobs her head.

"And Hayes Harris? What's he really like?"

"You know," Isabelle says, leaning back and pulling a long drag of her cigarette, "they're just like everyone else, they put their pants on one leg at a time."

I roar. Where did she ever hear that one? Stuart's eyes are bugging through his glasses. He seems slightly embarrassed by Isabelle's remark but also a bit titillated. He turns to me.

"Wasn't it a tragedy about Randolph Thoburn's untimely death? Did you read his obituary, that part about how when he was a young reporter he had interviewed the Duke and Duchess of Windsor and afterward had sent the Duchess just one perfect yellow rose?"

I'm cringing. It always embarrasses me when I read employees' obituaries in The Paper. I think it's corny when some reporter or copy editor gets the full treatment, picture and a full column filled with trivial anecdotes that are great when retold in the warmth of the city room but seem silly in cold print.

Funny, Stuart has brought up that one perfect rose thing

again. It was just this past Friday morning that the memorial was finally held. "It's such a rotten time, no one's in town," Sydney Sugar, the press agent, complained to me in the ladies room of the Shubert Theater before the service, "but it's now or never, I guess," she had added. "If you wait until fall when the new season starts, no one is interested in memorials, especially with a new critic to get to know." I had felt a twinge for Randolph then and whispered something appropriate to myself like "Sic transit" before finding my way to a seat.

Reporters and copy editors and executives from The Paper, along with some of the most celebrated theatrical names of the day, filed into the theater, filling up the orchestra. Roger Glickston delivered the eulogy. His appointment to Chief Drama Critic has not been announced officially yet but it is an open secret all over town. When they put it to him, now or never, it is said, he canceled the year at Oxford PDQ.

If I had been Betty I don't think I would have wanted Glickston delivering the eulogy, but she didn't seem to mind. She was brave, and magnificent in dove gray. I was surprised to see at least three women sobbing alone in the back rows. What was really startling though were the five bud vases, each containing one perfect yellow rose. They had been delivered separately from different florists, each of whom told Gil Gilchrist that the purchaser wished to remain anonymous. But Betty didn't seem troubled by it, so why should I be, I thought.

Stuart's a nice fellow, I think, why not give him a thrill.

"You know," I say during a lull in the conversation, "I drove Randolph Thoburn's wife to their country home in Nyack after his death. A charming Victorian house overlooking the Hudson."

Stuart laps it up just as I knew he would. "Really?"

"Did you hear that she wants to put it up for sale?" Isabelle asks.

I am shocked. "No," I answer, "I'd have thought they'd have to carry her out of there."

"She spoke to Judd about it. Apparently she wants to come back to the city and do something."

"Do what?"

"That's just it. Judd told her not to make any rash moves. She told him she can't bear to be there alone now. He told her that would pass and she would want the house again, it's all she has. She also told him she's stuck because she doesn't drive and he told her to continue to use the woman who drives for her now and to learn to drive herself in due time."

Stuart is captivated and doesn't even notice the waitress standing over him waiting for him to pay the check. It is midnight already and we are the last customers in the coffeehouse.

We gather ourselves together and leave, making our way back to the guest house along the quiet cobbled streets, empty now except for a bicylist or two and a couple here or there—two who connected?—headed perhaps for a late night party.

17

My head is throbbing and I lean back in the bus and shut my eyes. Stuart is absorbed in *Advise and Consent*. He had turned to it almost as soon as he finished The Paper. He spent much more time on The Paper than I did, reading through all the stories, reading stories that weren't stories, first edition bunk leads, full of fluff and yesterday's tidbits, written to hold the space for the *real* story that was to come.

To come. More to come. I must remember to tell Bill about that Lenny Bruce routine John Campbell was reciting the other day. "To is a preposition; come is a verb." To come. To kum. Lede to kum. Hed to kum. Those funny words scrawled on copy to say the lead or headline is coming. You're invited to my intercourse party. Everyone's coming. To come. To come is a verb. Everyone's coming. The rhythms of the Bruce patter and that old high school joke mingle with the rhythms of the bus as we churn along. My headache is vanishing.

I lean over and take my own folded copy of The Paper

out of the straw bag at my feet. Before I get very far in thumbing through the first section, Bill's think piece jumps out at me; he really worked that Bobby Kennedy poop, first with an exclusive sidebar in yesterday's paper and now this depth analysis. How nice that he trysted in Hyannis for the weekend.

He certainly sounded pleased about the piece this morning. At least he was pleased about something. Maybe it *was* the early hour, but his lack of enthusiasm about my returning to the city today sure put a damper on my hell-bent eagerness to blow Nantucket and get back to him. After talking to Isabelle until almost three o'clock this morning I decided that it had been a mistake to think I could enjoy myself on this vacation with Bill back in the city. Isabelle said if I felt that way the best thing to do was return. Why waste the money to finish the time up here, she said, especially since rain was predicted for the end of the week. My share of the room didn't come to all that much; it was food, if I had to buy my own dinners, that would add up. Isabelle, I think, was happy to see me go. Our relationship at the office and for occasional midweek dinners and ballet and theater did not travel well.

When I left the guest house this morning I bumped into Stuart, who was headed for the ferry too. I had no idea how I would continue after I got to Hyannis or what the plane schedule was. I asked Stuart if he would like to share a rental car with me back to the city but he declined. He was in no hurry to return, he said, he was still on vacation. He was continuing his exploration of famous American resorts. "I decided to give this summer to New England," he told me, explaining the methodical itinerary that had brought him to the Berkshires and the Maine coast in late July and the Cape Cod–Boston area in August. Last night Stuart had told us about his trips to Europe, but I hadn't realized he had gone every summer since 1956, clocking in England, France, both Paris and the wine country, Italy, Belgium, Switzerland, and Holland plus Scandinavia! Stuart is a chemist with the New York City Department of Health and gets something like three weeks plus accrued days every year.

We are on our way to Newport, the next stop on Stuart's itinerary. He had waited for me on the wharf while I telephoned Bill and when I came out of the phone booth I impulsively invited myself along with him.

"Fine if you want to," he said. "There are a lot of things to see in Newport and this is a good time."

"Well," I say, coming out of the rest room, "I feel better now, ready for a nice relaxing lunch in some elegant place. I hope lunch is still being served." He is standing at the news kiosk in the bus station where he waited while I washed up. He has already bought a Newport guidebook and is reading it intently. I suppose I should give Bill a buzz and tell him I won't be coming back to the city today after all, but it is almost ten minutes to two now and all I can think about is lunch.

"Lunch!" Stuart says sharply. "We don't have time for lunch. There's a bus at two-thirty that goes on Bellevue Avenue, stops at the Breakers, runs along the Ocean Drive and winds up at the Touro Synagogue. We just about have time to grab a snack over there, find a place for tonight, and make that bus."

Over there is a grease-slicked marble-topped counter along one wall of the bus station and the snack we grab is a cup of coffee and a cellophane-wrapped sandwich of white bread and American cheese. The sandwich sticks in my throat and I abandon it for a Snickers.

The Chamber of Commerce directs us to a guest house not far from the center of town where the landlady is more than happy to rent us two single rooms. The festival crowds are gone—the jazz riot wasn't all that bad, she tells us—and the yacht races haven't officially begun yet. "You're lucky," she says, "it's the midweek and midmonth lull. Starting tomorrow, I'm booked for the rest of the season."

We leave our bags locked in our rooms and start off to catch the Circle Tour bus. Stuart certainly is organized when it comes to travel. He doesn't waste a minute. Walking from the guest house, he pulls out his guidebook and we don't miss one historic building along the way.

I refuse to bury my head in the guidebook with him and instead I am drinking in the sights and sounds of the people weaving up and down the street. Now he must stop and study the façade of the old Newport Casino. A loud squeal from two guys looking into the window of an exclusive men's-wear shop attracts my attention. They let out another whoop and resume their stroll. I see their faces and my heart stops. Allan! Is that Allan on the left, walking with that fellow in such an intimate way? But they are around the corner and gone before I can be sure. Perhaps it was just the fellow's hair that reminds me of Allan.

Allan! Could he be a queer? A homosexual? Was he always? Is it my fault? What did I do wrong? He loved me and I failed him. But I tried. I wanted to. I even begged. It was his idea to lie naked and hold each other. I wanted to put the light on and talk about it but it was he who insisted on the dark. Maybe I was too forward. Did I castrate him? Am I a ball-breaker too?

"Something wrong?" I am startled by Stuart's head next to my face, his weak eyes straining at me through his thick glasses, doubled now with the green clip-ons he uses for the sun.

"No, I'm all right. Just a bit dizzy. Perhaps I should have more to eat. I feel weak. That happens to me sometimes from hunger. I guess the candy bar wasn't enough."

Stuart straightens up, relieved, I think, that I am not going to be sick and a burden to him.

"I'll run over to that store and get an apple or something," I say, checking my watch. "We have time." I look to him for confirmation but Stuart is staring past me. I turn. A white Rolls-Royce has just slid to a silent stop and an exquisite blonde in skin-tight orange pants and a hot-pink silk shirt tied above her midriff is languidly putting a gold thong onto the pavement.

It is that girl who was with Teddy Lowe at Peter Simon's on Fire Island. She puts her other foot on the pavement as I start to walk off it and our eyes meet behind her sunglasses.

"Hi," I say, sure she will not acknowledge me, sure she will avert her eyes, turn her head.

"Hello, Arlyn," she answers, a tight little smile playing on her perfectly formed lips.

My God! What a memory. But of course it is an unusual name.

"And you're . . ." How embarrassing! It's almost always the other way around with me, I remember someone's name while they draw a blank on mine. She is gracious as she tells me her name.

"June. June Rogers." She smiles easily. "Didn't we meet at Fire Island?"

"That's right," I tell her. "On the Fourth of July weekend."

"Are you here with that guy you were with then?" she asks.

"No. I'm with him." I turn to call Stuart closer but find he's standing practically on top of me, his guidebook closed, his eyes wide open, his green clip-on sunglasses raised. He is, as they say, gaga. After all the nagging about not having time for lunch he doesn't seem in such a big hurry now.

I introduce them and am amazed at Stuart. It is difficult to get his attention. He is entranced by June Rogers.

"Do you spend much time in Newport?" he is asking. "I'm thinking of extending my stay."

Is he kidding? Extending his stay. Ten minutes ago he was on the world's tightest schedule. He's beginning to get on my nerves.

"Stuart," I say, tapping his shoulder, "I think I'll skip that tour. I'll just grab a bite and hang around here, sit in the park or something. I'm much too tired and hungry for a bus tour now."

"You know," he begins, talking to me but looking at June Rogers, "I was just thinking, perhaps—" I cut him off just in time. I'm sure he's going to suggest we all have lunch together. The creep! All his talk about keeping to his itinerary and you know he'd drop it in a minute to be with some over-made-up sexpot like June Rogers.

"It's almost two-thirty now, Stuart, I wouldn't want you to miss the bus on my account. You'd better just dash for it. I'll see you back at the guest house before dinner, okay?" It is mean, but a guy like Stuart can sometimes bring out the worst in me. I turn my back to him, and June Rogers, taking the cue from me, does the same. She must want to get rid of him too.

"I guess I had better get going if I want to get on that bus," he says. "Nice meeting you. Maybe we could meet later, all have dinner or something."

I am stunned. The utter gall! How does he have the nerve? He's supposed to be shy, a schnook! It must be my presence that makes him so bold with June.

"Oh, that won't be possible," she tells him. "I have a dinner engagement."

"Too bad. Maybe some other time. How long are you going to be here?"

"Just till Labor Day," she answers and before Stuart can change his whole life I save him: "You're going to miss that bus."

"Yes," he says, looking at his watch as he turns to leave. He flips down his clip-on sunglasses and walks away. I almost feel sorry for him. I don't think he could ever get someone like June Rogers. Even for money.

The chicken salad is special, just as June said it would be, but I pick at it without joy. Seeing her sip only ice water makes me feel very fat, especially after her little speech about how I don't have to worry what with my fabulous figure and all while she, poor thing, has only to look at food to gain weight. She sits and babbles about the producer she is with this month. I have the feeling that she hasn't really talked much to anyone recently.

". . . and he won't be back from the city until it's time to go to this party I was tellin' you about. He's not bein' picked up at the airport until seven. If you like, I can take you for a spin out on the Ocean Drive. You really ought to see that. But first I have to have a fittin' and you can come with me, it's right in ta'n here, right next door."

It isn't just the slurred words and dropped g's that have crept into her speech as she talks, it's that way her voice rises and peaks in the middle of a sentence, the questioning tone of her statements, that peculiar way she says town—ta'n.

"Where are you from?" I ask suddenly.

I am not prepared for her reaction. After all, I'm not really prying. It's just a conversational question as far as I'm concerned. But behind the sunglasses she has kept on even in this dim tea room I can see her eyes narrow to slits. Ropes of muscles appear in her lovely neck and her speech is precise and finished again, exaggeratedly so, as she answers coolly: "The same place you are, Arlyn."

I am flabbergasted. I'm not sure what she's talking about. She still seems familiar to me but for some reason I can't place her. What does she mean? The same place as I'm from. Is she from Pittsburgh? I couldn't have known her there. I remember absolutely everyone I ever knew there.

"What do you mean?" I ask. I see the muscles in her neck relax. "You do look familiar to me," I continue. "Don't you recall I mentioned it when we met on Fire Island? You thought it was from some party but I had a different feeling. Now you seem to know me from Pittsburgh? Is that what it is? Do you know me from Pittsburgh?"

"You really don't know?" she asks.

"No. I'm sorry, but I can't place you. Did you go to Pitt?

And why didn't you say something about Pittsburgh when we met that other time?"

"Oh, but it was all so many ages ago," she says lightly. "Now I'm not even sure you're the person I thought you were. I guess I have you confused with someone else. But why bother with all that now." She picks up the check the waitress has left. "Shall we get out of here? How about that ride?" She drops a dollar on the table for a tip and sails for the cashier's booth before I have time to take out my wallet.

I follow her out into the street still trying to place her. She must have me confused with someone else. I'm sure we met at some party in New York. I would have remembered meeting her in Pittsburgh or Europe.

It is the sexiest dress I have ever seen. It is a slippery black satin that looks like an ordinary strapless in the front but dips in the back to about an inch below the crack in her buttocks. It is that inch of crack that must be so tantalizingly sexy. More would be too much. I can see now what men find so desirable about her. My first impression of her being so ethereal seems silly now. Today she strikes me as being almost earthy. Maybe that's the secret of her success, being able to project different moods. What mystery will she conjure tonight in this dress?

"It will be ready by five o'clock, don't worry," the manager assures June as she backs away from us with the dress carefully laid over her outstretched hands.

"She wasn't so nice when I first came in here," June whispers to me as we leave the shop, "but she knows me now, she knows I don't just look, you know, how some people do in expensive shops. I've bought several things here already."

Just as we step out into the street the Rolls makes a swift U-turn and glides up to the curb. I reach to open the door but June tugs at my shoulder. What a gaffe. The chauffeur is bolting around the front and in an instant he has the door open for us. June ushers me in first. Sinking into the deep red leather upholstery, I wonder about the producer. I want to ask about him and Teddy Lowe but I am sure that June would not appreciate questions now. Now she is the grande dame showing me the sights. It is not a difficult thing to fantasize, I think, while sinking into the soft cushions of the Rolls. She leans forward to give the chauffeur the directions and then sits stiffly back, barely touching the soft seat. She seems to take a special delight in pointing out the gigantic estates to me. I wonder how Stuart is doing on that bus tour. They call the mansions cottages here too but in comparison to these castles the homes in Hyannis Port are downright simple. These places are mind-boggling, to say the least. June seems eager to show me all the sights, telling me the names of the various places and the millionaires who built them. It is all very spectacular but somehow I am more excited about sitting in the Rolls with June Rogers. She puzzles me. I can't read her. "The same place you are, Arlyn." What did she mean? Was she talking symbolically?

She insists we stop at the Breakers. I look for Stuart among the tour groups milling around but he must be off to some other cottage by now; that, or he is in one of the other sixty-nine rooms in this one. In the library June steers me over to a group in front of a massive stone fireplace. "Catch this," she says as the tour guide begins to translate an inscription carved in French: "Little do I care for riches, and do not miss them, since only cleverness prevails in the end," the guide reads to the tittering crowd.

"Some nerve," June mutters as we walk away. "Don't you think that's the height of gall?"

"Actually," I say as we leave the library and head for the exit, "I think it's very clever."

She turns sharply and looks at me closely. "Do you really think so?" she asks.

"No," I assure her.

We get back in the Rolls and continue our ride. June has stopped pointing out the sights and instead is repairing a split nail. From a large straw bag with Capri sewn on it in red raffia she has taken a file and a bottle of Hardcoat. I watch fascinated as she undertakes the delicate operation.

"You can talk," she says, "it won't bother me."

"Didn't you love Capri?" I ask, thinking of my mad time there with Aldo.

"Oh, I was never there," she answers. I am mortified, but she seems unperturbed. "I was never in Italy, or in Europe at all, for that matter. A girlfriend gave me this bag. She was over there working on a movie. She had this bit part. It's fabulous, she says. I'm dying to go. In fact, I expect to be going very soon. This producer's making a movie in Rome and he says there's a good part in it for me."

Suddenly June points the nail file toward the right. I look out the window to where she has indicated.

"Over there," she says, "across the harbor is Hammersmith Farm. That's the estate of Jackie Kennedy's stepfather. Some farm." I try but I can't make out very much through the haze that is rising from the water.

"When rich people do it, it's okay," she says softly. "They get away with it."

"That's for sure," I answer, not quite sure exactly what June has in mind that rich people get away with, but sure that whatever they do, rich people get away with it. "It's really very clever of them, don't you think?" I add.

June shrugs at my little joke.

"Where will it be now, mum?" the chauffeur asks through his speaking tube. Did she send him some signal through the glass partition?

"Where to?" June asks me. I have the feeling that she wants to be free of me now. It is past five and she must want to go wherever she goes to prepare her body for that dress.

"Drop me anywhere. I really enjoyed the ride." I rummage in my bag for my notebook. "Let me have your address in the city," I say, "maybe we can get together sometime." Perhaps in another situation I can ask her some of the questions about her life that I've held back on today.

Maybe she would really like to talk about it with me. Look how she ran on today. There might even be a story in her, not for The Paper, of course, but maybe some magazine. I wouldn't have to use her real name.

June lifts her sunglasses for a minute and looks directly at me. "I enjoyed it too, Arlyn. Really I did. But I don't expect to be back in the city too long. Like I told you, I expect to be goin' to Rome for that movie."

I get the message and put my notebook away. Obviously June is not interested in seeing me in the city. I served my purpose, filling some dead time during a dull day in Newport. Now she is through with me. It's beginning to bug me. Did we ever know each other? Why can't I place her? But it's too late to bring it up again. The Rolls is squeezing through narrow alleys toward the guest house. I see Stuart has made it back. He's sitting on the steps, anxiously looking up and down the street. He is not reading the guidebook or *Advise and Consent*. He must be very, very hungry by now.

18

Ken Bancroft begins to tear the books of my sermon apart.

"Very good. Thank you, Arlyn."

I am dismissed. I had waited at his desk while he read it. There were no questions and now he is starting it on its way into tomorrow morning's paper.

"See you," I say as I walk away. I am at loose ends. It is the Sunday of the Labor Day weekend and the sermon was my only commitment between leaving work on Friday evening and returning to work on Tuesday morning. Isabelle went to some resort I never heard of for the last summer weekend. A much finer crowd than Nantucket, she said. Needless to say, she didn't urge me to go with her.

I do have a tentative date to go to a movie with Kit Rockwell but I don't feel in the mood to see her now. She's getting a bit much lately. "Billsy gone home to wifey for the weekend, Arlyn?" or "That sermon and a dime will get you a cup of coffee." I don't know why she's so sour. I really got angry with her the other day when I mentioned that I might work on that piece about the last cooper this weekend. Actually I can't since I've done all I can do until I check a couple of facts. She said it was silly. My stomach knots as I dial her number.

"I've been waiting for your call," she says.

"Kit, would you mind terribly if we didn't meet today? I'm in no mood for a movie. I have this awful headache and all I want to do is go home and sleep. Maybe tomorrow, shall we talk then?"

"I'm busy tomorrow," she says, "but I am disappointed about today. I'm making dinner for you and a friend." There is a slight pause. "I've told her all about you."

I am confused. Dinner with Kit and a friend? She hadn't mentioned that on Friday. We had just talked about a movie. And what on earth could she be telling her friend all about me?

The sky is cloudless, the air is sweet. Midtown is deserted. The cabbies are all at the beach today. Everyone is gone from the city, it seems. The streets belong to the tourists, the out-of-towners. Straggling up and down, they seem lost in the wide-open spaces of Broadway. Do they know it's a different Manhattan today?

I'll walk too, crawl slowly up the street, but instead of looking at the landmarks, I'll imagine lives. That family. Where are they from? Iowa, or perhaps Kansas? Does the woman know her skirt is too long? Is New York what they expected it to be?

I should have come out and done that feature when I had the idea even after Ashley turned it down: "Just go out and talk to tourists without a peg? Nothing exciting about that, Arlyn. Forget it." Now of course it's too late. The summer is over. Maybe I'll talk to the tourists at Thanksgiving or Christmas. But that's not really the same.

Thank God the summer is over. Funny I should say that, it started out with such a bang. But August has turned into a real drag. Everything was better before the trip. I should have canceled Nantucket.

Perhaps it was deceitful not to have called Bill from Newport when I knew I wouldn't be in that night. I suppose he is right about that. Subconsciously or not, I must have wanted to make him worry. But is he really telling the truth when he insists that he didn't even notice? "I worked late and had dinner and went back to the hotel and fell right asleep, sweetie. I assumed you got in late and bushed and just collapsed in bed too. I wouldn't have wanted to call and wake you." Was he telling the truth or was he paying me back for making him worry that night he waited in the motel room?

Oops. Sorry.

"Watch where yer going, lady. What's the matta, ya neva saw a Rolls-Royce before?"

It is at the Columbus Circle cabstand. June Rogers is getting out of the Rolls and into a cab, trailing a silver fox stole and the straw bag from Capri. The chauffeur is piling luggage on the front seat of the cab. As I run toward it calling to June I see the chauffeur stuff money into the cabbie's outstretched hand and before I can reach it the cab pulls away. Inside the Rolls I see the form of a large man sunk deep into the soft upholstery. He is puffing on a cigar.

On impulse I jump into the next cab. It is crazy and I feel so silly saying it: "Follow that cab, please."

The driver makes one twisted motion to eye me up and down before he throws the cab into gear and we lurch into traffic. We are off, through Central Park, doing what I have seen a million times in the movies, following a cab. But what will I do when we stop? *Hi, June, I just thought I'd follow you. I've been thinking about you a lot since we had lunch and when you didn't hear me call you I thought I'd just jump in this cab and follow you.*

I can hear her answer: *Thanks a lot, you big jerk. Did it ever occur to you that I heard you and ignored you? Don't I have a right to my privacy? Can't you mind your own business?*

I shudder at the thought of what I'm doing. The cab

leaves the Park and turns on Fifth Avenue. This is silly. I'll just redirect the cabbie to take me home. And she's not even going to her own place. She said she lives on Fifty-seventh Street. She's probably visiting someone who lives here on Eighty-ninth. Why don't I mind my own business?

At Third Avenue, June's cab shoots across but mine is caught by a red light. Terrific. That solves my problem. The meter reads sixty cents. "Here," I say, giving the driver a dollar. "This will be fine." He is amazed at my big tip but I don't even wait for his thanks. I jump out and run across Third Avenue. June's cab has stopped midway in the block. The cabbie is bringing her luggage—matched pieces in baby blue—to the pavement. I stop running and begin to stroll casually toward her. The timing is perfect. Just as I approach the cab she is getting herself out of it, silver fox, Capri bag, and all. I am surprised to see that her hair is matted, almost unkempt and her face is puffy, as though she was crying.

"Hello, June. Need a hand?"

She is startled by my voice. Something is wrong. Her eyes are dull, her lips hang slack. She is pale and without makeup and I wonder if anyone would call her pretty, let alone spectacularly beautiful.

"Arlyn! What are you doing here?" Am I imagining it, or is she happy to see me?

"I live in the next block." No need to tell her I followed her. "What about you?"

"I live here." She points to a four-story gray house.

"I thought you had mentioned something about Fifty-seventh Street," I say, picking up the suitcases the cabbie has just dumped.

"I stay there sometimes with a friend," she says, offhandedly. She leads me up the outer steps, dragging the third piece of luggage the cabbie had deposited on the pavement, a model's case.

"The bastard," she says, and I think she means the cabbie.

"He could at least have brought them up to the vestibule," I say.

"Not him, though he's one, too. But what did he care, he got his tip up front. I'm talking about Hilly, that's the name of the guy I was with, the producer I told you about. Some name for a fat guy, huh? A whole fuckin'—excuse me, Arlyn —a whole damn month in Newport and he decides in ten minutes we have to get back to the city. Just like that. 'Get your things together.' I was all set to wash my hair. I hope he croaks."

"That is something," I say, "spending so much time together, a whole month."

"Oh, we didn't spend that much time together," she calls over her shoulder. "He was away a lot. But he was always bringing people up for a day or two. Thank God. It was such a boring place to be stuck for a whole month. And so snooty."

"Why did he have a house up there for a month, anyway?"

"Oh, he had it for the whole season. He was going to make a movie around the festivals but after the mess with the jazz festival he lost his backers. Some really weird folk singers who were supposed to be in the movie were there and he let them stay until the folk festival was over. Then he asked me up. He liked me there when he came and he'd call me from wherever he was and tell me to get the caterer, the limousine service, people for a party, whatever he needed."

"That's a rented Rolls-Royce?"

"Rented or leased, he's got some deal. He loves that one. Always has to be that one and that driver. It cost him an arm and a leg to be driven all the way down today but I guess it's worth it to him. He's on his way to some big meeting, something with new backers."

We are climbing the narrow inner stairs now, the silver fox swinging into my face. As we round the landing on the third floor a dog barks ferociously behind a shaking door. June tosses her shoulder toward the door and hisses at me. "This fairy lives there with his giant dog. A real menace. It oughtn't to be allowed."

I follow in silence, wondering about the fairy. Ever since I thought I saw Allan on the street in Newport I have become more sensitive to homosexuals. Sometimes I find myself staring at one rudely, wondering if he was ever normal, ever the way I remembered Allan.

June opens the door to a tiny top-floor apartment and pushes ahead, dropping the stole and bag and model's case on a table near the door and rushing to a small bedroom to turn on an exhaust fan.

"Whew," she says, coming back and taking the luggage, "this place is an oven. How about some iced coffee?"

"Love it."

I sit down and watch her. She works quickly. I look at the long, narrow window behind me. It reaches from the floor to the ceiling and is only about two feet wide. I have never seen anything like it before.

"That's an unusual-looking window."

June laughs. "So, you've never been in a railroad flat before?"

"That's what this is?"

"The back end of one. It's been cut up. It's really not that bad except in weather like this. The only way you can get air from the airshaft window is with the exhaust fan. But I'm not here that much, so what does it matter? And I don't expect to be living like this forever. I'd rather put my money in clothes than in some fancy apartment I'm never in."

June stands and beckons me to follow her. "Come 'ere," she says, "I want to show you something." Along one wall of the bedroom she has three double-doored metal wardrobes lined up next to each other. There is barely room to walk around the wardrobes and the single bed and a card table cluttered with jewelry, makeup, and a large theatrical mirror with lights. We edge around the bed to the wardrobes and June opens all six doors.

"There's just one tiny, dark closet in this apartment, behind that wardrobe there." She points over the top of the wardrobe nearest the partition to the kitchen. Jammed into the three wardrobes are garment bags of various sizes, and plastic and cotton sheeting draped over outsized and odd-sized shapes. Shoes cover the bottom of each wardrobe.

"I'm getting a little crowded here, but I haven't had time to clear out what I don't want. I give all my old things to the Goodwill," June says proudly, "except for the designer outfits. You can sell really fine things, you know. Over on Madison."

I'm not sure if I'm expected to ask to see the contents of the garment bags and plastics or just admire the quantity. I'd love to see her clothes but I have a feeling she doesn't want to unwrap everything.

"If it wasn't so damn hot in here I'd show you some of my things," June says in answer to my unasked question. "I have this beautiful red suit with a real leopard collar, a pink cashmere dress with a mink-trimmed jacket, a lot of nice things like that but I hate to undo them, I have them put away so nice and tight, you know, moths and all."

"What about the silver fox?"

"Oh that. If you look close you can see that's shot. It was one of the first pieces of fur I got."

I wonder when that was and how many other pieces of fur June has. I'm sure June wouldn't appreciate that joke that girl at the Gladstone Agency used to tell about how her boyfriend was giving her a mink coat piece by piece every time he gave her yet another mink-trimmed sweater or headband or muff.

June carefully shuts all three wardrobes and we edge our way back to the kitchen.

"Do you get a lot of modeling jobs?" I ask. It's really a loaded question because I just can't believe she does. From time to time she has referred to herself as a model but she is never very specific about what she does. I knew a lot of girls in high school who said they wanted to be models but never seemed to know what a model did other than lead a glamorous life and look beautiful for the camera. I bumped into a girl from my neighborhood on Broadway once. She said she was a slip model in a Seventh Avenue showroom. She didn't seem too happy.

"Tons," June answers after lighting a cigarette, "I get tons of jobs. I have to turn jobs down, I'm very particular about what I do."

"What kinds of things do you do?" I don't see her as a high-fashion type, but she's not a Junior Miss or Judy Bond Girl either. "Do you work a lot on Seventh Avenue?"

"Some," she answers and suddenly she is evasive and vague. "Oh, I get so many jobs I can't even remember them all. It was before the summer. Now I'm concentrating more on acting. That's really what I want. I really thought that Hilly would do something for me. The pig!"

"And now you're sure he won't?"

"Oh, he still says he's going to send for me from Rome but I'm not going to hold my breath. What makes me so mad is if I wasted my time. And he used to be more generous. Jesus! A whole month. I should have remembered what my mother always said, a bird in the hand is worth two in the bush. But I thought I had this bird in the hand."

"Is your mother still in Pittsburgh?" I ask. It's a sneaky question. June has never actually said she was from Pittsburgh. All she said was, "The same place you are, Arlyn."

June doesn't seem to notice my trap.

"She's dead."

"I'm sorry."

"How about you?"

"She's living in Pittsburgh," I answer.

"And your father?"

"Him too."

"Gee, both. Are they still in the same house you grew up

in?" What a strange question. Did June live in the neighborhood? Where is her family now?

"No, where they lived is torn down now. They had to move a few years ago. What about you? Do you have a lot of relatives in Pittsburgh?"

"Only my little brother. He's not so little. He's over six feet tall. But he's younger than I am." June looks away and bites her lips. Maybe it would help her to talk about her mother.

"When did your mother die?"

"Four years ago. When I was nineteen." She lowers her voice and barely mouths the next word. "Cancer," she whispers, touching her left breast. Then her voice becomes stronger. "It was cancer. Definitely. Her heart wasn't all that bad."

"It must have been rough, your mother's death. Are you close to your brother?"

June is staring off into space. Really, I must be wearing out my welcome. The poor girl came home exhausted and here I am yakking away. "I guess I'd better go," I say. "You must have a lot you want to do."

Her head jerks as she turns back to look at me. "No, I'm not in a hurry. It's nice talkin' to you. I kinda feel comfortable with you, Arlyn. Like I don't have to comb my hair for you." She pats her matted hair. "But this is ridiculous, right?" We both laugh. For some strange reason I feel comfortable with June, too. I'm ashamed of my motive in following her here. I wanted to pry into her life and all she wants is to sit and talk. I certainly won't ask her any more leading questions now.

She lights another cigarette and pushes the pack toward me. "Arlyn, you really don't remember me?" There is a plaintive urgency in her voice. It's embarrassing not to remember someone. I take a long drag of my cigarette and stare at her hard. She is talking now, fast and very excitedly.

"I don't know why I'm getting into this now," she says in

a rush of words. "You really don't know who I am and I'm not sure why I'm forcing it. In Newport I dropped it right away and you never pressed."

I lean forward. Even if she wanted to back off now I'm sure I would not let her. Who can she be?

"There's really no reason you should remember me . . . Oh, Arlyn, how I used to envy you! You lived in that big house and we were in that horrible room with the toilet at the end of that long, dark hall and only a hot plate to cook on and we had to set our milk and butter in a box outside the window. I always remember that I once heard you had two fridges in your house. Is that really true?"

Two fridges. I start to laugh. She thinks it's because we were rich, like that girl in the Philip Roth story. What a thing to be envious of.

"It's true, June, we had two refrigerators, but not for the reasons you think, not for fruit or anything. We had them because we had them." It sounds funny the way I say it and we laugh.

"You see," I explain, "because of my father's job we had to move back into my grandmother's house and we brought our big new refrigerator with us. When my parents moved, there was a big stink because my father was supposed to live in the ward."

June looks blank.

"It's not important," I say, "it has to do with politics. Anyway, everyone did it, you know, kept a voting residence in the ward and lived somewhere else, but he had too many enemies, I guess, to be able to get away with it. Actually, I don't think he minded that much. He liked living there. It was his life. It was my mother who was upset. It was good to be back with her mother, she always said, but she would have liked a better neighborhood for us. Anyway, my grandmother wouldn't let them take her old refrigerator out of the kitchen. She liked it and it was still good, she said. So they put the new one in an alcove in the back hall. People actually told you we had two refrigerators? Where did you live anyway? I can't understand why I don't remember you."

"Across the street from you. But not for very long. We moved a lot, I can hardly remember all the places. We lived all over, but then mostly on the North Side. But I remember distinctly when we lived across from you. I was in second grade. It was 1944 and we'd just come from Youngstown and we didn't have any money. I used to see you, you're a couple of years older than I am, you're about twenty-six, right? I used to watch you all the time, how you dressed, those pleated skirts and those soft sweaters. You were like a movie star to me."

"But where did you live?" I can't remember June living across the street. I knew all the families from Mrs. Owen's up.

"In Mrs. Owen's," she answers.

"Mrs. Owen's? The rooming house?"

"Yes."

"Oh." I don't know what to say. I didn't know any young children ever lived there.

"Were you ever in there?"

"Not really." I didn't want to tell June that we were forbidden to walk on that side of the street, past Mrs. Owen's rooming house. It was always a strange and scary place to me, frail old ladies—biddies we called them—and shabby old men. Pensioners, my mother said. And that one guy who begged in town, skating his torso around on that wooden board. "Stepped on a mine in France," my father told me once. "But he does all right for himself," my father added, assuring me I didn't have to feel sorry for the guy. "He gets a nice pension and he makes out very well with his tin cup in front of the Mellon Bank, and every Saturday he has one of the neighborhood boys come with him to the State Store where he buys a case of Four Roses that he sells by the shot from his room on Sundays." On Sundays especially we had to stay away from Mrs. Owen's where a steady stream of shaky men came and went all the long blue day.

"Did your father live in Mrs. Owen's too?" I ask, sorry almost as soon as the question is out of my mouth. Now I remember June. A snapshot forms in my brain. It is of a dark-haired woman with bangs dragging two children and some cardboard suitcases down the street looking for Mrs. Owen's. Lucky I was sitting on my own steps that morning and I could run over and direct them to the right house. No wonder I didn't connect June Rogers with Mrs. Owen's rooming house. The person in front of me bears no resemblance that I can see to that scrawny, sullen little girl. No one ever saw them much or knew much about them in the short time that they lived in Mrs. Owen's but I can almost hear my mother talking about June and her brother, "those poor fatherless children."

"My father got killed in the war," she is saying, "but the government cheated my mother. She never got his money. They said he had another wife who was the legal one. But that was a big lie."

"Oh, how terrible." I don't know what else to say but June saves me from having to say anything more.

"Well, it doesn't matter. It was sad for my mother but I never really knew him. He enlisted in the Navy when I was too little to care. He was killed at Pearl Harbor. His ship went down. My mother should have got a lot of money and my brother and I should have got insurance and scholarships and all that. But she didn't get a thing. Only home relief. That's what we had to live on till we were old enough and she could go to work. She sold sheets and towels at Gimbels. Till she got too sick to work."

June stands up and walks around the room, straightening chairs, lining up the salt and pepper shakers on top of the stove, folding a dish towel. When she returns to her chair I can see that she has put her mother back into the niche in her mind where she stays, undisturbed, I imagine, most of the time.

"Whew, I really am bushed," she says, leaning back and extending her feet in front of her. The opalescent nail polish of her manicured toenails is chipped. "This party last night, it was fabulous. Went on all night. The police came *twice*. He should worry. He's leaving for Las Vegas tonight, right after that big meeting. Then Rome. He was supposed to go only to Rome. Then he got this call and his plans changed just like that." She snaps her fingers. "That's why we had to leave so fast." June seems to have gotten over her anger with the producer. His rushing her out on such short notice is almost justified.

"Do you see him a lot?" I ask.

"To tell you the truth, that was the first time I was ever with him. But like I told you, I did it because of the picture. I really hope I get a part."

"Do you have much acting experience?"

"No, but I heard it's not hard to learn. For the movies, that is. They keep stopping and doing things over."

June's eyes seem to be sinking into her head. She looks like she's ready to drop.

"Thanks for the iced coffee," I say, standing up, "it hit the spot. You look beat. You'd better get some rest."

She nods her head in agreement and doesn't try to keep me.

I pause at the door. "What's your number?" I ask, just to be polite. I remember how she reacted the last time I asked her. "Maybe we can get together again sometime."

To my surprise, June recites her number to me. I write it down. Is she just being polite too? Well, no matter. I'm sure I won't call her. June and I are like ships in the night. Every so often our paths cross, but really we have nothing in common. We lead such different lives.

19

Am I on to something, or is she really just a nut? I am sitting here in the cluttered one-room apartment of Carlotta Della Sandro the "Bohemian bassoonist," as Gil Gilchrist dubbed her, while she is giving me a spontaneous preview of the concert she will perform in Carnegie Recital Hall next Sunday afternoon. She means business and her seeming spontaneity is, as she said it must be to work, carefully structured according to the immutable dictates of so-called random choice. Whatever that means.

Many recitalists go into hock to book the Recital Hall, where, by tradition and custom, they are assured the reviews that will authenticate them in the music world. For most, it is their formal debut and perhaps their only solo concert before they either join the ranks of vocalists and instrumentalists in the orchestras and opera companies around the world or disappear. It is often a make-or-break situation and, for many, years of study and training, months of preparation for the debut, a seemingly endless outlay of money for the hall, accompanists, publicity, and advertising culminate in a three-inch review, not always kind. And some, through accidents and quirks of fate, even miss out on the three inches, and find the next morning that their debut is unnoticed and unrecorded.

There is no danger of that happening to Carlotta Della Sandro. She has seen to that. Her forthcoming Happens-Dance and ConcertAnti will definitely not go unnoticed. Proof of this is my presence here in her cramped West Fifty-sixth Street studio apartment this mild evening at the end of September.

Every day for the past three weeks Carlotta visited The Paper, patiently waiting in the reception room until she found someone to listen to her. The members of the Music Department ignored her from the start. Her recital, they said, will be covered in the normal course of events and if she is worth a story there will be time to write about her afterward.

It was when Carlotta shifted her campaign to Ashley that I became involved. She barraged him with letters, releases, telegrams, telephone calls. Finally one morning Ashley said I was being too polite and encouraging to her on the telephone. "She's outside now," he said, "go and see if you can get rid of her once and for all."

"Let me go," Gil Gilchrist shouted, jumping up and already running toward the corridor. "If she's the same broad I saw sitting out there a few minutes ago, she's a real looker."

Gil was back in three minutes, putting the kibosh on Carlotta Della Sandro for good it seemed.

"A real nut case," he announced, flinging a handful of flyers and press releases into the wastepaper basket. "The concerts of the sixties," he said in a high-pitched and sooo cultivated voice, "will extend beyond the time and space of the concert hall. My work is a harbinger of the time when artist and audience will be one in creation." He returned to his natural voice to add, "And she wasn't the broad I was talking about. That was one of Bob Mann's ladies, naturally."

It was a very funny bit and I forgot about Carlotta Della Sandro for the rest of that day. But early the next morning when the receptionist called and told me that Miss Della Sandro was waiting to see Mr. Franks, I put down my container of coffee and went out to greet the Bohemian bassoonist. I hated to leave my coffee, it was at just the temperature I like it, but why keep her dangling needlessly, I thought. I'll get rid of her kindly, once and for all.

She was sunk deep into the leather couch in the reception room directly under the glowing, softly lit portrait of the Old Pub. In the subdued light of the discreet reception room, where the walls are covered with the mats of those famous front pages of yesteryear, bronzed for eternity like a dear one's first shoes, Carlotta Della Sandro crackled like a flash of electricity.

Her large, almond-shaped eyes were made up as though she was about to dance the Black Swan, heavily outlined, with a thick glob of jade green shadow sweeping dramatically to her hairline. This sinister look was strongly contrasted with the full, soft, almost childlike lips, completely bare of even a trace of lipstick.

Between her colorful face and purple-clad legs, Carlotta wore nondescript black clothes, a skirt and a sweater and a shawl of some kind. I was at once shocked and captivated. Who would come to The Paper dressed like this? What was her game? Was she a nut or was she truly a serious artist, a graduate of the Juilliard School of Music, recently returned from California, a gifted bassoonist ready to embark on a career devoted to the stiff and proper black and white penguin world of the concert hall?

When I told him about her, Ashley was offended by her disrespect for the established boundaries of good taste and tradition. But I pressed him to let me do a story about her anyway. I was sure it would be good and once he saw how I handled it, I assured him, he would push to have it run in the paper. Finally, he agreed. Whatever else you said about Ashley, he recognized the new in news. He loved pictures of

David Tudor breaking up pianos with his hammers and though he called John Cage "that nut" he always complimented the Music Department when they ran an amusing story about him. But this unknown crazy girl was another thing. Of course I could have done the story and presented him with it afterward, but I thought it only fair to Carlotta to have some commitment before I told her my editor was very interested in her.

As it was, she seemed annoyed that it was I who would be writing about her and not one of the men on the staff. Suddenly she was all booked up, but we did finally make this date and once I arrived the interview began to go quite well. By now I have all the basic information, more than enough to satisfy the stiff rules of The Paper regarding names, birthplace, and all that: Caroline Palmer born twenty-three years ago in Brooklyn.

"Della Sandro is the original spelling of my mother's maiden name," Carlotta had explained to me, "and Palmer of course was Palmeri. I couldn't decide if my concert name should be Carlotta Palmeri or Carlotta Della Sandro so I threw the coins and Della Sandro won. Which do you like?"

I wanted to ask about the coins. I had heard vaguely about people throwing coins in some ancient Chinese ritual like reading tea leaves, but it was getting late and I probably wouldn't have room for anything like that in this story anyway. I made a mental note to check on it for another story. I would have to make my move soon. It was almost time for the Nixon-Kennedy debate to start. Carlotta, of course, doesn't have a television set. She is oblivious to the campaign. I would be very surprised if she knew anything about Kennedy and Nixon other than the fact that they are the candidates and Kennedy is a Catholic. Now I wonder if she even knows that, as I lean back against the massive black cushions propped on the bare floor and watch her bring her performance to a smash-bang-windup finish. *Smash-bang-windup finish*. Great, I think as I write the words in my notebook. That is exactly what is happening.

Carlotta is dressed as she will be on Sunday. Her black leotard is pulled down at the neckline and pinned with a big, silky yellow rose. A great part of her white bosom is exposed, jiggling now behind the bassoon that is slung across it. Her black, full skirt is pinned up at one side to reveal bare legs and feet.

With her left foot she activates the button on a tape recorder to accompany the sounds that she makes with her bassoon. It's like those records of famous concertos with the solo parts missing. Only instead of the orchestral part of, say, the Mozart Clarinet Concerto or the Grieg Piano Concerto, the sounds pouring out of the tape recorder are of garbage-can lids banging and pneumatic drills breaking sidewalks.

Carlotta's right foot is constantly busy as her toes run over a lute-like contraption fashioned from orange crates and thick rubber bands; intermittently the whole foot stomps the pedal of a drummer's cymbal and the heel scrapes through a box of kitty litter.

This is the finale of the ConcertAnti part of the program. Now comes the climax of the HappensDance. Suddenly, as I had been warned she would, Carlotta springs up to perch on the stool she had been sitting on. Removing the bassoon from around her neck and holding it aloft, she strikes various Ariel poses while beeps and bloops come from the tape recorder.

Gracefully jumping off the stool, she carefully places her bassoon on top of her cluttered bureau (which she has told me will be as is on stage) and does a headstand. Folds of black jersey fall around her head as her white legs stretch to the ceiling. Her legs, it turns out, are bare from the knees down, or the ankles up, however you look at it, for Carlotta is wearing old-fashioned pink cotton snuggies that cover her thighs. Snuggies! The kind my mother and aunt wore over their girdles on bitter winter days when it was just too cold for them to go pantyless as usual. I dimly remember having a child's size myself, but I don't, thank God, remember wearing them.

I am still in such a state of shock from the sight of the snuggies that for a second I don't recognize "The Star-Spangled Banner" coming from the tape recorder. It is the tune, of course, but it has been orchestrated, I realize, for bassoon with hammer on steam-pipe accompaniment.

A neat midair scissors and Carlotta is right side up. The performance ends as it had begun, with her sitting demurely on the stool playing some rather conventional notes on the bassoon.

"How about some coffee and cake?" she asks, leaving her mask of solemnity with the performance. "That's all I have." Her manner is easy and friendly.

"I'd love to," I tell her and mean it, "but I have to run." Bill must be getting impatient waiting for me. In any case, I probably shouldn't stay. This is an interview, not a social call. I have to sort all my thoughts and read my notes. If I can get the piece written tomorrow and show it to Ashley on Wednesday he will be able to schedule it for Friday if he likes it. Friday is always a good day for feature stories.

My stomach is churning as the cab lumbers through Central Park. I wish Bill weren't waiting at the apartment and the debate wasn't tonight. Anyone would think I was crazy to hear me say it, I know, but that's really the way I feel. *Never satisfied. What do you want?* It's true I had been looking forward to this evening for days. We would eat at my place and watch the debate together. Now I'm itching to get right to my notes, to work on the story, to see what I have, what I can come up with. I'm starving, but a tuna fish sandwich would be more than enough. I'm not even in the mood for steak. The steaks! My God! I rushed to work this morning and forgot to take them out of the freezer.

He is sitting in the black Danish chair with a glass of bourbon at his side. He has pulled the television set up close. His shoes are off and his feet are on the coffee table. His tie hangs loosely around his neck and he is smoking a big cigar. I hate his cigars so he hardly ever smokes them in my presence, but tonight of course is different. It's a special occasion. I had talked to him just before I left the office and I know he wrote a think piece about the probable impact of the debate and it stands a good chance of being on the front page. He deserves to fill the room with the smoke from his cigar, it is a night for a smoke-filled room, and I am glad it's mine.

I walk toward him and he pulls me down. I slide onto his outstretched knees, my legs straddling his, touching him lightly, just grazing, bracing myself against the floor. He pulls playfully at the turquoise-colored beads that flap on my breasts. I look down. Half-moons of perspiration have sprouted under the arms of my white blouse.

I straighten up, feeling very cruddy. "What's happening?"

Bill seems relieved that I have removed myself from atop him. "They'll be starting soon," he says. "Are you hungry?"

"Starved. Just let me change and I'll fix the dinner. How'd it go for you today?"

"Sen-sational. It's down for the front page. It should stir a lot of shit." Since the Hyannis trip Bill has begun to write about the campaign.

"I had a terrific interview with Carlotta Della Sandro. My head is swimming. I wish I could get to my notes right now."

"Oh yeah, the nut. I know how you feel. But your notes will keep. Especially a story like that, all feature details, no analysis or depth interview."

A vise is tightening on my chest. I say nothing but he must be aware of what I am feeling for he speaks again before I can answer.

"Aw sweetie, I didn't mean to disparage you. It sounds like a wonderful story, it really does. It's just that a soft story is a soft story and I'd really be insulting you if I pretended otherwise. Harbinger of the sixties, indeed. What do you call that thing she wears?"

"A leotard," I answer as I drag myself into my kitchen.

But what's this? I am cheered already. Bill had taken out the steaks and even popped the frozen baked potatoes into the oven. He is a dear. I'm not crazy about these frozen baked potatoes topped with the frozen cheese swirls but he loves them. He introduced me to them. The first time we ate here I messed up completely. I had to wait until the potatoes were baked until I could broil the steaks in this dumb stove. The salad wilted and the potatoes got cold and the next day Bill arrived with the countertop broiler and several packages of frozen baked potatoes. He likes everything done at the same time, he said, and it is all a matter of organization and planning, the reason, he said, his barbecues were the most successful in his whole neighborhood.

My clothes are sticking to me and my feet burn. I put the lettuce to drain and reach for the steaks. "I'm putting the steaks on now and I'm going to take a quick shower," I call to Bill. "I should finish before they do but keep an eye on them."

"Righto," Bill calls back.

Deep in the couch now, we sip coffee and watch the end of the debate. Bill is wild-eyed. Kennedy really excites him. "Yeah," he is saying, "yeah, go, baby, go." His hands are underneath my robe, his fingers are like tongues of flame licking my bare belly. I open his belt and loosen his pants and the flickering light from the television and the stabbing staccato voices become soft and muted as I root around in his dark places.

Bill just wants to see the lead stories on the nightly news before we go down for the papers. On the street the night air is clean and sweet. All the exhaust fumes have gone wherever they go. The sky is bright with stars.

I flip through the movie magazines at the newsstand on Eighty-sixth Street while Bill buys the papers. A touchy business, the buying of the papers. When he buys one set we will return to my place and sprawl over the couch, reading and commenting, drinking beer and making love until he groggily lets himself out. When he buys two sets I know that he will see me safely back to the apartment, kiss me gently, and return to his hotel.

It has nothing to do with his marital situation, he insists, but only with the circumstances at hand. We are both tired, he might say, or we're both busy, or the next day will be a real bitch, or I need my rest or he's bushed. And of course since the summer ended there are all those nights he has to go to this or that event with some editor or other. Still on the surface we are the same. He is just as crazy about me as ever, he says every day. To tell the truth, I'm often just as happy that he doesn't come back upstairs as often as he used to. The late hours were taking their toll on me and I'm often just as happy to kiss him good-night well before midnight.

His daily call to JoAnn is from the office late in the afternoon. When a man is pulled away from his family The Paper expects that he will call her regularly and keep the ties strong. Bill will be in New York longer than originally planned. He won't be returning to Washington at the end of September but will be staying through the election. It's not exactly clear why. He has a hunch it has to do with the good impression he's been making. He's delighted. It not only means he's on his way on The Paper, it forestalls the dreaded time when he will definitely have to speak to JoAnn. Needless to say, I'm only happy about the first part of his reasoning.

I'm more than upset about his lack of movement where JoAnn is concerned, but there's not much point in arguing about it, I guess. A man needs time to breathe, free of all pressures, he has told me many times, and I guess I agree. "I've spent my whole life making important decisions when others wanted me to," he said, "let me have a few months for myself. You know," he always adds, "I'll never give you up."

He has bought two sets of papers. "I'm thirsty," he says, "how about you?" We cross Third Avenue and he orders a papaya juice and sips it slowly as he reads his story on the front page. I watch his face, the satisfied smile that spreads over it. I feel great pride at this moment. I want to pull him to me. Do all these people hurrying home with The Paper know that the story they just read or are going to be reading, perhaps first, was written by W. B. Hallam, my man, this man here, this man who loves me?

We kiss good-night on the threshold of my apartment. He hands me my paper and I gently close and bolt the door. I can still hear his footsteps on the stairs as I run across the room for my purse and take it with me to the still-uncleared dining table. I sit down and take my notebook out, pushing the dinner dishes away without looking at them. I am engrossed in my notes. I can see the story taking shape. I can begin to see the lead in print. And above it:

By Arlyn Crane

20

Today is the day. Today I definitely talk to Purledge. Strike while the iron is hot. Today with my feature on Carlotta Della Sandro blazing across three columns I'll show him the sermons and the travel piece and ask about my chances.

I turn on Third Avenue and walk faster. It's a perfect day for this new Anne Fogarty wool and mohair jacket dress. And the soft rose color looks better on the street than it did in the store. I'm so glad I went shopping last week and found it and didn't wait the way I usually do until everything good is gone from the stores. Two short blocks. Two short blocks to the newsstand, the newsstand where thousands of copies of the Friday paper are piled high, each one with my by-line.

Last night after we went out for the City Edition we returned to the apartment to celebrate. Bill was very sweet. He had a bottle of champagne stashed away in the back of the refrigerator. He had brought it in with him earlier, rolled in his raincoat. He had hidden it on ice while I showered. That explained why he hadn't let me buy a drink at the papaya stand. "Come on," he had urged, "let's get back."

We were at the newsstand where we had just opened The Paper to find my story. When I saw it, my heart jumped. A three-column picture of Carlotta Della Sandro playing her bassoon while one bare foot scratched around in a box of kitty litter. Under the picture a headline—"BASSOONIST PLANS UNCONVENTIONAL RECITAL"—and under that—"By Arlyn Crane."

Bill and I read the headline together and after we said "By Arlyn Crane" simultaneously he turned and kissed me on the nose. That was too much for the news vendor, who at that precise moment just had to rearrange his stacks of papers, squeezing between us and the stand, bumping my hip with his groin and forcing us to move.

"I'm thirsty," I said, "how about you?" I started to cross Third Avenue but Bill pulled me toward him and headed uptown. "Come on," he said, rather brusquely, I thought, "let's get back."

I was very disappointed but I walked in silence. Two and a half whole blocks to walk before I could read my story in print. How often I had imagined the two of us standing at the papaya stand, slowly sipping juice and savoring a story I had written.

Pop! It was our first bottle of champagne together. He tossed the cork to me and I carefully placed it on the bookshelf.

"A first by-line in the daily paper is an auspicious occasion," Bill said, sitting down beside me with two wineglasses brimming over with champagne. I took one from him and we touched the glasses. "To many, many more," he said, kissing me gently on the forehead.

After a few sips of champagne he took the glass from my hand and set it down on the coffee table alongside his. We drew close and kissed and then undressed each other. Neither one was in the mood but the ceremony seemed to call for it. Lovemaking was part of the ritual of celebration. Later I was only dimly aware of his leaving.

Buying my own copy of The Paper this morning is even more exciting than it was getting it and reading my story with Bill last night. Just a quick look to see that it's lasted uncut through to the Final Edition. It has. It is still there, in the same place, picture and all. My heart is pounding wildly now as I walk to Lexington Avenue. Rushing down the subway stairs all I can see is The Paper, folded under a dozen stiff arms. In seconds each one will be on the platform and then on the train, The Paper opened with my by-line leaping out in front of each jostled reader. Many readers will spend time on the front page, of course, the hard news, the aftermath of the debate, the big bash at the UN, the flap about Castro moving up to Harlem after being slighted downtown, but sooner or later the picture of Carlotta Della Sandro will catch their attention and they will look at it and then drop their eyes and see My Name. And My Story. Hey, you'll be seeing my story, I whisper under my breath to the pin-striped, silver-haired man stepping on the train ahead of me.

I sit down and look to my right. A jacketless young fellow is reading the *Daily News*. How disappointing! I wanted to study my subway neighbor's reaction to my story. On the other side of me a woman in white gloves is trying to turn a page of *Advise and Consent*. My neighbor with the *News* turns his page, away from Khrushchev and the beer-swilling Fidel and . . . what's that? I catch my breath. That picture. It is June Rogers. No mistake. There's the blond hair, the delicate features. What is her picture doing in the *Daily News*? I lean closer to the young man. "EAST SIDE MODEL MURDERED. Assailant Unknown. 'Never saw so much blood,'" according to Patrolman Frank Malloy of the something precinct. The print gets smaller, but I am still able to make out words: ". . . model . . . luscious blonde . . . ice pick . . . repeatedly . . . crushed skull."

A sourness rises in my throat. I gag and swallow it. I

quickly thumb through my copy of The Paper but I find nothing by the time the train arrives at Forty-second Street. I get off and weave dizzily through the crowd to a newsstand and buy the *News*, and the *Mirror* too. Right now I have a need for the tabloids, always better on this kind of story

I stand at the newsstand and devour the accounts in both papers, impervious to the nudges from the vendor, who arranges his already arranged papers in an attempt to sweep me away from his stand. Really, there is not much more to read than what I had read on the subway. June Rogers, identified as a luscious blond model, was found yesterday by the super of her East Eighty-ninth Street apartment after she failed to keep a date with an unidentified friend at a Fifty-seventh Street address. The apartment was "blood-soaked." Robbery did not appear to be the motive. According to the *Mirror* it was the superintendent who said he never saw so much blood.

Walking through the underground passage to the shuttle for the West Side, I feel dank and heavy. The mohair is itching around my neck. The black leather gloves I am carrying seem ridiculously superfluous. I jam them into my bag. I see the doors of the waiting shuttle begin to close and automatically run and join in the mad dash to squeeze onto the three-car train.

John Campbell is sitting in the first car reading The Paper, carefully folded lengthwise in front of him. I squeeze myself beside him, drawing curse-filled mumbles and glares from the man on the other side as he sucks in his breath. The ancient wicker of the seats snags my stockings. John closes his paper and looks at me, yelling above the screech of the train:

"You should have seen what I did last night. I went up to the Theresa Hotel. It was great. Those guys are really something, the way they stomp around. And Fidel. He's too much."

"I've just had the most terrible shock," I yell back.

John looks puzzled.

Suddenly I realize I don't want to talk about June now. I don't want to scream over the shrieking of the subway wheels, to quickly explain it all to John, to give him a summary in minutes, tell about the lunch in Newport, the drive, the visit in her apartment, the way I feel now thinking of her dead. John is looking intently into my face, waiting for my answer, but I shake my head. When the train comes to its stop I say as brightly as I can, "I'll explain it all some other time. Tell me about Castro. Does he really have all that sex appeal?"

John shakes his head condescendingly. "Arlyn, you disappoint me. It's more than mere sex appeal. It's a whole attitude toward life. You should know that. Speaking of sex appeal, I see Big Bill has analyzed the Kennedy appeal." John raises his eyebrows. I don't answer.

"Say," he continues, "aren't you going to ask me why I'm taking the shuttle this morning?"

"Why?" I ask, suddenly curious. Is John living on the East Side already? He was just promoted to news assistant, for God's sake!

"I didn't get home last night," he is saying proudly. "I was with some of the out-of-town reporters. They are something else, believe me. What a blast. I ended up sleeping on the floor of a room in the Commodore and I haven't the slightest idea whose room it was."

I am relieved when John peels off at the corner of Broadway to stop for a container of coffee. He is already dashing across the street when I realize that he didn't mention my story. Him. John Campbell. Of all people. He would most certainly have said something about it right away. If he had seen it. I am dumbfounded. People will read The Paper this morning and not see my story. They will be so busy reading about the circus at the UN and the endless analyses of the dumb debate that they will not get back to the cultural pages before their trip to the office is over. And how many will get back to The Paper on their lunch hour or on the way home? Not too many, I know. Unless it rains, which isn't likely today, they will spend their lunch hour walking around the blocks where their offices are and for their trips home in the evening most will want to doze or read different papers, ones with lots of columns and gossip. But how could John have missed it. Why didn't he at least notice Carlotta's picture? And my by-line?

Am I crazy? June Rogers is lying dead and here I am worrying about everyone in the world seeing my story. Poor June. How awful! That lovely body, punctured with ice-pick holes, bled dry. Ugh. I shut my eyes to black out the sight. I wonder what happened to the body.

Gil Gilchrist is waiting for the elevator. "Good story today, Arlyn," he says, sweeping off his hat. "Congratulations!" I thank him warmly. Good old Gil. You could always count on him. He didn't miss anything. He is truly a Reporter's Reporter. Should I tell him about June? Maybe he can tell me the quickest way to find out what happened to her body. But something keeps me from mentioning June to Gil. Somehow I know that he will just make some nasty remark about her, refer to her as some looker, and then he will no doubt leer and say in his own quaint way that she probably got what she bargained for, paying the fiddler and all that. I know a lot of people will think that. I can just hear them. "Nobody forced her to get into that kind of life, Arlyn. She could have done an honest day's work." What's the difference what she did, she didn't hurt anyone, and she was such a friendly person. I shudder to think of her punctured body.

Isabelle is in the Ladies Lounge. She lets out a long, wolf whistle when she sees me. "It's stunning, Arlyn. Absolutely stunning." I gratefully spin around so she can admire the dress from all angles. Slowly I unbutton each frog button and gracefully remove the jacket, dangling it from one extended hand as I plant the other on my hip and strike a model's pose. June flashes into my mind and I stop. I am sickened at my actions, but it is too late. Isabelle is smiling at me from the couch. The door opens.

"Da da da da da da . . ." It is Kit Rockwell who has come in and is humming and waving her arms in the manner of an orchestra leader. My body crumbles and I head for the couch, dragging the jacket behind me. Kit stops humming and exaggeratedly tiptoes toward the washroom. I must remember to say something to her, to assure her that it was not her sudden appearance or the humming that caused my change in mood.

Isabelle is looking at me strangely. "What's the matter," she asks, "did that one upset you?"

I wonder if Kit has heard Isabelle refer to her as "that one."

"No," I answer, "it's something else. I told you about June Rogers, didn't I?" Isabelle nods.

"Well, she's dead," I say, hardly believing my own words. "She was murdered. Yesterday. Look. It's splashed all over the *News* and *Mirror*." I hand the two papers to Isabelle.

Isabelle is stunned. "June? The one you met in Newport? Stuart told me about her. Murdered!" Isabelle is dating Stuart regularly now. They met again at a Kennedy rally sponsored by the Lexington Young Democrats right after Labor Day and things look good. Just yesterday she told me she had finally convinced him to at least talk to her plastic surgeon. "For his own sake," she insisted, "it's for him, it will make him feel better."

Now she has finished reading about June and puts the papers down. "Soooo," she says, rather too archly, I think, "the glamorous life is snuffed out. You have to pay the piper, that's for sure. You live by the sword, you die by the sword, or should I say ice pick?"

I stand up, smooth the wrinkles in my dress, and change the subject.

"This is my big day. Did you see my story? That feature on Carlotta Della Sandro ran this morning."

Isabelle jumps up and reaches to pat me on the shoulder.

"Mazel tov. I'll run right out now and read it." She is gone.

I remain behind to straighten my stockings and tidy up. Christ, I feel grimy already. What a day. I must try to see Purledge as soon as possible.

21

I hear reproach in Bill's voice. Why is he so angry? I waited until ten-fifteen to call. He should be up by now anyway.

"I have to talk to you right away."

"My God, what is it? Are you okay?"

"I'm fine. It's something else."

"For crissake, don't do this to me." I hear the crinkle of the cigarette pack and the intake of his breath as he lights up. He had once told me that I could call him anytime anyplace if I was in even the remotest kind of trouble or danger. But please, he had said, use your discretion and don't upset me with ordinary, everyday crises. If I frightened him too much with trivial emergencies, he had warned, he would begin to think of me as "the girl who cried wolf." Now his voice is hoarse. "What happened?"

"June Rogers is dead, she was murdered." The word clings to me, clammy and cold.

"June Rogers?"

"The girl I told you about, the one I met in Newport."

"Oh yeah." Bill is sounding more awake now. He clears

the phlegm from his throat. I would recognize that sound of his anywhere. "When?" he asks.

"Yesterday. She was found in her apartment last evening. An ice pick, lots of blood. And her skull was crushed."

"Do they have a suspect?"

"Unknown assailant. I wonder if there's something I should do, you know, get in touch with the detective, find out what's going on, maybe I can help, maybe I can—"

Bill's voice is tight when he breaks in. "Don't do a thing until we talk. I'll meet you in the cafeteria in forty minutes."

Sharipp. Sharipp. The mail is heavy for a Friday. The cultural scene has really heated up in the last few weeks, the season is now in full blast. Carlotta Della Sandro is lucky she got all that space today. Another week or so and it would be out of the question, a flaky, young unknown like her. I must think of someone who would be considered more newsworthy for my next story. I scan the releases for an idea, but it is difficult to come up with one. Feature space is tight, a waste of newsprint, some people think, though others feel The Paper is on the right course in running more bright writing and light pieces. I wouldn't be trusted with any of the sacred cows, as we call them around here, of course. They would have to be written about by one of the top men, dispatched to the Great One not as an inquiring reporter but as an ambassador from The Paper.

I had delayed going for my container of coffee, intent on finishing the mail before meeting Bill, and now I must be feeling caffeine deprivation. It is very difficult to keep my eyes open. Oops. Almost opened that letter for Lowell in error. He has been getting a lot of mail this week. Last Sunday his essay questioned whether the Emperor (Jackson Pollock) really had any clothes and shouldn't we all pause a moment in the beginning of a new decade and take stock of what we have been so unabashedly praising in the last decade.

Ashley loved it even before he knew it would bring so

many letters. "It's about time someone said it," he had told
Lowell. A lot of the people in the art world were outraged,
while many apparently agree with Ashley and feel the re-
evaluation long overdue. It's been rumored that a slew of
letters—pro and con—have been received in the Publisher's
Suite as well. Lowell is pretending to be taking it all in
stride. "I've been around this business too long, Arlyn," he
told me, "to get excited over the periodic rise and fall in my
popularity with my readers," but the general consensus is
that he's come back slugging after the low blow of having
been passed over for promotion. Since Tony Weather and
Gil first told me about how Lowell expected to get Ashley's
job, I have paid particular attention to Lowell. I've tried to
imagine him as Cultural News Director and I just don't see
it. Good as Lowell is at what he does, I can't see him running a forty-man-plus department. Still, I suppose he should
have had the chance to try; plenty of others around here
shouldn't be running departments either. But as a critic/
newsman he's the best. About that there can be no doubt.
This latest flap is a case in point. If he survives unscathed,
it is said, and the bets are that he will, then he's really
made. He will have taken on the giants and won. He will
be a leader instead of a follower, a taste-maker himself instead of a mere chronicler.

Jean Blake ambles over and leans on my desk, planting
her palms firmly on it.

"Say, Arlyn, that was a marvelous story this morning. You
really captured that girl's nuttiness. I broke out laughing on
the subway." Jean's cigarette is disappearing into an ivory
holder. With practiced yellowed fingers, swollen from years
of typing, she removes the minuscule butt and flings it to
the linoleum floor, where she grinds it out.

I am pleased with the compliment but distressed by
Jean's comment. "I hope I wasn't too hard on her," I say. "I
hadn't wanted to make complete fun of her."

"Oh no, dear, you didn't," Jean reassures me. "That's the
beauty part."

This is a problem, I am learning, how to write a story that shows you off to your best advantage without abusing the subject. It is tricky.

A tap, tap, tapping of insistent high heels reverberates in the corridor that leads from the city room. Jean and I look around to see Ernestine Herbert heading straight for my desk.

"I'm off to lunch with Kennedy mère and her enceinte daughter-in-law," Ernestine says, somewhat out of breath, "but I just had to stop by and tell you that your story this morning was first-rate." Ernestine makes a circle with her thumb and index finger to punctuate her words. "A real piece of work. You really skewered her. We must talk."

Ernestine nods acknowledgment to Jean and turns, tap, tap, tapping back out of the Cultural News Department. Jean wordlessly continues on her way to the supply cabinet behind me for a shorthand notebook and then as she walks past my desk again she pauses briefly:

"Never lose your heart or surrender your soul to The Paper," she tells me, tossing her brittle bleached head toward the corridor that leads to the city room, echoing still with the sound of Ernestine's high heels.

I smile weakly at Jean and slit open another envelope. I wonder about Jean, who is nearing retirement. Her only life seems to be her job as the secretary in the Radio Television News Department and the care of her invalid mother, who can't even go away in the summer anymore.

Sharipp. I have an appointment with Purledge at two-thirty. Ginny slotted me in and said unless something comes up she is sure he will see me at that time. *Sharipp.* Ernestine Herbert has an exciting job but everyone knows she doesn't have much else. She's too tough and ambitious. Bill is right. All the softness and femininity have been wrung out of her. I wonder if they had ever been there. Her high heels and tiny waist fool no one. She is steel inside. And when she does win an award for best woman reporter from one of the journalism societies, she invariably turns up at the awards dinner with one or the other of the bachelor or widowed or divorced executives, an arrangement strictly business, it is said, no matter what happens afterward. Sometimes I envy Ernestine the excitement of her job and the sense of accomplishment it must bring, but just as often I feel sorry for her.

> *There's only one thing worse*
> *In the universe*
> *That's a woman*
> *I said a woman*
> *I said a woman*
> *Without a man.*

Sharipp. Sharipp. But you can't have it all, that I know. Dame Fortune never comes with both hands full. *Sharipp.* That is the title of my novel if I ever write it: *Both Hands Full.* But would the heroine have it all? How could she? Not all at the same time. This is a problem and one of the reasons I never get too far with the novel. Even Bill wasn't much help when I discussed this with him. "Depends on how your character develops, Arlyn. You are, after all, master of her fate, but you have to make sure the reader is not surprised. You have to prepare us for whatever fate befalls her." In the early days of his marriage Bill had been working on a novel about his war experiences but he eventually gave it up. He says he had spent so much time devouring books about how to write a novel and what makes a good novel that he never had time to write it. That's a good joke but a poor excuse. I've read those books too. They don't prevent you from writing. What prevents you is not knowing how much you can give your heroine and still remain truthful.

"Good morning, Miss Crane."

"Arlyn, remember?" I smile as warmly as I know how to Roger Glickston but it still doesn't do much good. He pads silently to his cubicle and shuts the door. The newly appointed chief drama critic of The Paper, it is generally agreed, is well-meaning but a tightass if ever there was one.

> *He walks like he's carrying eggs between his legs.*
> *They'll eat him up. One season on Broadway and they'll eat him for breakfast.*
> *His ideas aren't bad, but his vocabulary . . . Marone!*
> *Let's give the guy a chance. After all, wouldn't most of us be nervous in academe?*
> *Shit no. Academia is a snap compared to the pressure here. That's the problem. He's never had to put it on the line, day in and day out.*

Naturally, starting so suddenly, Glickston wasn't expected to carry the kind of load that Randolph had. That problem was solved by moving a man over from movies to be the Number Two man in drama, a lateral slide with a bit more prestige but less in the way of "fringe benefits," as it was whispered in quotes.

I often wonder if being *on the tit* is really as common around The Paper as some say it is. And if it is, what does it really amount to? Tickets? A night on the town? A vacation with the wife or girlfriend? A weekly envelope? A weekly bottle? It's said that certain press agents own certain reporters. Is that really true?

But there is another side. Press agents can give a tip or a story that shows the reporter off to good advantage, and if the reporter is lazy or drunk they have even been known to get the story written for the reporter, especially out of town. A lot of the press agents are worms right out of *Sweet Smell of Success,* but there are just as many who are not that way. A lot are really just like reporters only they are paid by clients who want publicity instead of by publishers who are providing it. There are some press agents I can't stand, but there are a few I really like very much. And look at Betty Thoburn, Randolph's widow. In just these few short weeks she's been showing her mettle and everyone in town is talking about her. She's not only doing the job that was handed to her out of pity by one of the bigger theatrical agencies around, she pulled off the biggest stunt in recent memory. A real coup, it was, everyone agrees, cooking up that contest for the preview audience to rename that sinking musical extravaganza *Land Ahoy!* It didn't really save the show, it's closing Saturday, but it did extend its life long enough for the producer to realize some of his investment. And Betty is credited with doing it single-handedly. Of course she has no other life, works day and night, eats and sleeps her job. But it seems to be agreeing with her. She looks quite good these days, she's thinner and clear-eyed. She's brisk and cordial with me and seems to want to forget the afternoon we spent together when I drove her back to Nyack after Randolph died.

Sharipp. Thank God! The last of the morning's mail. It is almost time to meet Bill now. I still have read about June only in the *News* and *Mirror.* It's time to check the other papers at the big library table in the rear of the Cultural News Department. But there's one thing I must do first, even before I read about June. I must look at my own story circled in red by the Music Department secretary and hanging with the other cultural stories of the day on the wooden frame. There it is. My heart leaps! Will I ever be blasé about it?

It takes awhile to find any mention of June in The Paper. But it is there, for the record, buried in the back, a staid paragraph with the deadest of deadhead headlines. But why not? June Rogers alive or dead is of no importance to The Paper or its readers. It would be different if she had made her mark, starred in a show, married the producer.

Armed with clippings about June, I go to meet Bill. These puny accounts from the responsible morning papers will carry more weight with him than all the eyewitness stories and enlarged photos splashed across the tabloids. I flick my eyes to the big clock on the pillar above me. In half an hour or so the p.m.'s will be distributed. The *Journal-American* should have a field day with June Rogers. Would-be actress, sometime model, blonde, beautiful. Their kind of story. Is it big enough for Dorothy Kilgallen?

I am surprised to see the Publisher's nephew on the elevator. Teddy Lowe is usually seen only late in the afternoon lounging around the executive bullpen waiting to go out on the town with one or the other of the bon vivant executives. Nights of wine, women, and song, they are called. Once Bill was invited along. "Never again," he told me. "It is too dangerous for a man in my position. To be blind drunk is one thing, but to lose control around the bosses is just plain dumb, even though they were falling-down drunk themselves," he said. "Guys who consort with bosses too much lose their edge. Socializing is fine, but you have to draw the line. The fellows a man roisters with are not necessarily the fellows he wants to take with him to the top. Remember Prince Hal." Bill prides himself on his knowledge of Shakespeare and I love to hear him cite a character or quote a phrase as an example of man's duplicity or inhumanity or whatever, especially when we are talking about someone we know.

I study the Publisher's nephew now, his face closely shaved and imparting that special glow of the rich in New York, a face from which the dirt of the day and the impurities of the night before have been purged. He nods a brusque greeting to me. He seems unusually serious and sober this morning and I notice that he sucks in his breath as he gets off at his uncle's private floor.

Bill is sitting at a table for two by the window cradling a cup of coffee in his big hands. I pass the steam table and quickly take a pot of coffee and a soft roll from the end of the counter. The cafeteria is almost empty, with more employees than customers at this hour. Luis is cleaning off a table near the cashier's booth. He does not look at me as he sloshes his wet rag over the Formica. My initial concern about what would happen when I saw him after that disastrous Sunday in his loft has proven unnecessary. Nothing happened. For a while I ducked him, doing without coffee or coming up here to buy it, and then one day he surprised me when I was sitting at Ashley's desk going over some dictation. Ashley bought me coffee and Luis went about his business as though I didn't exist. Ice. And that's the way it's been. He serves me but ignores me, and I am relieved and delighted. I wonder if his schedule's been changed and he will be working up here regularly now.

Bill watches me approach. It seems like a long time since he's looked at me this way. Familiarity does breed more than contempt and children. It breeds dullness. Here we are only in the third month of our grande passion and it takes a new season and a new dress to start the sparks going.

"Smashing, you look absolutely smashing. As befits the writer of the best feature story in the paper today."

I put down my tray and shuffle a little curtsy, clasping the folds or what I can grab of my pencil-slim sheath dress, and sit down smiling. I push the clipping across the table toward him.

"Here, I brought you these about June." I pour my coffee and butter my roll while he reads.

"Poor baby," he says. "Your big day and it's being spoiled by a dead slut."

I straighten up. The knife clatters to the floor. I am stunned.

"How can you say such a rotten thing?"

"Now, now," he begins, reaching over to stroke my arm but stopping almost before he can begin. Nervously he pulls his hand away. What was he thinking about to touch me in public? Through everything, no matter what is or is not said about us, we have tried to remain discreet.

He is talking now, that soft, comforting slur blanketing me. "I'm sorry, sweetie. I didn't mean to be harsh." He urges the uneaten roll on me. "But these girls who live this kind of life, they sort of ask for it, don't they?"

"What kind of life? Who asks to be murdered?"

"Now don't get on your high horse. You know what I mean. Actress. Model. How about that producer, if that's what he was? Hmmmm?"

"And the Publisher's nephew. I just saw him on the elevator. Strange, isn't it? A little early in the day for him."

Bill is horrified. He leans across the table as close to me as he can get and strains as he whispers gruffly: "Are you crazy? You met him with her at a social event several months ago. You'd best be sure you don't blab anything about him around the office to your secretary pals."

"I didn't say he did it, I just said . . ."

Bill stands up. He is uneasy. "Let's drop the whole thing. You keep out of the detective business. Leave that for the pros and the police reporters."

I follow him out of the cafeteria. We pass the Publisher's niece, sitting with the gang from the Women's Page. How does this proper matron feel about her brother's peccadillos? I wonder. How much does she know about his night life? What would Daddy say about Teddy's indiscretions? Poor Daddy. He must be spinning.

At the elevator bank Bill's face is expressionless, but his eyes seek mine when he speaks. His voice is low, his lips hardly move.

"Your meddling in this wouldn't do either of us any good. These things have a way of getting out of hand. Especially when one's own house isn't exactly in apple-pie order."

The minute hand drags. It is like sitting in high school mesmerized by the impossibly slow crawl of the minute hand past the Roman numerals of the big wooden clock in every classroom. Only here it is the large, clear-faced, modern clocks prominently placed on the pillars that surround us. One minute. Another minute.

I am washed and freshly made up. At twenty-eight minutes after two I will stand up and begin to wend my way to Albert B. Purledge's desk in the executive bullpen. The prospect of talking to him about my future on The Paper has made me tense enough, but right now I am ready to jump out of my skin because of something else.

The entire Cultural Department, it seems, is clustered around Tony Weather's desk a few feet from mine, rehashing June Roger's life and death, making it all sound like a stag movie. Dorothy Kilgallen came up with a scoop and it is all over the front page of this afternoon's *Journal-American*. June was definitely not a model or an actress, but a much-in-demand call girl who worked out of a swank East Fifty-seventh Street apartment leased by a Hungarian refugee who is said to be vacationing in Venezuela at the moment. If the list of June's Johns was ever made public, Kilgallen says, a collective shiver would issue from a number of blue-blooded members of the Social Register as well as a slew of politicos and industrialists.

Everyone has something to say. Jokes about Pat Ward and Mickey Jelke and his call girl ring are resurrected. It is all very boisterous. They cannot outdo each other fast enough with whores-I-have-known (or, in the case of most of these bigmouths, read-about) stories. Lowell has even dragged in a gory tale of a famous nineteenth-century beauty whose bed of sin was set on fire after she was, in his words, "done in." It was the *scandale* of its day, he said, and pulled the failing *Herald Tribune* out of the red, starting it on its august rise to its present glory.

Finally it is time. I pick up my purse and leave the nest of magpies chortling over June's death. Yes, I know I'm being too hard on them. If I hadn't known her personally I'd probably be right in the middle of the group, laughing as hard as anyone.

In the corridor Bob Mann stops me.

"I was just coming to look for you," he says. "There must be something wrong with your phone. It doesn't ring. How've you been?"

What is this all about? Mann, whom I have hardly seen

all summer, is now leaning up against the wall, prepared, it seems, for a leisurely chat.

"I'm in a hurry," I say, continuing to walk toward the newsroom.

His fingers circle my wrist. "I have to tell you something. It will only take a minute. You read about that model who was murdered yesterday?"

"Yes."

"You may not remember but you met her briefly at the Simons' last summer. She stopped to say hello to Ed Hart. She had posed for him once, a fashion thing. I'm on the story."

I am dumbfounded. Does he really believe that in three short months I could forget that June stopped in with the Publisher's nephew and not to see Ed Hart? But remembering Bill's warning, I say only, "I was so startled when I saw her face in the papers this morning." Then I can't resist adding, "I remember her vividly."

Bob looks at me sharply. "Strange you should recognize her face so quickly. The picture was an old one. Don't you think she looked different last summer?"

"Well, I recognized her name, too," I answer. "Actually I remember meeting her very clearly," I call as I hurry away.

Albert B. Purledge looks up from his ever-present manila folders as I sit down in the straight-back chair alongside his desk. At this moment, I know, the movement is being registered throughout the entire west end of the huge room, much as a seismograph registers the slightest earth tremor; and just as the news of the earth's shifting is relayed to observatories all over the world, news of Ashley Franks' secretary sitting at Purledge's desk is relayed around The Paper. Of course my sitting here registers only a minor tremor, say a mere two or three on the Richter scale, not the nine or ten that a Foreign Correspondent or Star Reporter would score. Still, my presence raises questions that need to be answered for those who find the answers to such questions important to their day: Why is she there? Is she being promoted?

Fired? Transferred? Chastised? Warned? Threatened? Besides being Ashley Franks' secretary, I must be known by many to be W. B. Hallam's *good friend*. Just what am I doing sitting in the hot seat on this Friday afternoon at the end of September? Is there a scandal involved, some must be thinking. But no, didn't you see her story in today's paper. Oh, sure, that's it. Maybe she'll make it to the Women's Page. Not bad-looking.

". . . and so, Mr. Purledge, I would like to know if I can expect to be considered for promotion toward a writing job within a reasonable time."

Purledge begins with his little dry cough. While I was talking he had pushed the folders to one side, including, I noticed, one marked EMPLOYEE PERSONNEL FILE: CRANE, ARLYN. PRIVATE AND CONFIDENTIAL, and reached into his right-hand drawer to pull out a long yellow legal pad.

Purledge hears me out, then he begins: "That little story this morning was quite interesting, Arlyn. You do show some ability to get a story and put it down. And I hadn't realized that this unsigned piece about the barrel maker was yours. And these sermons here, I wasn't aware you were doing them. But Arlyn, you should know, doing sermons and writing a feature story or two is a long way from staff."

"I know, sir, but it seems that this is what's done. When Peter Olsen was promoted to news assistant from copyboy everyone remarked on his feature stories and said he's a comer who shows initiative and drive."

"But Arlyn, Peter Olsen is a qualified young man who was hired as a copyboy with impeccable credentials. He is a graduate of Columbia College."

"I'm not asking to be promoted to the reportorial staff immediately, Mr. Purledge," I say, though I am sure I had made this point clear before. "I'm asking if I can have any hope of being promoted to a clerk's job and a news assistant's job and can be in line for a reporter's job."

Purledge leans back in his chair. The rimless glasses glitter. Why does he make me feel like an interloper? Is it really very pushy of me to be here? Purledge coughs again. "Arlyn, there's more than one way to cross a river. If you know what I mean." His voice is kindly as he reaches back and takes a piece of copy paper from the typewriter table behind him. With a thick copy pencil he illustrates his remarks as he talks:

"If you're here," he says, drawing an X, "and another fellow is here"—another X—"and you both want to get here" —he draws a circle—"and this is water"—three long wavy lines—"now the fellow can cross here"—a direct route—"but you may have to go here first." Another X, this one indicating me, is on the other side of the X that represents the fellow who has just crossed the river. "From here," Purledge says, tapping the X that is me, "perhaps you can still make it across the river to another point. Sometimes these things take a little longer, that's all."

He looks at me triumphantly and smiles. He tears the pages he has just written about me off the yellow pad and staples them together. Along with the Crossing the River diagram they will go, I know, into my folder. He hands me the manila envelope with my sermons and feature story and stands up, beaming down at me proudly. "You're working out very well here, Arlyn. You're an asset to the Cultural News Department just as I knew you'd be when I chose you to be Ashley Franks' secretary."

Clumsily gathering my purse and the envelope with my clippings, I stand up. My face is burning hot and my palms are like ice. I am not sure what has just happened. Was the interview a success or a failure? I feel Ginny's eyes on me as I walk away. Ginny, I know, will never say a word about my chances for promotion to me or anyone else. Ginny, as Purledge has said, is truly a perfect secretary. Trustworthy, loyal to her boss, and discreet. And she does look like one of the Seven Sisters even though she never went to college. That Peck and Peck suit is *class*. Walking back to the Cultural News Department, I wonder if the rose mohair is perhaps a bit too garish for the office.

22

"I don't understand," Mom is saying, "does this mean you won't come for Thanksgiving?"

"I'm not sure." I feel stuffed already. Why did she have to make pancakes? My favorite, she says.

"I hope it's nothing that would embarrass me." Dad has been nervous ever since I told them the purpose of my surprise visit.

"How could it embarrass you?" I say, rather too cruelly, I suppose. "The Pittsburgh police aren't the ones dragging their feet on this one, it's New York's finest who can't find the murderer."

Mom shudders and Dad sighs. He begins reviewing again the problems facing the police today.

It's been five weeks now since June Rogers was killed and the police are no closer to solving the murder than they were the day it happened. For a while they pinned their hopes on a would-be actor on-and-off delivery boy from the Daitch Shopwell Market who lived in June's building and disappeared around the time of the murder. But he was finally tracked down the other day and his alibi is ironclad. He definitely was not in Manhattan the day June was killed; he was in jail in Albuquerque. He had run a red light on his way back from Los Angeles and was arrested for possession of marijuana.

When Bob Mann told me this yesterday morning, something dropped out of the pit of my stomach. I have become obsessed with June's murder. I have a file of every clipping about the case and I check Bob regularly for all the scuttlebutt that doesn't get into the papers.

I was sure it was the actor-delivery boy. It's so ironic, I had thought, June being killed by a guy who lived right in her building. "Not a customer after all," I told Isabelle with relief. "Let's wait and see," she answered and now it looks as though she could be right.

Bill was even harsher when we discussed the case. "She was probably toying with some man, Arlyn, or worse, trying to blackmail him. That could make a fellow desperate. You know, sweetie, you should lay off this. When you play with fire you get burned. It disturbs me that you spend so much time and energy worrying about this whole sorry mess."

Bill would really be disturbed if he knew why I came home. I just told him I was going to visit my parents and he accepted it. Maybe he was happy with the prospect of my being away for a couple of days. There has been a strain between us lately and neither one seems to want to acknowledge it. On the surface we still laugh and talk and jump into bed the way we always did, but there is tension.

On the plane it occurred to me what is really wrong. We never mention JoAnn anymore. I avoid asking what the lawyers are saying, or even if there really are lawyers. All I know is that in July he told me they both made appointments. And there is something else we don't talk about. Bill was originally hired for the Washington Bureau and his three-month New York orientation period has been lengthened until after the election. He's sure he will be offered something good in New York. A few weeks ago, I know, he was leaning toward accepting. The offer, he said, if it comes as he expects, will be "too seductive" to ignore. Now he's talking about getting back to the "hub of things" in Washington.

Ashley was surprised that I wanted my Columbus Day holiday time so suddenly but okayed my request without discussion. Tony Weather and Gil, however, couldn't let such an unusual occurrence pass without comment. While I was clearing off my desk I caught snatches of their animated conversation: "sudden" and "Pennsylvania" and "humanitarian doctor."

The idiots! I thought. They assume I'm going to that abortionist near Chambersburg. Why else would a girl take sudden time off work? And of course to them Pennsylvania extends from Philadelphia through Bucks County to the Dutch country and ends there.

"I don't know when I'll be back," I tell my parents. "Probably for dinner, but I'll call you."

Mom looks horrified. "You're going to be gone this afternoon, too? Karyn is planning to come for lunch. With the baby. You haven't seen him for six months. He talks a streak now."

"I told you this trip wasn't a family visit."

"But your own sister. And your nephew."

"Won't they be here tonight? I'm sure I'll be back tonight."

"Of course they'll be here tonight. With Bernie, too. But she's dying to see you this afternoon. I don't know what it is, the way you treat her. Sisters should be friends."

Now Dad stands up, brushing his shoulders and adjusting the huge Kennedy button hanging from his lapel. No one paid any attention to his defense of the Pittsburgh police so he's for sure not going to have any discussions about love between sisters. It's time for him to get down to the Court House where he's appreciated.

"I'll wait on the porch," he says.

"Be careful," Mom tells me as I button my coat. I had

vaguely outlined my plan to them when I arrived unexpectedly last night. I would start with the high school. Maybe if I flash my Newspaper Guild Press card I can look at June's record. Then I would try to find people still in the neighborhood who knew her. The *News* carried a picture of her brother identifying the body, "Bereaved Brother of Bludgeoned Blonde." I'll want to talk to him. There are a number of Douglas Rogers in the phone book.

I suppose the caption was accurate in essence; in addition to the ice-pick wounds, her head was bashed in. Bludgeoned. And more. The New York newspapers are cooperating with the police investigation and not divulging all that is known about the murder. All the stories hint at the "sick" mind that has to have committed the murder, but not one of the papers has ever reported the bizarre details that are common knowledge around their city rooms. RAPED AND TAPED. I know some of the papers are dying to use that headline and print the story of how poor June was found with her vagina sealed shut with layers of shiny black electrician's tape, the stuck snatch, one wag said, but the police asked for self-censorship of the details. Holding back information often helps the police flush a confession out of the perpetrator. The press has complied so far.

In Pittsburgh, June was a two-week wonder until she was bumped for the Carnegie Child Stalker. Three little girls from Carnegie had been raped and brutally murdered within ten days of each other and that, of course, is a running front-page story.

Since yesterday the New York police have found themselves in a real bind. When the actor-delivery boy didn't pan out, reporters from the less responsible papers put it to the Police Commissioner: Either get to the Johns List or let us go with the Raped-Taped angle. In fact, the *Daily Mirror* is said to be ready to go with some juicy tidbits, though everyone knows they don't have the complete story. But that isn't important; they have to do something for their circulation. Everyone says they're in real trouble.

The responsible papers have a different interest in the case, of course. The murder of a young woman in a cut-up railroad flat in Yorkville is basically of no interest to the powers in the city; June was not living in the kind of building that one would expect to be secure from intruders. It would be different if the murder had taken place in that swank East Fifty-seventh Street apartment where she worked.

The only interest June Rogers and her murder hold for the responsible papers and their powerful readers lies in the little red leather Mark Cross notebook found in the victim's purse. This notebook, dubbed instantly the Johns List by Kilgallen, has up to now not been used by the police in the investigation of the murder. It is unlikely, they reason, that any name on this list would travel to a fourth-floor walk-up to stab June with an ice pick and then leave the notebook, easily retrievable from her alligator bag. The list is in code, but apparently the phone numbers are correct.

While many of the reporters covering the case agree with this reasoning, they also know that the police are being derelict in their duty by not questioning the names on the list. Who cares about the presumed innocence of these men? Just imagine week after week of pictures and bios of some of the city's most powerful men. Circulation could go through the roof. Everyone wants to read about pillars of the community caught with their hands in the cookie jar, as Bob Mann so aptly put it.

At the streetcar stop Dad finally speaks. "Arlyn," he says, "be careful. A girl like you has to watch what she gets herself into. Your mother didn't sleep all night for worry. And I myself think it's no business for you."

"Don't worry, Dad. I'll be okay."

23

The Vice Principal is impressed with my place of employment. It is his Sunday pleasure. He has a standing order at the Hilton newsstand. His first love is the theater, he confesses. He and his wife vacation in New York every Christmas, managing to see about ten plays in seven days. He was really shocked by Randolph Thoburn's sudden death and isn't sure yet about Glickston. He's really not supposed to let me look at June's Permanent Record Card without proper authorization from the Board of Education, but, as he says, what the heck, I'm from New York. What difference does it make, really. He knows I'll be discreet and, after all, the Pittsburgh reporters got to it. "To be truthful," he says, "there's really nothing much of interest on it, but I know you want to see that for yourself." He disappears into a file room and returns with that familiar large yellow-orange card.

JUNE VICTORIA ROGERS entered Forbes School in the Pittsburgh Public School system on March 10, 1944, when she was seven years and two months old; she had completed six months of the second grade in Youngstown. She lived with her mother, Dorothy Ann Rogers, and her brother, Douglas Andrew, who was eleven months her junior, at 7 Epiphany Street. Her father, John Victor Rogers, was deceased. June had been vaccinated, had measles and chicken pox and was a Methodist.

It's funny to think of June being in Forbes School when I was there. But of course I was in fifth grade when she was in second.

The Epiphany Street address is scratched through for one on Bluff Street and then one on upper Fifth Avenue. But she didn't stay in Forbes School long. The Fifth Avenue address and Forbes School are scratched for addresses and schools in the West End and on the South Side and finally over to the North Side. By this time June is in high school. There are a number of changes of residence through tenth, eleventh, and twelfth grade but there is only one school.

Her record ends on April 18, 1954, two months short of graduation. There are many notations and addenda about this. She was an above-average student, with an I.Q. of 116. She was not a discipline problem. All she would tell the guidance counselor was that her reasons for quitting were personal.

There is a tiny notation at the bottom of the card about an incident on 3/28/54. There was an altercation at her locker, it says, between June and her brother, Douglas, 10B, H.R. 102, Miss Stutz. The origin of the incident, it says, is unknown, but June's sweater was torn and she was given permission to go home to change clothes. Douglas was warned about fighting on school grounds.

The Vice Principal has returned to his little cubicle but his eyes never leave me. When I look up questioning, he walks over to where I am standing.

"Well," he says, "you can see. An average student, destined for an average life. Then boom. Who knows what life holds in store?"

"Was she beautiful then?" I ask.

"What?"

"Was she stunningly beautiful like, say, Marilyn Monroe?"

"Well, you know, a lot of our girls like to dye their hair and wear heavy makeup, if you know what I mean, but Marilyn Monroe . . ."

"I mean, did she stand out from the other girls?"

The Vice Principal clears his throat. "To tell you the truth," he answers, "I don't think I could tell you. I can't quite place her. The girls' guidance counselor would have dealt with her and, as I told you before, poor Miss Shannon died last spring."

"How about Douglas? Do you remember him?"

"Douglas?"

"Her brother. He was a student here."

"Of course. No, I'm afraid I don't remember him either. You see, the way we work it here, my special interests are the college-bound."

"Would it be possible to see his card?"

"What? Whose card?"

"Douglas Rogers. I'd like to see his Permanent Record Card."

"Hmmh." The Vice Principal looks at me with a steady gaze. "That would be highly irregular, you know. These cards are entrusted to us to be kept in strict confidentiality. The poor girl is dead but the young man is just beginning his life. I would think not."

"Just for a minute. There's something that interests me personally. Perhaps I didn't make it clear. You see I'm writing this as more of a personal reminiscence, not really a news story or anything like that, and I noticed that June went to Forbes School when I did. I want to check to see if Douglas was the little boy I always remember her picking up at the kindergarten. If he is, I helped them cross the street. They were so cute. I'm a stickler for facts even though this is just two girls from the same school in the big city and all that kind of feature fluff. I'm even thinking of writing a play about June and me as children."

"That sounds good. You're not really writing about the murder or anything like that. Why not?" He disappears into the little file room again and my heart is racing.

I quickly scan the entries on the Permanent Record Card of Douglas Andrew Rogers, who was out with scarlet fever most of the first grade and had to repeat it. The addresses and schools all correspond with June's but there is something different on the top portion of his card. Methodist is scratched out and First Church of New Christian Vision is written in with an asterisk next to it. I find a note at the bottom of the card: 10/22/53—Douglas is to be dismissed on Wednesdays at two for Religious Instruction and Service. Douglas was an average student and was graduated in June 1956.

I return the cards to the secretary and ask for the yearbooks. She points to a high shelf behind me and I take both 1954 and 1956. For some reason I'm not sure of, I open 1956 first.

DOUGLAS ANDREW ROGERS. "Doug." My God! My head feels like it's going to explode. That face! I could never forget it. Douglas Rogers is that kid who stood in front of the Art Cinema on Wednesdays and Saturdays railing against sin. "Why, he's no more than a child," Mom would say, "it oughtn't to be allowed." He's who June reminded me of. That's why she seemed familiar to me.

Images tumble in my brain. The time I dragged my sister, Karyn, to see that double feature of an English film and the Stars of the Russian Ballet. Karyn was mortified to be seen going into that movie house, but I finally convinced her that it was all right because the movies we were going to see weren't dirty.

Give your sins to Jesus. Awake! Repent. Spit on the devil! His face was inches from mine, the smeary paper flapping above his head. Karyn tugging at my coat. "Let's not, Ar,

let's go to the Penn instead." I, ignoring her pleas, marching
resolutely toward the box office.

"You must not buy a ticket," he is screeching into my
ears. "You will be punished if you give your money to these
agents of the devil."

Karyn had disappeared into the Fashion Hosiery store
doorway as I stood my ground, blurting out in almost inco-
herent fragments my carefully rehearsed question: "Don't
you find a difference," I shouted, "I mean, why are you here
when it's Noël Coward or Trevor Howard being noble and
patriotic? Don't you see any difference between them and
Hedy Lamarr writhing in ecstasy or Betty Grable when she
wakes up screaming?"

"Sin, sin," he squeaks in my face. "Sin. Communism and
adultery. It all comes from the devil to weaken man. This
house of the devil must close. Do not let them profit here
with your money so they can spread more sin on the people."

My hand is shaking as I close the yearbook. I turn to see
if the secretary is watching me but she is busy lining up
some pink cards on her desk. The Vice Principal has gone
for a smoke.

JUNE VICTORIA ROGERS. "Junie." No wonder the
Vice Principal doesn't remember her. I said Marilyn Monroe
thinking of June's recent evocation. I should have said Kim
Novak. The short, clipped, bleached hair in the duck's ass;
the plucked eyebrows; the seductive yet plaintive look in
the studied bedroom eyes. Other girls in the yearbook
tried to look like Kim Novak too, but only June made it.
June's Ambition: To be a model. Favorite Saying: "That's
for Darn Sure." Best Friend: Helene Saunders.

I flip to Helene Saunders. "Sandy." Ambition: To be Mrs.
R.M. Favorite Saying: "Good Things Come in Small Packages." Cheerleading Squad.

On a hunch I flip through the "M" boys. There are three

"R.M." possibilities. Robert Madulavich, Ronald Marin, and Richard Matthews. Madulavich was a Westinghouse Award Winner, Valedictorian, and active in the Latin Club, the Physics Club, and the Orchestra. He is also chinless with glasses. I rule him out. Both Marin and Matthews played Varsity football but Marin's ambition was to cut a hit record and play for the Pittsburgh Steelers while Matthews wanted to become an engineer.

"Excuse me," I ask the secretary, "do you have a phone book I could look at for a minute?"

She slides it across the counter to me muttering about the phone book at the pay phone in the hall. There is no listing for the First Church of New Christian Vision. Ronald Marin still lives in the neighborhood, a few blocks from the school, right on Federal Street. There are two Richard Matthews listed. I jot down all the numbers, return the phone book with thanks, and dash to the pay phone in the hall.

The woman's voice is small.

"Sandy?"

"Yes."

"Is this Sandy?"

"Yes, this is Sandy."

"Sandy, you don't know me, my name is Arlyn Crane and I was a friend of June Rogers' in New York and I'm here doing something on her and I know you were good friends and I wondered if I could talk to you."

"She told you about me? June did?"

"Yes," I lied.

"Well, okay."

"Shall I come over to see you, or do you want to meet somewhere?"

"I guess you'd better come over here. The baby's still nappin', so I can't leave yet. You know how to get here?"

"Yes," I answered, lying again and hanging up the phone. Another minute and she might change her mind, the baby might cry, who knows what could happen.

24

"Please don't bother," I say, but Sandy ignores me as she opens a long bakery box and removes a luscious-looking apple strudel. Even as I lust for the strudel I have the sick feeling that she left the baby alone to dash out to buy it.

"The bakery's just down the street," she says, as though to reassure me.

She's really very nice, this peppy little ex-cheerleader, Helene "Sandy" Saunders Marin, née Sandowski, with the Kennedy button on her blouse and the scrapbook of clippings about June.

"I guess it was kind of silly of me to do this," she says, "but it kind of kept me from thinking about it too much. For a couple of days I even went over to the Hilton and bought all the New York papers. My mother says June was always a tramp and got what she deserved and my husband says I should forget about her. He says I have to get rid of the scrapbook before Kimberly can read. What do you think?"

"You know," I say, lighting a cigarette, "I wasn't nearly as close to June as you were and I had the same obsession. Still have it."

Sandy nods her head appreciatively. She feels justified keeping the scrapbook. As she talks, I see her motives as somehow purer than mine; she wants to keep some memory of her friend alive. What do I want?

I want to see June's murderer arrested and punished. I really do. That's true. That's why I came to Pittsburgh. But I also want to be a heroine in all this. That I have to admit. I want to be the one who finds the murderer, I want to be covered in glory, to be rewarded, to be . . . But what's so terrible about that? Is it my fault the police have been unable to find the murderer? Can I help it if I'm the best person for the job? Why should I feel guilty about the glory I don't have yet?

"We were close friends only when we were seniors," Sandy is saying. "Something happened to June during the summer and when we came back for our last year she was, well, she was a knockout. Before that hardly anybody knew who she was. We became friends right away, almost in the first gym class of the semester. I remember it clear as if it was yesterday. She walked me to my locker, we had gym last period, and Ronnie, my boyfriend, he's my husband now"—she turns and points her pert nose toward a large framed wedding picture hanging on the wall of the small living room behind us—"Ronnie was waiting for me with Frankie De Vita. Frankie was the sharpest boy in the school, maybe the neighborhood, and he took one look at June and flipped his wig."

Sandy leans back now and closes her eyes. A sweet smile forms on her face. "What a time that was! We were seniors, big deals and all that. Boy, did we have fun! The four of us. Frankie didn't play football but he came to all the games with June. And afterward. Wow. June was always at my house. My mother says she was a tramp because she says she saw her coming out of the Fort Pitt Hotel one morning with a man who put her in a taxicab and paid the fare. I don't know nothin' about that. If that happened, it happened toward the end, right before she went up to New York."

Sandy jumps up to turn the gas on under the coffeepot on the stove behind us. She picks up a sponge and begins wiping tiny spots off the shiny white porcelain top of the stove.

"What did happen?" I ask carefully, afraid of breaking her reminiscent mood.

"Even Frankie came to me," she continues. "'What's wrong with June?' he asks me and I say, 'Whatya mean?' but I know what he means. First she starts missin' a lot of school, and I mean a lot, not like most of us a day here and a day there. Frankie never went to her place, they had this arrangement where she called his house, asking for him the way the bookkeeper in the shoe store where he worked did. At first June called him when she wasn't comin' to school and he would meet her when he could, but then she even stopped callin' Frankie and in a couple of weeks she was gone."

"How come Frankie never went to her home?"

Sandy looks at me with a clear and steady gaze. I realize that she is debating with herself whether to answer my question.

"June didn't tell you?"

"Tell me what?"

Sandy sits down and traces crumbs along the table top with her index finger. "June really had a lousy life," she begins. "Sure she looked like Kim Novak, and her boyfriend was the sharpest guy in the school, and the two of them together were like the king and queen when they came into a room, but that's all she had. She had nothin' else, believe me. I hope she found some kind of happiness after she left, though I wonder about that too."

Sandy has found a crumb of strudel on the table and is in the process of fingerpainting it into concentric circles.

"What was her life like?"

"Huh?"

"I mean, what was so terrible about it?"

"Well, I don't know, her mother was this religious fanatic, she practically lived at Kathryn Kuhlman's. That wasn't the worst of it, I guess, when you think about it. That wasn't so bad except that her mother was always at the lectures. You know who Kathryn Kuhlman is?"

I nodded my head. Everyone in Pittsburgh knew about Kathryn Kuhlman the evangelist and her miracle healing powers, so called.

"But Dottie Rogers wasn't the whole story," Sandy continues, "even though she was enough to drive you crazy. It was that brother of June's who made her life miserable."

"How'd he make her life miserable?"

"Oh, he was always pickin' on her and naggin' her and embarrassin' her in the street. He was younger but he acted like he was older. I always felt like he hounded her into it."

"Into it? Into what?"

Sandy looks at me without revealing her thoughts.

"You know, into whatever she got into. And what he said at Dottie's wake. I couldn't believe it. I was standin' right there. He blamed Dottie's death on June. Can you imagine? Everyone knew that the poor soul was eaten up with a cancer, but he made June feel terrible over it. He said it was the Lord's wrath and all that junk. June just broke down and cried and cried."

"It must have been terrible," I say, thinking of June being harangued at her mother's funeral.

"It was. It was the last time I saw June. At the wake. She came in from New York. Really looked terrific. So sharp. She said she had this good job as an elevator operator in a building on Park Avenue where all the operators were blondes. She said Hollywood producers were always looking the girls over and it was a good place to be spotted. She touched my stomach the night of the wake and then I had the miss."

Sandy stands up to get the heating coffee. "I don't think

there was any connection, I really don't. Ronnie and my mother said I should be careful who I let touch my stomach. But I had two more misses after that and I never let anyone get near me."

"I'm so sorry."

"Oh, that's okay. Kim's healthy as can be, thank God, and the doctor says I'm two months gone now."

"Congratulations. How do you feel?"

"Good, but I have to take it easy. I did with Kim, too. Even with the pills the doctor gives me I have to be careful. I was going to paint this kitchen for Christmas but it will just have to wait no matter how much it needs it."

I flick my eyes over the gleaming kitchen in wonder that anyone would find it needing a coat of paint. I ask Sandy about June's mother and brother.

"No one really knew them too close," Sandy tells me. "They moved a lot, mostly in these furnished rooms. For the last couple of years they had this small apartment across from the Planetarium. That's where he still lives, where he runs his church."

"Is that the First Church of Christian Vision?"

"Something like that. He's the pastor. Twenty-two years old and the pastor of a church. That's what they call it—a church. He started it almost as soon as he got out of the Army. He says he was discharged on account of his asthma. Who knows? It's a wonder they took him in. He's got the gift, they say."

"The gift?"

"You know, to preach God's word and all that."

"The newspaper said he worked for the post office."

"He does. That's where he gets his money. There aren't too many members to his church."

"How many?"

"Oh, I dunno. Maybe twenty or thirty. Maybe less. My mother says five or ten. Who knows? No one pays any attention to them except for my aunt, who lives around the corner and kind of sees them goin' in. She says she's seen as many as thirty at different times. My mother says it's the same ones."

"Who are they?"

"Mostly old ladies. A few young girls. Maybe one other man. All weirdos, if you ask me. My aunt says they left Kathryn Kuhlman because she lost the way, was becoming too big for her britches. Then Douglas started his own church from that one."

"Tell me about the time her brother fought with her in front of her locker."

Sandy is genuinely surprised at my question.

"Wow! She told you about that? I almost forgot all about it. I'm surprised she told you. She was so mortified. I didn't think she'd ever mention it to anyone. I don't think I would."

"Were you there?"

"Right next to her. We were all there, Ronnie and Frankie and June and me. It was the lunch period and we never ate in the cafeteria you know. We waited until they opened the doors and let us out for the last ten minutes and we ate at the Dog Shoppe. June was putting her books away and he just comes out of the blue and socks her."

"Just like that, without saying anything?"

"Oh, I guess he said somethin', but it was somethin' about the path of wickedness. Like that."

"The path of wickedness?"

"Yeah. I remember her tellin' me about it later. One of the last times I saw her, I guess. She told me he was always buggin' her about sin. That's when she told me all about her miserable life. I didn't know it was so bad until then. He was really like— You know, he used to stand downtown and . . ."

"Yes, I remember him. I recognized him in the yearbook."

"You saw the yearbook? Where?"

"At the school."

"At the school? What were you doing there?"

"Oh, I just stopped by. Then what happened, after he hit her?"

"I think she told him to get lost or somethin' like that and before anybody knew what happened he walloped her one in the mouth and reached out for her sweater. It looked to me like he was trying to hit her in the bust but she moved and his hand grabbed her at the neckline and she pulled back and the sweater ripped. What a sight! That pink sweater split down the middle and her bra showing and the seed pearls bouncing all over the floor."

It was a vivid image. I look at Sandy, waiting for more of the story, but she is silent.

"Then what?" I finally ask.

"I can't remember. I guess I screamed or made some loud noise. Frankie and Ronnie lit out after Doug but he disappeared down the hall. Then I remember June put her coat on over her torn sweater and I went with her to the guidance counselor's office and she got permission to go home and change. Come to think of it now, I don't remember her being around school much after that. Oh, I'm sure she came. I remember talking to her and all but it was never the same with us. Like I said, Frankie tried to get in touch with her but then he never mentioned her again. We were all busy gettin' ready to graduate."

"Is Frankie still in the neighborhood?"

"Poor Frankie. He got killed in Korea. An accident."

"What a shame."

"Yeah. It's like she had some kind of bad luck with her, isn't it? Makes you kinda wonder. My misses, her mother, Frankie, and now her."

"Do you know how I can reach Douglas?"

"*Him?* You want to talk to him?"

"Yes. Why not?"

"He scares me now. When I see him on the street I turn my head." She is reaching for a white leatherette address book. "I have it here, if it's the same telephone as when June lived there. The address is the same. What are you using all this for anyway, all that stuff you've been writin' down."

"Oh, just a little background story I'm putting together. I'll be sure and send you a copy. Thanks so much for all your help."

I extend my hand and we shake tentatively. Suddenly Sandy seems uneasy. She stares at my notebook as though she is seeing it for the first time.

25

I look around the living room for vestiges of June and her mother, but the room, the main parlor and meeting room of the Second Church of New Christian Vision, seems too stuffy and overbearing for June to have ever lived in it. Her lightness and beauty would dry up in this somber atmosphere. Heavy red-velvet drapery and lacy curtains obscure what must be a stunning view of the Planetarium across the street. At one time this place must have been grand indeed, but now an air of cramped seediness pervades.

I am seated at a round oak, claw-footed table that is too large for the truncated parlor. I can imagine the apartment next door with the other half of the parlor beyond that thick plaster wall. This side has the full triple bay windows and the marble mantelpiece. I wonder what the other side got.

Across from me sits the Reverend Douglas Andrew Rogers. He is slapping his big hand with the long, well-shaped fingers on the silk-embroidered tablecloth to punctuate his words. The blue stone of his class ring sparkles in the light of the chandelier overhead. I am playing, I realize, with one of the pale green fringes resting in my lap. I quickly move my hands back to the table. I have left my notebook in my purse for the duration of the short interview Doug has reluctantly granted me.

At a respectable distance three women sit quietly, worn Bibles open on their laps. They have their eyes downcast and appear to be reading, but I can tell they are straining to hear every word between their young pastor and me. The drapes and curtains, I am sure, are their addition to the parlor. I have interrupted a study group. It is highly irregular, but what could they do? I appeared flashing my Guild card and Douglas was forced to let me in, saying he could give me only fifteen minutes.

He didn't want to, of course, but my sweet smile and little dip to the ladies must have disarmed him. "Would you like a cup of tea, child?" one had asked, thinking, I'm sure, that I had come to be saved. At first Douglas waved her back, but as I stepped inside the room he quickly changed his tone.

"Yes, certainly I'll talk to you, but no more than fifteen minutes, you understand. We are in the middle of the Lord's work and cannot be interrupted. And, this is just between us. It is not for you to use in your newspaper. I have declined calls from the press for interviews and I am only talking to you out of common courtesy."

He must have the gift, I think, as we sit down where he indicates. Forget about his young age. He's so sure of himself and in such total command of the situation.

My time is almost up and I realize that I have heard little more from him than a droningly endless monologue about how Angel June is now sleeping peacefully in heaven with their dear mother in the arms of Jesus. "Whatever my sister did," he is saying, "is between her and her Maker now and I know He has forgiven her. Indeed, He wanted her to rest with Him," Douglas tells me.

I get this image of luscious June snuggling up to rest with her Maker but stifle the thought. My attention is fixed completely on Douglas as he assures me that God is not vengeful and did not take June to punish her for her wicked ways but to give her the peace she was never able to find on earth.

His lips quiver as he talks and the pale gold hairs above them are damp with droplets of perspiration. His blond hair is slicked back along the sides and lifted into a slight pompadour. His eyes are striking: a paler blue than June's with short, thick lashes that are almost colorless. A bloodless version of his sister.

"Now you can tell me something," he says, drawing himself up and pushing his chair away from the table. I know that once I answer his question he will stand up and I must leave. "I've been wondering," he says, looking me directly in the eyes, "how the police investigation is going in New York. Have you heard anything interesting?"

Is he pulling my leg? "Don't they keep in touch?" I ask.

"Why should they?"

"Well, you are her next of kin."

"They have their duties and responsibilities. As I have mine. When they have something concrete to tell me I'm sure I'll hear. I was just wondering if you heard anything, you know, around the Newspaper Guild."

I check my impulse to laugh. What can I say? It worked. He was, as we say, not unimpressed with the card.

"You know," I say, "the prime suspect was tracked down the other day and he turned out to have an ironclad alibi."

"No, I hadn't heard," Douglas Rogers answers, standing now.

"You know, the delivery boy who lived in her building?"

"Oh yes, him. I never thought it could be *him*."

I am not sure what he means by this. Is he telling me God would never have chosen a delivery boy from Daitch Shopwell, an out-of-work actor, to bring June to nestle with him? But I see I am not going to have a chance to pursue the matter. The Reverend Rogers has stood up and the interview is over.

"I'd like to use your bathroom if I may."

He seems exasperated but waves me in the right direction. "Next to the kitchen," he says, adding, "Please try to hurry. We do have our work to do here."

I hear a bustle behind me as the ladies move to the oak table. I try to see as much of the rest of the apartment as I can but it is not easy. The kitchen is small and dim. The musty smell of the parlor is compounded by the heavy smell of recooked grease. Across from the kitchen a flowered curtain conceals an alcove where a black raincoat and two light suits neatly hang alongside a few white shirts and a laundry bag. I let the curtain drop and skim my eyes over the shelf above. A suitcase and an umbrella.

The bathroom is even smaller than the kitchen and the bulb above the sink can't be more than twenty-five watts. I flush the toilet and run the water immediately. I have to tug to open the wooden medicine cabinet. The usual. Shaving cream, razor, Mennen's after-shave, Band-Aids, and some old dried tubes of ointment and a couple of bottles of prescription drugs. I lean close to read the labels: "*Walgreen's Drugstore, Greyhound Bus Terminal, New York, N.Y. #734583261. Mr. Douglas A. Rogers. One tablet as needed. Sept. 29, 1960.*" *September twenty-ninth, nineteen sixty!* That's the date! The date June was murdered. Or the night she was found, in any case. That Thursday night.

I shut the cabinet quickly and lean against the sink. What should I do? I've been in here too long already. I flushed too soon. I flush again. They'll think I'm sick. I copy the number of the prescription down. That's all I can do. Maybe that's enough.

What was he doing in New York on that day? He didn't identify the body until two days later. Her brother from Pittsburgh, the papers said, they didn't say he was visiting her or in New York at the time.

Douglas stops reading when I enter the parlor. "Everything all right?" he asks.

"Yes, thank you," I say, dipping slightly to the ladies. "I'm

·

all right now." I tiptoe to the door. "I'll let myself out." We all smile with relief.

On the street I begin running. I must get back to New York. I can't believe my luck. I am positive Douglas killed June. I must tell someone right away. Who? Bill? Bob Mann? Find out who the detectives are. How to get in touch with them. Bob would know. But first I must find a bathroom, before I explode.

26

"Arlyn, stop with the telephone. Come. Sit down and eat. Your dinner's getting cold. Whatever it is, it can wait." For Mom nothing is urgent except having the dinner she's cooked eaten before it gets cold.

"Who's she calling that it's so important she has to jump up in the middle of a meal?" asks Karyn.

"Leave her alone, at least she's here. She was talking about going back to New York this afternoon but we talked her out of it." For Dad negotiation and compromise are all.

The officer comes back on the line. "Sorry, Miss, but I still can't locate either one of them at this time. Your best bet is to call tomorrow if you don't want to leave your name and wait until someone from the detective bureau gets back to you."

"But I did that this afternoon," I remind him, "and the detective who called me said I had to talk to Detectives Kelly or Ambrose anyway."

"That's because you didn't want to make a formal statement."

"But how could I? I only want to talk to them, to find out if they know a certain thing, to tell them—"

"Listen, lady, I hate to cut you off but we are kind of busy here now, so if you don't mind . . ."

"Thank you," I murmur and he clicks off.

I'm sure I'm right in feeling that I shouldn't tell just anyone about Douglas Rogers and the prescription. It has to be the detectives who are working on the case. I don't feel comfortable babbling an accusation of Douglas to just anyone. And anyway, isn't that slander? I'd better be careful and just wait.

When I called Bill this afternoon he was sure my information would hold until Monday. "I'm not saying it isn't interesting, Arlyn, but it doesn't sound like anything that can't wait. From what you tell me, that Rogers isn't going anywhere." He's probably right. And I'm sure he was right about my not calling anyone at The Paper.

I return to the dining room and take my place at the table in front of a plate of cold pot roast and potatoes and string beans. All conversation has ceased and all eyes are on me.

"I think I'll get some hot food," I say, starting to rise with my plate in my hand. My mother is up and around the table in an instant, taking the plate from my hand and disappearing into the kitchen. "We didn't know you'd be on the phone so long when we served you," she says, apologizing for my cold food.

This is too much for Karyn.

"Daddy said you were thinking of going back before we got here," she says icily, "that you were going to leave without even seeing the baby."

"But you don't understand, Kar, this is not really a visit. If I had gone right back this afternoon I would have come in again on Thanksgiving."

Mom returns with a new plate of food for me. She never sets food on the table family-style but serves from the stove so it's always hot.

Karyn does not give up. "You mean to say now you're not coming in again on Thanksgiving?"

"It does seem silly to come in again so soon, doesn't it?"

"This meat is delicious. Girls, your mother worked all afternoon cooking and the family is together. Let's enjoy it. No arguments. Right, Buster boy?" Dad leans over and tickles fourteen-month-old Keith, who at this moment is busy picking up string beans from his high-chair tray and sucking them into his mouth like a vacuum. Everyone in the family thinks I'm jealous of Karyn, my little sister, and her husband and her baby. That's not true. I like Keith well enough for a nephew, but he's too round and jolly and easygoing like his father, Bernie, for me to be envious. When I have my child I know he will have more personality than dumpling Keith.

Keith responds to Dad's comment by halting the movement of a bean from the tray to his mouth and tossing it away. He then smashes his fist into his potatoes. Ugh. I can't understand how Karyn lets him do things like that. My child wouldn't, I know. Now Mom is wiping his face. "Little piggy," she is saying, "Grandma's little piggy." He grins and sticks his finger in her eye. "Lil' pizzy," he repeats and everyone howls and applauds. Another new word. Our little genius.

Karyn is flushed with happiness at the attention that her son has taken from me. It has been established. She is the one with the husband and the child. But as far as I'm concerned it's all in her head, or hers and Mom's together, for I fully expect to have a husband and child someday. I haven't given up yet even though they may have for me. And when I do he won't smash his fist into the potatoes, I can assure you.

It is Bernie who brings the conversation back to me. "Arlyn, will you please tell me what's going on?" he asks. "I heard you blew in last night and have been out all day. Something about that North Side girl's murder."

Though Mom and Dad have heard the story of my day

and they told Karyn about it while I was showering, all is quiet around the table as I bring Bernie up-to-date.

"I still don't understand," he says. "What do you expect to do here? You're not going to get mixed up in this thing personally?"

A perfect opening for Mom. "That's how I feel. This is no business for her, it's a messy business and she's liable to get hurt. You agree with me don't you, Bernie?"

Bernie shrugs, but Mom plunges on.

"I can't see what she's going to find here, can you? All that poor girl's troubles started when she left Pittsburgh. Of course she didn't have such an easy life but her mother was a good woman. I used to say hello to her."

Mom stands up to take Bernie's plate and as she walks to the kitchen to get him his seconds she keeps talking.

"That girl, I can't even think about it, the men she went with. It always ends up bad, that kind of thing. Why? What for? What did she have to do it for? She went to high school, she got a good education, she could have got a good job in town without any trouble, I'll bet. I heard the secretaries at U. S. Steel do very well."

Mom hands Bernie his plate, sits down, and leans toward me. I know what's coming.

"And you, Miss Busybody, what business is it of yours? What's she to you? So you're both from the same city and she lived across the street from you for a short time, and you bumped into her a couple of times in New York. So what? That's all in the past now. Forget it. Keep your nose out of other people's business."

"Arlyn always was nebby," Dad says. "Remember the time she nearly set the house on fire trying to steam open those envelopes." Everyone laughs at the memory. I am amused at my father's word for my inquisitive nature. It has practically dropped from my vocabulary since I left Pittsburgh, but every once in a while it creeps back. I try to say nosy instead these days.

"I don't even remember that girl," Karyn says. "I looked

at those pictures in the newspapers and I still couldn't remember her."

"Neither did I," I say. "That's what was so weird. I knew there was something about her that was familiar but I just couldn't place her. Then it hit me . . ." I stop. They are all looking at me, waiting for me to tell them what hit me, how when I saw Douglas' picture in the yearbook I realized that when I met June on Fire Island and in Newport it was her brother whom I was reminded of, that otherworldly fanatic teenager who stood in front of the Art Cinema denouncing the devil. But I stop myself. When I told them all about my day I left out the part about Douglas.

"What hit you?" Mom is saying. "Look at her, look at the circles under her eyes. She's not sleeping, she tells me."

"You're losing sleep over this?" Bernie asks with genuine interest. There can't be too many things that would keep Bernie up past his ten-thirty bedtime. Karyn once told me you could set a clock by his habits.

"Yes," I tell him, "I really have. I've really gotten involved in this thing."

"It must have been awful," Karyn says, "I could hardly read about it in the papers."

"That's what I say to myself when I wake up at night. 'It must have been awful.' Then I see the whole thing reenacted in my mind, pieced together from what I read in the papers and heard around the office. I see the tiny apartment, I was there, you know, it's what they call a cut-up railroad flat, and I see the nick in the door. You know about that?"

They all nod their heads. They have read about that in the papers, the police theory that the nick was caused by the victim throwing a pepper shaker across the kitchen at the murderer. "I remember the pepper shaker on the stove," I tell them, "and I see that open bottle of ammonia in the kitchen sink." They are blank about the ammonia. I explain. "The police deduce that whoever did it wiped away all fingerprints. They never recovered the cloth that was used. I guess that wasn't in the papers."

Bernie looks puzzled and Karyn reminds him that I had visited June Rogers in her apartment. I wrote about that in a long letter home after the murder. While they are reminding him of my relationship with June I decide not to tell them what else I see when I wake at night. Why burden them with the image of the trail of blood leading from the air-shaft window where the police believe she cowered in terror—Oh God!—to the bed where she was found spread out, dried rivulets of blood crisscrossing her lovely body, her silken hair matted to her splintered skull, her legs slightly parted to expose the strips of shiny black electrician's tape. HIM. DOUGLAS. HER BROTHER! What could she have thought of when she saw him approach with the ice pick raised? Her little brother. Poor June. It must have been awful.

"Oh, this is all too morbid to be talking about," I tell my family. "I'm getting a headache from it. Can we talk about something else?"

Everyone seems relieved, especially Bernie.

"What time do you want me at headquarters tomorrow, Lou?" Bernie asks Dad.

"Early as possible," Dad answers, looking at his watch. "And we'd better get down there now. I told the boys we would stop by after dinner. I want to go over the schedule of watchers once more. And you'd better find out where you're scheduled on Tuesday." He stands and buttons his vest. He looks at me. "You wouldn't want to come down and work a few phones, would you, Arlyn? This Kennedy has brought a lot of young people out. Karyn was in the other night."

One thing about Dad, he never gives up. But why hurt his feelings, why tell him what I think about what he does, how I believe that people shouldn't have to promise to vote for and work to get a politician elected just to get what is their right, whether it's a fair shake in the police lineup, a broken sidewalk fixed, a scholarship to college, or a government job. Why start? He will only cough and get upset as he defends the system that in his words "makes this country the greatest in the world" and "keeps everybody honest." My college texts have much the same thing to say about patronage, but maybe the professors who wrote those books never overheard the kind of telephone conversations I grew up overhearing, tales of fixed parking tickets, reduced sentences, plush appointments to Orphan's Court or the Sheriff's office or the Coroner's staff.

"No, Daddy," I answer, "not tonight."

"Maybe tomorrow," he says, brightening, "it's the most important time, the Saturday before election. We could use you."

"I don't think so. In fact," I say, making my plans as I say them, "I'm returning to New York tomorrow morning."

"Tomorrow morning. But it's Saturday," Mom wails. "What's the use of rushing back on Saturday? I thought at least you'd stay until Sunday."

"It's settled, Mom, let's not discuss it." I start for the telephone. I'll get that nine o'clock plane and be in the office by eleven. I'm sure I can figure out what to do from there.

27

The receptionist in the lobby gives me a sleepy nod. Since I began doing sermons, he has become accustomed to my coming in on weekends. The elevator operators are off today so I must take the automatic elevator. My heart is pounding.

The city room is almost empty. Pools of light play checkers with pockets of semidarkness. On weekends the reporters and editors have to light their own way without benefit of the services of lobster-shift porters. It is only a few minutes to eleven and the big push of the early Saturday deadline, constantly moved up to accommodate the enormous logistics of getting that massive Sunday paper out to the suburbs and beyond, is still hours away. The dominant sound around the office now is the continuous clicking of wire machines and the lone peck of a typewriter. A quick glance toward his clean, closed desk tells me that Bob Mann isn't in. That's good. Since he is assigned to June's murder investigation he would be the logical person for me to tell about June's brother. I am relieved that I can take my information to someone else.

No one of importance is in the city room yet. A few clerks and news assistants are hovering around the City Desk. Telling one of them about June's brother would be foolish, I know. "Yeah, sure, Arlyn, I'll get right on it. Sounds like a real Pulitzer for sure." Or worse, the earnest ones, the Future Editors of America types. "Thanks very much, Arlyn, good of you to think of us and if we need any further information we'll let you know."

Either way I'm nowhere. Better to wait until I find the right person. I wish Moe Greenside worked weekends. I can see that Lennie Morse is somewhere around. His desk is open, his typewriter pulled up from its well. A sheet of paper is rolled into his typewriter and a soggy coffee container is sitting next to it. He might have an idea. I go in search of him and find him at a long table in the morgue, poring over a fat envelope of fragile, carefully folded, yellowing clippings.

"Hi," I say, sitting down across from him. "Can I talk to you for a minute?" I lean over the table close to him.

"Sure." His look is expectant. What does he think I want?

"Have you heard anything about that June Rogers case?"

"Chet Price is now on it officially," he says.

"Price?"

"Why are you so surprised? He's been working on it from the beginning unofficially. Now he's on it officially. He's doing a story for tomorrow's paper. A warning."

"I don't understand."

Morse's smile is crooked. "He's the gumshoe, you know, the spy? Chet Price is more than just an old fart sitting out there diddly pooing with the advanced obits. That's only one part of his job. The other part is to keep tabs on the, quote, friends and enemies of management, end quote. That's the main part. In fact, there's talk of putting someone good on advanced obits."

"Friends and enemies? I don't get it."

"Actually, he mainly snoops on the staff, but sometimes he is called upon to dig up dirt on city officials and the police."

"But why? Why would he snoop on another reporter? And what kind of things does he report?"

"Oh, things like a reporter or editor's affiliations, political leanings, secret romances, that sort of thing."

"Secret romances? Are you kidding?"

Lennie's eyes narrow and I can't read his expression. Is he playing with me, teasing me, warning me, or just answering my question? "Well, for one thing," he says, "it's a form of control, it keeps us from getting too, too self-righteous. It keeps the Guild from really getting strong, some say. How can we organize within or get on our high horses and force The Paper to take a crusading stance, blow the whistle on some corruption outside, threaten to expose The Paper's hypocrisy if our own underwear is dirty? Almost everyone has something to hide from someone."

"I understand," I say, even though I don't really. "But why has Price been put on the June Rogers story?"

Lennie rolls his eyes. "To gather ammunition in case it gets hot for you-know-who."

Now I understand. "I heard it was hot for him already. How can Price help him?"

"Price's story tomorrow probably won't make any sense to you, but certain officials and Police Commissioners will read it and quake in their boots. They might restrain some eager detective a bit longer from questioning some material witness, including, of course, Teddy Lowe. They might have to release the Raped and Taped story to stall for time. One more day, and another, and another. Who knows? It might all blow over, something might happen and Lowe will be off the hook. Not even embarrassed with the messy business of being questioned. Sometimes it's important to buy time."

"You know," I say slowly, "the funny thing about all this is that I'm sure Lowe had nothing to do with the murder. Why would he be so afraid of being questioned?"

"He can't afford to be dragged through the tabloids in this mess. It's one thing to play around with someone like June Rogers, it's quite another for a man to be linked with her in the public prints. Even though he's separated, he does have a wife and children. Think of them, her connections, the children's school. And what makes you so sure he has nothing to do with the murder?" Morse adds, but signals me immediately not to talk. Chet Price has just come into the morgue and is walking importantly to the counter behind us. He has no time to kibbitz with me today, I can see. No "Did I ever tell you about Monty" stories now. Now he is all business and to emphasize this point he is drumming his fingers impatiently on the counter while the morgue clerk rushes off to the forest of file drawers to find the envelopes of clippings that Price has requested.

I have picked up one of the clippings Lennie has spread out in front of him. What on earth is Lennie doing with Ed Hart's By-Lines Folder? The clerk hands Price several bulging envelopes and he returns to the city room nodding brusquely to us as he passes.

"Why are you going through Ed Hart's clips?" I ask. "He didn't die, did he?"

"Au contraire," Lennie answers, wiggling his eyebrows. "He has just begun to live, as they say. I guess you haven't heard. Hart and Mimi Simon went off together. Into the sunset." He grins as he walks two of his fingers across the table toward me.

I am shocked. Although I haven't seen Hart since that weekend in July, Mimi is often at The Paper waiting for Peter to finish and we have chatted frequently in the Ladies Lounge. Just last week she was showing me a travel folder for Puerto Rico, where, she said, they were going for Christmas.

"Ed Hart and Mimi Simon? I find it hard to believe."

"So did everyone else," Morse says, "including Peter. Apparently things were strained between Peter and Mimi for a long time but this was a complete surprise to him."

"What could have been the trouble between them? They seemed very well suited to each other."

"Oh, in a lot of ways they were," Morse says. "They got along together, had the same sense of humor and all that. But evidently they weren't really making it."

"She just left like that?" I wonder how it is done. How does a couple formally end a marriage?

"Yep," Morse answers. "Just like that. It was only the other day. Peter was very broken up about it. He managed to get an out-of-town assignment. It's a terrible blow, losing your wife to a loser like Ed Hart."

"Loser? Why do you say loser? Ed seems very nice, he—"

"Oh, come on. A broken-down drunk ending his days as a p.r. flack. The deal is that Mimi'll save him, resurrect the artiste in him. They're moving to the country, away from the rat race, y'know, there to produce great art. Mimi got an assignment to ghost a diet book and that should hold them for a while until he connects with the best-selling novel that is in him fighting to come out."

Lennie's harshness surprises me. "Maybe he will," I say in Hart's defense, though I am not sure why I'm defending Hart. "Maybe he just needs an understanding woman to draw his best work out of him."

Lennie Morse snorts. "Judging from these clips of his he needs more than the love of a good woman. That's why I'm here. I was curious to see just what he did do."

"What about Ed's girlfriend?" I ask. "I met him with a girl on July Fourth weekend and as I understood it they were a steady item. Janet something. Do you know who I mean?"

"Janet . . . do you mean Janet Dugan?" Lennie Morse leans back and chuckles. "She made out all right. Don't worry about her. She's sailing in the Bahamas right now with a dying art director."

"Dying?"

"Well, perhaps that's a little dramatic. The story is that he reached his fifty-fifth birthday, heading his own agency, all the money he could ever want, and he had his first heart attack. He decided to live a little before he died and what better companion for his adventure than Janet Dugan. But enough of this chitchat. Tell me, why are you so sure that Lowe is innocent?"

I take a deep breath and look Lennie Morse right in the eye.

"I'm almost sure I know who did it."

"Who's that?"

"Her brother."

"Her brother. Arlyn, for crissake, don't you think the police would have checked out her brother? What makes you think it was her brother?"

"I talked to him this weekend, in Pittsburgh. I was there. He's the leader of this nutty little church that meets in his living room with a bunch of old ladies and he's only twenty-two and he's got the gift and when he was a teen-ager he used to stand in downtown Pittsburgh railing against sin and now he runs on about his angel sister and . . ."

As I talk I can see that Lennie Morse is containing his laughter. Finally, when he breaks in, he is composed. "Arlyn, Arlyn, take it easy. What are you running on about? So the kid's religious, maybe a nut, that doesn't make him a murderer."

"But he was in New York that weekend. I saw the—"

"And besides, I'm sure the detectives working on the case know all about him."

"The papers said only that he works for the Post Office."

"That may be all that was in the papers, but I'm sure the detectives know more. They always know more. You should know that. I know you like to feel like Lois Lane, but believe me, Arlyn, as a friend, don't get yourself in deeper than you can handle. This isn't a comic strip, it's real life. The last thing you want to do is look silly accusing some poor jerk of killing his sister when he's innocent. You really can't be too careful. What were you doing in Pittsburgh?"

"That's where I'm from. I was visiting my parents."

"And somebody in the family knows this guy, fixed it up?"

"Something like that. You don't think I should tell anyone, Bob Mann or Price or the City Desk?"

Lennie Morse slouches back in his chair and sticks his pencil behind his ear. If he were wearing an eyeshade he would be adjusting it, pulling on it. "What can I say, Arlyn? You have to do what you want. Just don't get carried away with this."

28

Ernestine Herbert is sitting in a leather lounge chair sewing a button on her turquoise coat. A cigarette is burning in the ashtray beside her.

"Hello, Arlyn," she says, without dropping a stitch, "what are you doing in today? A sermon?"

"No. I'm kind of easing off them, only if I'm really needed. I'm trying to do other things now."

"Good idea. And you do them so well."

"Ernestine?"

"Yes?"

"Ernestine, I need your advice. You know that call girl who was murdered in Yorkville?"

"Yes, what about her?" Ernestine looks at me coolly, squinting slightly.

"Well, I met her, you know."

"You did?"

"Yes. Several times. And she's from Pittsburgh, where I'm from, and I just came back from a quick visit there, ostensibly to visit my family but really because I'm so obsessed with the murder. Oh, Ernestine, I know it sounds crazy, but I think I found the murderer."

I am sitting on the edge of the couch across from her and I can feel my face burning and my windpipe closing. Ernestine has stopped sewing and is looking hard at me as I recount it all: June at the Simons' with Teddy Lowe, meeting her at Newport and our lunch together, the visit in her apartment, the trip home this past weekend, visiting the school, and the record cards and yearbooks, finding and talking to Sandy and Douglas. Her intelligent attention has helped me tell the story smoothly and, I think, coherently. When I am finished she takes a long drag on her cigarette and speaks.

"You've checked the clips and know everything that's been written about the case?"

"I have a complete file at home. I saved every story from every paper. I even have clippings from the Pittsburgh papers."

"Her brother was never a suspect?"

"No. Officially, at least. He arrived to claim the body. That's all."

"You have no hard evidence, Arlyn."

"The prescription. How about the prescription, dated the same day she was killed, and filled in New York, what about that?"

"But he did come to claim the body. He was in New York."

"But not until two days later. Didn't I make that clear? The prescription in his medicine cabinet was filled the day she was found dead."

"Humn," Ernestine says, shutting her eyes tightly. "It isn't impossible, of course." She lights another cigarette. "Let's go back and take it apart, piece by piece. Now, you say that on the Sunday of July Fourth weekend you first saw this June on Peter Simon's deck and she was accompanied by someone we both know." She winks as she says the last phrase and I catch on. We are not going to be mentioning the name of you-know-who.

Methodically and with great care we examine every piece of information I have about June. I repeat all I can from the lunch in Newport and fill Ernestine in on details of the crime and its follow-up that she wasn't aware of or had forgotten. And I carefully reconstruct, as best I can, all my conversations in Pittsburgh with the Vice Principal, Sandy and Douglas Rogers. Then I explain about going to the bathroom and opening the medicine cabinet. Ernestine doesn't move a muscle while I am talking about this, so I have no way of knowing whether she approves or disapproves of what I did. I know a lot of people would disapprove. How many would approve?

After we have finished, Ernestine goes over all the details again. I am thrilled at her response. Her persistent questioning has forced me to sharpen the focus of my story and she is ecstatic that I copied down the prescription number. Lennie Morse had cut me off so fast I wasn't even able to tell him about the prescription.

"That prescription number, Arlyn. That ought to do it. What you should do now is go to your desk and write as full and complete a memo as you can, leaving out nothing. You never know what incident or fact you may think is insignificant that the police will find very valuable. Write it for the City Desk but don't just drop it there. Moe Greenside is coming in today to coordinate the local election coverage. Make sure you give the memo directly to him. Tell him I suggested it, that I thought what you told me was very, very interesting. Make sure you keep a copy for yourself, and it wouldn't hurt for you to send one to the legmen at the police shack. Just mark it F.Y.I. It might help to insure you get credit if anything does come of all this and it will definitely make you a friend. These guys feel so forgotten out there it's wise to include them in when you're working on a police story. They'll break their neck to help you when you need it."

My heart is racing. I am standing now, looking down at Ernestine. She is on the edge of her chair, ready to fly to her desk; just a few more stitches through the button and a firm knot and she breaks the thread deftly.

"Thanks so much, Ernestine, you've really been such a help. I know you have to get going today and I held you up, but I don't know how I would have—"

"Nonsense," she breaks in. "I did nothing. You did it all. If you're right and this can forestall or quash the Johns List investigation scheduled to begin tomorrow, I'm told, a lot of people around here will be very, very grateful to you."

29

My hand is shaking as I put the receiver back into its cradle. "Can you stop by and see Mr. Purledge at two-thirty?" Ginny had asked, no comment in her voice. The perfect confidential secretary, as always. If I had pressed her, could I have trapped her into revealing some little clue? Just a hint to know what he wants to see me about? A promotion? To the city staff? Not impossible, of course, but very improbable. No doubt it's just some routine business, something to do with the automatic Guild pay increase that I must be due for about now.

How can I survive until two-thirty, three more hours, on this day of days! Getting promoted would be the only way to top the morning. Only getting married could be more exciting.

I light another cigarette and savor again the sweet sensations of the past few hours. The first inkling of what this day would hold came when I walked into the city room and Greenside rushed up after me calling, "Nice going, Arlyn, that was a really nice job."

I turned and looked at him, not knowing what he was talking about. After the hectic pace of the trip to Pittsburgh and spending most of Saturday writing and then thinking about the memo, yesterday I was pretty wrung out. I had spent most of the day in bed, and I was still not fully with it when Greenside called out to me. He must have been taken aback by my blank look.

"You heard what happened? Somebody telephoned?"

"Telephoned?"

"Christ, I can't believe it. No one called you? The two detectives flew to Pittsburgh Saturday night. Almost as soon as they read your memo."

I am stunned. They actually responded. And so fast.

Greenside continued, "When I read it I thought there might be something to it so I sent it out to the shack. The guys there passed it on."

"But there's nothing in the papers about it, is there?" I had managed to skim The Paper on the subway. I suppose I had held out some dim hope that something would come of my memo.

"Oh, not yet, Arlyn. Tomorrow. It's not that urgent a story. Now that the murderer is known. It was when the murderer was unknown that our readers were eager for news of the case." Did he wink, or did I imagine it?

"And they flew right out?"

"Almost immediately, as soon as they checked the prescription number. A brilliant move, Arlyn, getting that number. It's all the tangible evidence there is, really. The poor schmuck got off the bus from Pittsburgh that morning thinking he was having an asthma attack. He carried an emergency prescription and had it filled right there in the drugstore by the bus station. In addition to helping catch him, it makes the whole thing look premeditated, though he denies that."

"And they're sure he did it?"

"Absolutely. He's a pretty cool character, from what I hear, a tough nut to crack, but they did it. Finally got him to break down and confess. Then he recanted and then he confessed again. It's been like that. Onagain, offagain, onagain, Finnegan. But they brought him back. They're holding a press conference this morning."

"This morning?"

"That's right. Eleven o'clock. Mann's covering."

"Good show, Arlyn." I looked behind me to see Harvey Kassell.

"Hey, Arlyn, congratulations." It was Sid Schwartz. And next to him Damon Crewes was beaming and talking very animatedly to Schwartz. Others soon joined the crowd, smiling and congratulating me. And that's the way it's been ever since. Every few minutes a new crowd surrounds me, offering me the symbolic laurel wreath for my victory. It is my day. I won the race, came in ahead of the pack, I am the Champion, the city room Star. Today. Tomorrow will belong to someone else. But today is mine. And I love it. Even more than I thought I would. It beats everything. Really.

It's taken forever to open the mail. Everyone in the Cultural News Department has had something to say, hanging over my desk, beaming and bestowing on me their best wishes. Ashley seemed especially proud. "Told you I have the best girl on the floor," he said to Lowell.

I called Bill as soon as I could, but the switchboard operator wouldn't put me through. "He's not taking calls this morning," is all she would say. I was incensed. Doesn't she recognize my voice. *Hey, don't you know me? I'm the one who calls every morning.* Please, I kept telling her, please try. Tell him it's Miss Crane from The Paper. But the dumb bitch only responded in her most robotlike voice: "Sorreee, but Mr. Hallam is not taking calls this morning."

I just reached him on his desk phone a few minutes ago and he did seem genuinely delighted at my good fortune today. "That's terrific, sweetie," he said. "I wish I could see you for a drink this afternoon, but with the election tomorrow you know how tied up I am. We will celebrate on Wednesday, though. You can be sure of that."

The call left me numb. What is going on? Not seeing me tonight. Of all nights. And it's Monday night. Monday has become almost a ritual night for us. His decompression chamber, he calls it; the time when he relaxes with me after the tensions of the weekend at home. Is it only because of the election that he isn't seeing me tonight? And tomorrow? What about tomorrow. He knows I'm working the election crew. Won't we even be able to have a drink together?

Even before the phone finishes its first ring I know it's Bill. What was I imagining? Of course we'll have a drink together. That he can always squeeze in no matter how tied up he is with the big guns up from the Washington Bureau for the election coverage.

"Arlyn." It is Isabelle. I can hardly contain my disappointment as I mutter a hello. "Arlyn, are you there?"

"Yes, Isabelle. What is it? I'm kind of busy."

"Arlyn, I just heard. Looks like they're putting you in for some kind of Publisher's Prize, some special category, something new to encourage the ranks."

A Publisher's Prize! Me! A special category. I'm feeling faint and I don't even notice Ernestine Herbert poking her head into the Cultural News Department from the corridor that leads to the city room.

"Got to dash now, Arlyn," Ernestine calls, "but I just had to say how pleased I am that it all worked out." She makes the okay sign. A blessing from Ernestine Herbert. "We'll talk soon," she calls as she walks away.

"Getting pretty chummy with the Iron Maiden, aren't you, Arlyn?" It is Tony Weather standing behind my desk. "Yeah, Tony," I say, "we're best friends." I want to get him off my back so I can rerun what's just happened. First Isabelle's call. Publisher's Prize, a special category. That must be what Purledge wants. Not a promotion after all. I am disappointed, but nothing can really dampen my spirits today. After a Publisher's Prize can a promotion be far behind?

At first I hear only the buzz. Then I look up. A florist's delivery boy is carrying a huge vase of one dozen long-stemmed American Beauty roses and, following Jean Blake's outstretched finger, he is heading right toward my desk. Half the Cultural News Department is in his wake.

"Secret admirer, huh, Arlyn?"

"Holding back on us, eh, Arlyn?"

I sit in stunned silence as they kibbitz around me. There is no card. It has to be Bill. His way of saying how proud he is of me. And how unhappy he is that he can't be with me tonight because of the pressure of planning for the election coverage. But why anonymous? That doesn't make sense. He could easily have used his code name for our messages and notes to each other: Mr. Mash, from all our jokes about the distillery.

"Someone is very appreciative of your memo, Arlyn."

I look up to find Damon Crewes smiling at me. What does he know? Has he heard something or is he only surmising? A hunch? The most appreciative person would be Teddy Lowe. Would he send roses? Hardly. That would only call attention to his role in the whole mess. The detectives? I had done their job, figured out the murderer. Now they would get citations. But why would they remind the world of my part in their success? The reporters at the shack? No, not them. Greenside? He certainly looks good for not spiking my memo. But roses? Ernestine? She doesn't get roses when she does her job. Don't reporters help each other and the police and editors and owners all the time? Why the fuss?

"Where ya taking the roses, Arlyn?" Gil Gilchrist follows me as I move the vase over to the sill of the nailed-shut, painted-over window.

"I'm allergic to roses. And anyway there's no room on my desk for a vase of roses."

Purledge is beaming at me through his rimless glasses. I sit down and he leans forward fingering the manila folder in front of him.

"Everyone is pleased with what you did, Arlyn," he begins. "You showed real initiative and real promise and you know how we reward that around here. I only have a few minutes now because I have to see the M.E. as soon as he's free but I wanted you to know that I'm recommending that you be promoted to a Group Ten position."

Group Ten. The highest group. The Reporter's Group. Purledge pulls open the top left-hand drawer of his desk and takes out a worn copy of the little blue book containing the 1959–60 New York Newspaper Guild Contract with The Paper. He opens to the page of salary scales and with a pencil lightly underscores the six-month step up in Group Ten. That is the salary I will start with since my present Group Six salary as secretary to Ashley is $3.00 per week more than the starting salary for Group Ten.

"We can go over this all some other time, Arlyn, but for now just let me say that Mary Beth Collins is leaving the Women's Page. She's retiring into motherhood"—Purledge coughs dryly—"and I thought we might give you a trial up there. It will be rough for you, of course, going from being a secretary to a Group Ten job, but I have faith that you can do it. I'll be counting on you not to let me down. I'm going on the line for you so you'll have to be on your toes. And, as you know, if it doesn't work out there will always be a secretarial place for you somewhere on The Paper. That's in the contract."

My heart has slowed down, but my head is spinning. Who is Mary Beth Collins? Should I ask? Group Ten. A promotion. But what does Mary Beth Collins do?

"Thank you, sir. I won't let you down. But if you don't mind my asking, just exactly what is the job?"

Was that smart or dumb? I know soon enough.

Purledge coughs and draws himself up. "Mary Beth Collins is a very fine girl; Frank Collins' daughter and a graduate of Smith College." It was dumb. If the job was good enough for the Real Estate Editor's Ivy League daughter, as Purledge tags those girls, it is certainly, in his mind, almost

too good for me. "It's a real break for you, Arlyn," he is saying. "You're lucky to be considered, but, as I said, I'm going
out on a limb for you. And of course your six-month trial, as
stipulated in the contract, will be very closely monitored."

"I appreciate that, sir. Just what does the job entail?"

"The makeup for the special Sunday supplements. The
Children's Fashion Parade has been Mary Beth's baby. It's
one of the most successful of the recent supplements, you
know. The last back-to-school number was almost two hundred pages and broke all supplement advertising records.
And you'll have a chance to break into the Women's Page."

The Managing Editor's private secretary slips behind
Purledge and discreetly whispers into his ear. The interview, I realize, is over. Purledge nods at me and follows her
into the M.E.'s wood-paneled office.

My head hurts. Do I want an aspirin or a drink? Group
Ten.

Makeup on Sunday Supplements. Children's Fashion Parade. Ugh. That's one of the first sections of the Sunday
paper I toss into the trash can, lightening the load to carry
home. The Women's Page. Ugh. The latest chintz in Alt-
man's model rooms; how to restore luster to worn parquet
floors; Givenchy's new look for spring.

Now I tune in Mary Beth Collins. The slim blonde always
standing at a stone in a far-off corner of the composing
room, spending her day telling the makeup men where to
put the bits of copy cunningly placed among the two hundred pages of full-colored pictures of little girls in in-
decently innocent undershirts. I see her there when I help
out Music or Drama or Dance or Movies when they're short
a man and need an eagle eye to read proof on their Sunday
pages. That's kind of fun, finding the errors, making the cor-
rections, rushing them to the copy cutter's desk and sometimes waiting until the linotype operator types the new line,
taking it to a printer, what we call a makeup man, and
watching as he deftly removes the lead slug with the error
and replaces it with the new one. But Mary Beth Collins'

job? I often see her looking very bored, standing at the stone with one shoeless foot resting on the other in its fashionably slim pump. It really is such a good break. Why do I feel like crying?

30

"Oooooooooh!" I press my face into the leather cushions and draw my knees up to my chest. Here it comes. Pow! Damn! The spasm travels its tortuous route through what that last doctor called my plumbing. It explodes in a mind-shattering paroxysm of agony. Ahoooooooooo!"

"Whew. When it's like this," I say, opening my eyes to look at Isabelle, who is standing above me, "I feel as though I'm being split completely open."

Isabelle is small comfort. "I can't understand why you don't do something about it. You don't really have to suffer like this in 1960. You could get a shot or a hormone, and I told you about my cousin Seena's operation. It didn't cure her problem completely, but there is some improvement. You have Blue Cross."

"I hate to start with hormones and shots and operations," I say. "And besides, that last gynecologist I saw said I'm perfectly healthy and there's nothing wrong with me that a husband and babies won't fix."

"That goes without saying," Isabelle answers, "but what

about your monthly agony?" She bends close to me. "Seriously, can I do anything for you now?"

"No, thanks. I think the paregoric I got in Medical is beginning to take effect. I should be all right soon." I turn my face toward the wall and Isabelle tiptoes out of the Ladies Lounge, flicking off the overhead light as she leaves.

The spasm is muted this time. If only the clot would push its way out. I want to reach in and grab it but the thought repels me. Instead, I tuck my hand under my chin and curl my knees up to my chest. Come on, clot. Out. Out, out damn clot.

Is Mom right? Am I really the only one in my high school class who isn't a mother? And what about college? Most of the girls must have delivered by now, cuddly packages of blue and pink presented to proud fathers and doting grandmothers. Like Karyn, they haven't disappointed their parents. But not me. Not this month. And this one would have been Bill's, not the result of a dismal encounter with some creep I couldn't wait to get away from.

Snap. The overhead light shines in my eyes. I sit up crankily.

"Oh, I'm so sorry." The petite woman stands in front of me, embarrassed, out of place. Her stomach heaves, proudly poking out of the slim pale-green wool sheath.

"That's all right." I look at my watch. I must have dozed for a few minutes.

The woman drops into one of the big chairs opposite me.

"I just had a tour," she says. "No matter how much you hear about it you really do have to see it to believe it. I was even in the composing room. Look. For my children. The type's still hot."

She leans over and opens her hand, showing me two slugs, hot off the linotype machine, resting on her dainty palm. "I guess you take it all for granted, working here every day."

I nod and the woman continues. "It must really be exciting. I've been to other newspapers but there is something special about this one indeed." She takes some Saltines out of her purse and begins to nibble on them. I wonder which reporter or editor's wife she is. I have pegged her as such immediately; the pushy tummy, the little black velvet cloche with the teeny veil, the white gloves. I usually bump into these wives in the Ladies Lounge at the end of the day when they have come to The Paper to pick up their husbands for the trip home after a matinee or a shopping spree or before an evening on the town. Sometimes I am jealous of them, of their wifehood.

It seems a bit early in the day to find a wife in here now. I grind out my cigarette and stand up. I'm a little shaky, but anxious to get back to work. As it is, I'll have to eat lunch at my desk to get everything done so I can have a decent supper before reporting for Election Night duty. I make a move toward the washroom but the woman has not stopped talking. It would be rude to just walk away from her. I try to leave at appropriate breaks but she is too fast for me.

". . . and I am pooped, let me tell you. This one seems to be taking more out of me than the other two. Only in my third month, you know, but it's been misery from day one. Morning sickness all through the day. We thought a change of scenery would do me some good. Never have been away from my husband on a presidential election night since we first met in 1948 at the Harry S Truman headquarters in Lou-ville."

My knees begin to shake. I feel faint.

". . . we took the shuttle up yesterday afternoon, had us a nice dinner at this Eye-talian restaurant, Bar-betta? Ever eat there? Sure is some delicious food."

I turn and start out the door.

"Nice talking to you," the woman calls, "I'm JoAnn Hallam. Do you know my husband, Bill?"

"I know him," I manage, but I doubt that she hears me. I am rushing to the elevator bank. First, a stop in the ladies room outside the cafeteria to put on a new face and then a container of hot tea to take to my desk. That ought to do it. I must pull myself together. Where is that damn elevator?

The door from the city room opens and I turn my back. Is it apparent that I'm so agitated? I haven't actually cried yet but my eyes must be swollen. They burn from holding back the tears.

"Arlyn." I shift my head and find Bob Mann standing beside me, his long fingers solicitously rubbing my back. "Arlyn, what's wrong? You look awful. Can I help?"

I look awful. My God. I rush away from him and bolt through the heavy door that leads to the fire stairs. He follows me.

In the stairwell he pushes me gently against the wall and tilts my chin up toward his face. "Relax," he says, in a cheerful tone, "you're with me now. Come, I've got just what the doctor ordered. What you need is a little schnapps, eh?" He takes my hand and leads me down the stairs. Sniffling, I follow, away from the news floor, away from the Ladies Lounge, away from JoAnn Hallam.

We are the first customers in the Theater Bar for lunch. The midmorning tipplers are just leaving, those who can, at any rate. Here and there in the dark corners I see vaguely familiar pates but I am not really interested at the moment in which editor does or does not need a prework cocktail.

Bob orders two martinis, very dry, and tells the waitress we'll both have the strip steak. "How do you want it," he asks, "rare or medium rare?"

"I'm not sure I want it, I'm not that hungry."

"Sure you do. Just what you need now. Rare?"

"Medium rare's fine," I say, "but I don't think I want a martini, I'd rather have—"

"Bring her scotch and water," Bob tells the waitress cheerfully. "Sorry," he says to me, "I forgot you're not a gin drinker. Now," he says, reaching across the table and taking my two hands in his, "Uncle Bob's here to help. I've been watching the drama unfold and I can't say that I'm surprised at the denouement."

I pull my hands away. *Denouement.* Why does everyone use words like that at the worst times in people's lives? I reach in my bag for a cigarette. Bob grabs the match and lights it and then takes my hand again. My left one.

"Arlyn, you should be the wife, the ring should be on your finger. You are not cut out to be the other woman, the office woman."

The other woman! The words sting. It's not like that Bob, really. I want to tell him how it's different with Bill and me, how special it is with us. Instead I just take a sip of the scotch and a drag of my cigarette and ask, too coyly, I think, "What are you talking about?"

"Arlyn," he begins, stroking my hand, "Arlyn, don't try to hide it from me. I know Hallam's wife is in the building. He introduced me to her five minutes ago. I know you don't think I'm a great genius at understanding the workings of great and sensitive hearts, but as soon as I saw you I figured out what happened. You were crumpled up, not standing tall the way you usually do."

I take another sip of the scotch, then another. I am just downing it now and Bob signals the waitress for more. Finally I speak. "Why should that upset me, her being in the building?" I suppose it is brave of me to attempt to be nonchalant but I can't pull it off. By the time I have finished the sentence I am dissolved in tears, my cigarette hand pushing my upper lip into my nose.

Bob gives me his handkerchief.

He's right. I should be the wife, not the . . . the other woman, the office woman. My God! Is that what I am? Why didn't I ever see it that way before? Apparently everyone else does. Am I the only one who believed he would leave JoAnn?

The cramps have subsided, helped by the scotch. I had forgotten about my period but now when I think of Bill and realize it is over with us, his leaving me gets mixed up with the blood that is leaving my body. "Ohooooo." I feel so bereft.

"That's it," Bob is crooning, "get it all out. How about another drink?" I try to shake my head but the waitress who is putting our steaks in front of us rushes off for another scotch. Have I really finished two already?

I blow my nose, stuff the crumpled handkerchief in my lap, spread the stiff crimson napkin over it, and begin to cut the meat.

"That's the girl," Bob says. "Nothing like a good steak to cure all the world's ills. Once I remember in Hong Kong I was showing the Publisher and his wife around and I had made reservations in the best restaurant in the city—Mandarin and exquisite, let me tell you. Well the Pub was sick of eating cut-up food with chopsticks, and his wife was too. 'You know,' he said, 'what I would really like is a nice, juicy steak, one I can sink my teeth into. Can you find me one here?' I didn't know it at the time but they were having a bit of a spat, you know, some domestic quarrel, that kind of thing." Bob winks at me broadly as though I should know what he is talking about. Or care. It turned out, of course, that the Pub's wife had learned of the latest cookie the Pub was nibbling between meals and she was, in Bob's words, understandably upset. Needless to say, our hero, the dashing Foreign Correspondent found them a first-class steak restaurant and before you could say well done both the Pub and his Mrs. were feeling a lot better.

And much to my surprise, so am I. While the Theater Bar's strip steak may not rank with the world's or even the city's best, it is juicy and tasty and satisfying. I am beginning to feel filled up again, restored.

"I really appreciate this, Bob. I know it's too early for you to have lunch, but it is helping me. I'm beginning to feel a lot better. It was a jolt, meeting her like that. You were right, of course. It was meeting his wife that threw me." Bob is smiling as I talk.

"Has it been all over the office about Bill and me?" I ask.

Bob shrugs. "You know how these things are, Arlyn. Your romance was a three-day wonder. And then, like everything else around The Paper, it became stale news. It's taken for granted. But not by me. No matter how you feel about me I still think a lot of you, Arlyn, and I hated to see you get yourself in that position with him. I could see the changes in you early on. All this business of your trying to get on staff. The sermons and your involvement with this Rogers case. I could see you turning into one of those hard-assed bitches and I knew it wasn't for you.

"A girl like you, Arlyn, you have a lot to offer, you could do very well for yourself. Any man would be proud to have you for a wife. You make a great appearance and you fit in anywhere. You're an asset. You're smart, you can talk, you have a good sense of humor. You should capitalize on what you have. Believe me, you're not doing yourself any good fooling around with a guy like Hallam."

"You mean I'm becoming damaged goods?" My sarcasm is lost on him.

"No, nothing like that. It's just that you had your little affair, now you have to make sure you just don't keep falling into the same kind of thing. Once, okay. Twice, people begin to wonder. To see a pattern. And you yourself will begin to lose your softness."

"Hardhearted career woman?"

"It's no joke. You have to be careful. All this running around, this pushiness, sermons, features. Your naked ambition shows, Arlyn, and it's not the most attractive side of you."

"I still feel like me. I don't feel any different. And, anyway, what have I done? A few extra stories and a trip to Pittsburgh . . ."

"And that was terrific. It was absolutely right of you to follow your intuition and go visit your parents the way you did last week. I was really proud of the way it all turned out for you. By the way, you haven't thanked me for the roses."

"The roses. You sent the roses?"

"You didn't know?"

"They were anonymous."

"Damn! And I worked so hard on the card. It must have dropped out. ROSES FOR REMEMBRANCES AND THESE ARE STREWN AT YOUR FEET IN HONOR OF YOUR VERY SPECIAL FEAT, that's *e a t*. Like it?"

"It's very nice." I guess he doesn't know that I moved them to the windowsill and threw them out at the end of the day. "You heard about my promotion?"

"No, when, what?" Am I imagining the tenseness in his voice?

"Purledge told me yesterday. I'm replacing Mary Beth Collins. Her job is to oversee the makeup of the pages for the Children's Fashion Parade. Purledge says it's a good way for me to work onto the Women's Page."

"Congratulations. What's happening to Mary Beth Collins?"

"She's retiring into motherhood."

Bob lifts his glass and winks. "To following in Mary Beth's footsteps."

As I raise my glass I think of Mary Beth's aching, shoeless foot resting on its mate. The Children's Fashion Parade! God, that job seems awful. I wonder how far along she is in her pregnancy.

31

"Jesus H. Christ," Kit Rockwell mutters. She has just dropped another card.

It is Kit's first time working on the big Election Count Board too. I am too confused and exhausted to answer her. We are the center of attention, the pivotal people in the hub of all the election night activity, and I, at least, haven't the slightest idea of what's going on.

All eyes are on us as we run up and down the wooden platform in front of the board slipping the foot-long oak tag cards with the latest returns we have scribbled on them into the appropriate slot next to each state and its electoral number. Behind us at a long wooden plank table the top editors and political writers are puffing on their pipes and sucking their cigarettes down to their toes as they shrewdly calculate the meaning of each new set of figures. At a respectable distance behind them, a large semicircle of curious onlookers fans out to encompass the whole breadth of the huge city room.

This is the nerve center. Off in another corner giant

rented computers are spitting out the tallies faster than I can climb the platform. The computers were brought in as an experiment on the advice of the new technological wizards who are infiltrating The Paper at every level—much to the chagrin of many people. It's all very well to look to the future, some say, but our job is to report the here and now. A lot of people don't trust the computers and are going about the election night coverage in the time-honored way. Only grudgingly do they peek at the television sets placed strategically around the room.

Isabelle had often told me that working election night was like going to a giant birthday party. She loved it, she said. "The glamour and excitement, the celebrities from Broadway and Hollywood and Wall Street and Seventh Avenue, the proud executives showing off The Paper in its shining hour."

When I signed up to work on the election night crew I thought I'd be sitting at a desk somewhere helping one of the reporter-editor teams collate and tabulate returns. But Isabelle, who was scheduled to work the Board, bugged out just this afternoon. She just had to be at the Lexington Young Democrats Headquarters with Stuart tonight. Paddy O'Connell, who really thought he was doing me a favor, assigned me to the Board.

What is it with Isabelle, liking this so much? Birthday party my foot. My sore foot. I'm even too tired to give a damn about that dirty old man from the telegraph desk who has positioned himself in such a way that each time I run up the steps of the platform he can look up my skirt.

This is definitely for the birds. Oops. Sorry. That's the fourth mistake I made in the last half hour. Bill caught the first and commented on it even before I got the card in the slot. Sitting at the command post below, he saw instantly that I had too many zeros coming out of Oregon at twenty minutes to twelve EST.

"Ready for another break, Arlyn?" It is Paddy O'Connell. This time it's Merrilee Spaulding, the willowy teenaged

daughter of The Paper's comptroller, whom Paddy is intro-
ducing. Merrilee is one of the score of top management's
children who come to The Paper on big election nights to
watch and wonder and work a bit. I hand Merrilee my
heavy black grease pencil and show her how to copy the
figures from the smeared strips of wire copy that teams of
copyboys are bringing to Kit and me in increasing numbers.
Merrilee is eager to begin, but if she is anything like my
other stand-in, Susan Apthorpe, the Legal Vice-President's
daughter, she will quickly bore of the tedious chore.

Teddy Lowe is standing at the coffee urn talking to Aus-
tin Spaulding. Spaulding very graciously pours me a container of coffee and signals Luis to bring his large platter of
sandwiches over to me.

"You look tired," the comptroller says to me. "This will
help." He hands me the coffee and bends to remove a stack
of copy from a nearby chair. "Sit," he says.

I am very appreciative. I am so dizzy I could drop. Thank
goodness this isn't a bad period. Spaulding doesn't seem to
remember me from his visits to the Publisher's Suite. He is
merely being kind. Lowe, who certainly knows who I am,
has turned his back so that he doesn't have to acknowledge
me. Fair enough. I am at this moment doing the same to
Luis.

It is after midnight and the picture has begun to change.
Nixon seems to be pulling ahead. There is much pipe-biting
and cigarette-chewing at the long wooden table. And well
there should be. All over the city room early editions of The
Paper are proclaiming in eight-column banner headlines that
Kennedy will win the election.

Bill is gesticulating angrily, trying to get someone to listen to him; the Managing Editor, the chief Washington col-
umnist, the Publisher, the Bull Pen editor. Anyone. He is
waving his hands and stomping his feet. That's when he's
great, when he's embroiled in a political discussion, aroused
and animated. We haven't talked since yesterday's phone
conversation. JoAnn is sitting on the rim of the spectators'

semicircle as an honored guest. Strange, but the meeting with her just this morning only registers dimly on my brain. I guess we do have all those defense mechanisms the analysts are always telling us about. And it's just as well. Merrilee Spaulding has had it and is waving wildly to me.

Now things have really heated up. Every return from the West Coast causes more agitation at the long table. Voices rise. I catch the words "unwise," "premature," "foolhardy," "big mistake." There is even talk of stopping the presses.

I ease myself back into the rhythms of copying the figures, running up the stairs, and slipping the oak tag boards into the slots. It's neck and neck. Someone will win and someone will lose. Kennedy or Nixon. Which will it be? Arlyn or JoAnn. Which? Someone will win and someone will lose. And what of the other alliances being made or broken?

"It's the sexiest night of the year around here," Gil Gilchrist told me when I announced that I would be working election night. "Liaisons are started that would be unthinkable in the ordinary course of events. It's the kind of night that makes people break out of their good gray lives."

"And a lot of lee-a-sons are ended, too," Tony Weather chimed in. "I remember in 1952 when the whole city room was practically in tears and Jean Blake said maybe Eisenhower wouldn't be so bad, maybe the voters were right, maybe he would bring the boys home, and her friend from sports threw a container of coffee into her face and went back to his wife."

It is well into Wednesday morning when Paddy O'Connell tells Kit and me that the City Editor will soon be giving good-nights. JoAnn has long vanished with most of the other spectators. The city room is now occupied by editors and reporters, copyboys and clerks, secretaries and assistants, many already in their coats and hats, clustered in congenial groups, waiting to be dismissed. It is an eerie sight; the frenetic pace of the early part of the evening has now been slowed. Here and there a bottle is uncorked and paper cups filled with whiskey are passed around. The strict dictum against whiskey bottles being visible is relaxed on this occasion. As the City Editor moves from group to group, people begin to shuffle toward the elevators. Arrangements are made to share cabs, food, beds. Kit and I decide not to join some of the others for coffee. We will share a cab straight uptown. She has just told me that she is giving notice at the end of the week. She and her roommate, she said, plan to live in Europe for a while. "There is nothing for us here," she told me, "we're not ready to settle down yet. We both have the wanderlust." She has seemed more like her old self in the last few weeks, since she made her decision.

As we all pile out of the elevator I am surprised to see Bill in the lobby leaning against a tall, marble pillar. Surely's he's not waiting for *me*. It must be someone from the Washington Bureau. With JoAnn in town and me surrounded here by all these busybodies he wouldn't dare.

"I have a cab waiting," he barely mumbles as he steps between Kit and me.

"Kit? Can we drop Kit?" I ask. But she is already walking away.

"No, she'll find a way," he answers without turning around.

In the cab he lights a cigarette for each of us and leans back. "That sure was some kind of night. I do hope I didn't make enemies. They were wrong to call it so early. It was too close. They got ahead of the news. But they wouldn't hear me out, they—"

"I met JoAnn today. Congratulations on the new addition."

There is stone-dead silence. He is shocked that I said it just like that. Good. Screw him. Talking about Kennedy and the Great W. B. Hallam's news judgment is not what I want to do at this moment. Who cares about the election? I want to talk about us. I want to talk, but it is obvious that Bill doesn't. He is leaning back, dragging on his cigarette, looking out the window at the sporadic predawn traffic.

"How could you?" I say. "Do you know how hurt I feel, how . . . ?"

His profile slowly turns toward me. The words come from between clenched teeth.

"Not now."

"Why not now? When? Do you know how it felt . . . ?"

"I said not now." His big hand reaches over to squeeze my wrist as though that will keep me quiet.

"I can talk anytime I— Ouch! You're hurting me."

"I'm asking you to hold it. We'll talk. But not now."

What's the use. I give up. The ride continues in silence.

32

On the stairs I turn. "I'm surprised you didn't keep the cab. Why are you coming up if you aren't talking?"

The voice is icy. "I don't discuss my most intimate feelings in taxicabs."

Inside the apartment he pours himself a bourbon while still in his coat and hat. I refuse a drink and rummage in the refrigerator.

"Come out here," he calls. "What are you hiding for? Now we can talk and you're avoiding it." I am surprised at the nastiness of the crack. I grab an apple and walk into the living room to see that he is sitting on the opened, unmade bed, still in his coat. I hate that and he knows it.

"How come you're sitting here with your coat on when you know how much it annoys me?" I say, walking past him on my way to the Danish chair. He grabs my waist and pulls me down on the bed next to him. He bends to kiss me but I back away, knocking his hat off with my upraised arm.

"How could you?" I shout.

"How could I what?"

"Don't play games. You know what I'm talking about. How could you make love to both of us at the same time. It's so awful!"

He takes a big gulp of the whiskey and leans back laughing.

"Arlyn, sweetie, sometimes you disappoint me. Now you're sounding just like every other woman. I thought you were different. Surely you understand." He stands up to take off his coat and he sits back down next to me on the edge of the bed.

"Understand? Understand what?"

"Understand that JoAnn is my wife. A man sleeps with his wife from time to time. You know that."

"But the baby. The new baby. What am I to make of that? Amy and Heather and your love for them, that I can understand. In fact, how could I love a man who didn't take his responsibilities to his wife and children seriously? But now another child? Doesn't that really foul everything up? I mean, Amy and Heather are almost in their teens and here you are starting all over again."

He falls all the way back on the bed and runs his hand over his face, stopping at his eyes. Is he blocking out the sight of the third child?

I go on. "I mean, it's humiliating and demeaning. You conceived this child after you knew me. It would be different I suppose if it had happened before."

"I know," he answers softly. "The timing is wrong."

"Timing! Is that all you have to say. Timing. And what kind of people are you, anyway. Isn't it a little irresponsible for the two of you to be bringing a child into the world?"

"I'm sure it is." He is barely whispering as he answers. His voice is hoarse and choked with emotion. I want to hold him and comfort him. "But JoAnn would not hear of an abortion and I'm not sure I wanted her to have one. That is my seed, my flesh and blood inside her. Of that I'm sure. It's another human life, an extension of me. Maybe a boy."

Are those tears in his eyes? My desire to comfort him is leaving fast.

"But didn't you use anything? How did it happen?"

He shrugs helplessly.

"That's all you can do is shrug? Didn't you use any protection?"

"What's the use of talking about that now, crying over spilt milk. It happened."

"Spilled seed is more like it. You, I know, would never use a condom, hating the damn things as you do. But what about her? Doesn't she use anything? You should have a dozen kids."

"Sweetie, what's the use. It happened. These things happen. You want me to blame her, to accuse her. She says she didn't do it on purpose and I have to believe her. Anyway, what difference does it make now. In any case nothing's changed between us."

"What? You mean that? Everything's changed."

"Why should it? I had two children, now I'll have three. I had to think about the two, now there's one more."

"You're very cavalier about this new life, this seed of yours."

"Well, shoot, maybe I do want it, too. But that still has nothing to do with us. I've thought about us a lot, too, and I was going to tell you my plan this week anyway, right after the election. I'm really sorry it happened the way it did, you seeing JoAnn and all. I didn't think you'd talk. Was it in that Ladies Lounge?"

"Yes. Did you try to keep her away from it? How considerate of you to plan to tell me yourself."

"Honey, this is no time for sarcasm and nastiness. I truly have been thinking about us, and I think I've come up with a fair solution."

"A fair solution! For whom?" My sadness is gone, the tears welling up in me have backed down. The son of a bitch. How dare he? I hate his guts at this moment and want him out of the apartment, out of my life.

". . . and as you know there are pros and cons working in both places. I have suggested that I be attached to the National Desk out of New York and cover Washington and the rest of the country as a roving reporter. It's being done that way on a lot of papers now and it makes sense. The Paper is too rigid about that sort of thing, having a man live and work from one city. Guys are flying all over now. I could hit the civil rights stuff in the South and monitor what's happening in Washington and what have you. It's under consideration. I didn't want to tell you until I was sure. I didn't want you to get too excited about it."

"And JoAnn? Where is she in all this?"

Either my sarcasm escapes him or he purposely misses it. "Someone was telling me there are some mighty pretty areas on Long Island. Maybe there. Or maybe Westchester or New Jersey."

"I see. When you're not roving the country you'll be with JoAnn and Heather and Amy and the baby in the suburbs. Sounds great. And me? Where do I fit in? Quickies before you dash for the eleven-ten?"

"Honey, I can understand your anger. Believe me, I can." The earnest look in his eyes almost makes me believe what he is saying. "And I guess I'm a little bit glad you're reacting so strongly, too. But I have been thinking about us, I really have."

"When you weren't plotting your roving reporter scheme?"

"Oh, you do mean to be difficult. A man has to carve his career. How many times do we have to go through that? But I have been thinking of how to fit you in. And I think it will work. When I'm traveling you could easily fly out and meet me. Wouldn't that be great fun? And of course I would still see you here."

"I was right about the eleven-ten. And my job. What about my job? If I'm doing all this traveling, what about my job?"

Bill looks at me with exasperation, telling me by his look that he thinks I'm being spitefully obtuse. "Weekends," he answers. "Weekends. A couple a month. And days off and vacations. You'd be surprised how much time together that is. I know of cases where it works out very well. For all concerned."

"You're kidding."

"Kidding? No, I'm not kidding. Why do you think I'm kidding?"

"You've got to be kidding."

"Baby, I'm not. I'm not saying it will all work smoothly and perfectly right away, and that it won't be rough for a while, but you'll see. It will work out."

"And me. What about me? What about my life, my future?"

"Well, that's the other part of it. I've thought a lot about that. The way we're going, seeing each other so much, you don't have a chance to get around. And I understand that you have to. Much as it hurts me to think about it, I understand it. You have to be perfectly free. A beautiful young girl like you. In fact, I want you to start getting around more." He grins and slaps my thigh. "But not too much right away, eh?"

This is incredible. If I heard it second-hand I would find it difficult to believe. This man, this man I have given my very being to has worked out a way to squeeze me in on alternate weekends. Now the tears are flowing wildly. I couldn't stop them if I tried. And why should I try? Let them come. Tears to kum.

"Aw, sweetie." He is stroking my arm. I pull it away. He moves closer and puts his lips to my ear. I begin to shiver. "My darling, I hate to see you hurt like this. If only I could undo it, but I can't. You are so special to me, you are so rare. I wish I could bottle you and keep you just as you are, but I know I can't. I know you have your life to live and I can't stand in the way. But can't we try to save something of what we have, it is so sweet, so special, you must admit that, can't we just—"

I move to stand up, to get away from him, but he yanks me down.

"No."

"No?"

"Let me up." My words are smothered. He is over me, covering my face with kisses, licking the tears off my cheeks, sucking my ear, taking it into his mouth. I am sobbing now. He leans back on his knees and removes his suit jacket and shirt. It is like a dream. How many times have we done this? How many times more? He slithers out of his clothes and quickly undresses me. I see him in a blur, bits and pieces of his face and chest, as though I am turning a prism away from the light, as though I am looking through a mirror that is cracked, broken, shattered.

When we are finished I am sore. We have been at times tender, passionate, jolly, matter-of-fact. This time we were mean. It was hard and furious and I wanted to tear his flesh off with my fingernails and swallow his tongue and smash his nose with my butting head. A soiled Tampax is wadded up in a tissue on the floor beside us. No time for niceties, no putting in of the diaphragm to catch the blood. The whole business is messy.

We lie quietly, our breath returning to normal, coming down. I am in the crook of his arm as usual but there is no unity between us. We are separate.

The phone wakes us. I look at the clock radio as I answer. A quarter to ten. We really must have been knocked out, both of us. Bill jumps up and looks at his watch. He dashes to the bathroom and I hear the shower.

"Hi, is this the daughter of the crony of Davey Lawrence, Kingmaker?"

"Who is this?"

"Sorry, couldn't resist the joke. Arlyn, this is Dan Roth. Do you remember me? That night in Hyannis Port?"

"Dan Roth. Of course I remember you. How have you been?"

"Terrific. Everything's terrific. And you?"

"Good. Everything's good." I say. "How did your Hyannis Port pictures turn out?"

"Great. I went back the next day and slipped right in. A breeze. I sold about four of them. One to AP."

"That's sensational."

"Yeah, it was pretty good. And I got other jobs from that. How about you? Did anything good come out of that night for you? Are good things happening for you at The Paper?"

"Well, a lot has happened. As a matter of fact, it started just after I left Hyannis. Remember I told you I was going to Nantucket? But it's a long story."

"I want to hear all about it. Can we get together? I'm only in the city till tonight now. Any chance of seeing you today? Lunch? Drinks? Dinner?"

"You're leaving tonight?" Bill has returned to the room and is beginning to put on his clothes.

"Yes. But I'll be back for good. I'm moving back to the city."

"You're going to live here? You and your wife are moving back?" Bill has tried to pretend he hasn't been following my conversation. But my last question was too much for him. He's sitting on the edge of the bed, one sock dangling limply from his hand.

"Just me," Dan Roth says. "My wife and I aren't together now."

"You're divorced?" Bill hurries with the sock. And the shoe.

"Almost. She'll be going to Mexico in a few weeks."

"You don't have children, do you?"

"No, thank God. That would really be a mess."

"Yes. It would be a mess." Bill is squatting in front of the wall mirror to put on his tie. The old familiar posture, legs spread, pants open and sliding down his thighs. In a second he will neatly tuck his shirttails around his body and pull up his pants.

"I'd love to see you today, Dan. Lunch is out, but drinks or dinner is fine." Bill throws a sad look in my direction. A chill passes through me. I pull the sheet and blanket around my naked body. Bill starts toward me, coat and hat in hand, come to kiss me goodbye. I turn away abruptly. I hear him let himself out of the apartment.

"So," Dan Roth is saying, "what, where, when? You tell me."

"Can you pick me up in the lobby of The Paper at six-thirty?"

"Great. Can't wait. And I want to hear all about your promotion. What did you say it was?"

"It's makeup for the Children's Fashion Parade, you know, the magazine supplement? And it's a chance to eventually work onto the Women's Page."

"Oh." I can hear the disappointment in Dan's voice.

"I know, that's how I felt too. But I have a different attitude now. I figure if I work hard and show my stuff I can get back down to the city room in a year or two. That's where I really want to be. I broke a murder case, you know. That's how I got the promotion. But I'll tell you all about it when I see you."